Say What Now?

JG Foster

Also by JG Foster

- Jessie Grean - A contemporary Young Adult book
- Her, Him & I - A rom com novella

A First Time for Everything

Week 26

A First Time for Everything

<u>Wednesday</u>

The airplane touched down at Boston's Logan Airport. Relief lightened my heart. After months of waiting, planning, and being all by myself—well, sort of—I disembarked from the metal bird. My limbs ached from the nine-hour flight. Actually, from the whole journey.

I had locked my front door back in Potsdam around 7:00 a.m. The sun wasn't even up yet, but by the time my flight landed, the sun had already set again back home. However, the clock in Boston only struck four in the afternoon. My eyes, head, arms, and legs just wanted to curl up on a soft bed with a blanket.

I waddled to the baggage pickup area. A mob of people already waited. The luggage carousel idled. I suppressed a groan. I shifted my weight from left to right for almost thirty minutes.

"Please open your bag," ordered a throaty voice behind me.

The shortness of the woman's tone made me look up. As I lifted my gaze, my eyes followed a dark blue, one-inch-wide, woven nylon extension leading down from her left hand. At the end of the leash, a beagle waited for his next command in front of my backpack. Taken aback by the dog, I snatched my carry-on up from the floor. My eyes zeroed in on the officer.

"Did you bring any food items into the country with you from your place of departure?" The officer scrunched up her forehead.

"Food?" I exhaled, as if the word was foreign to me. Technically, English was foreign to me as my mother tongue was German, but I had acquired the meaning of this word during third grade. I understood what the uniformed woman meant.

Reactivating my brain, the contents of my bag flickered through my mind: my phone, a charger, my computer, a book, a water bottle, headphones, my wallet, my passport, a spoon, my bullet journal, a pencil case with fine liners, a fountain pen, and washi tape.

"No," I insisted. Still, the dog fixed his pupils on me.

"Please open your luggage," instructed the woman.

Stunned, I wanted to refuse. Just because someone ordered me to follow their demand didn't mean I mindlessly obeyed. What if the woman was trying to pull a con on me despite being in a uniform? Airports provided loads of opportunities to get robbed. After all, people hurried quickly from one point to another, causing travelers to often submit to authority figures immediately to decrease their delays.

I covered my mouth with a yawn to conceal my hesitation. If the woman was for real, noncompliance could lead to detention. *Do they employ translators here?* I could not deal with an interrogation in a second language. Without a doubt, I could not even sustain an interrogation in my mother tongue either. Only *yes* and *no* would worm out of my mouth. Regardless, experiencing this kind of confrontation immediately after I crossed the Atlantic for the first time was not on my to-do list.

My back hurt, my forehead pounded, and my eyelids sagged. I just wanted to go home—to my new home, for the time being—to shower away the long flight. My shaky hands unzipped my backpack, hoping for the best but expecting the worst.

The woman shuffled through my belongings. Annoyed, I bit my lips. I didn't have anything to hide, but I feared that my wallet would vanish right under my nose. Wouldn't that be a fantastic welcoming present?

The woman pulled out a zipped-up transparent plastic bag from my carry-on.

"Oh, I had yogurt." My response echoed back in my face when the dog shifted his attention from my backpack to the woman's hand—a spoon dangled from her fingers.

She returned the silverware to me. "Have a nice holiday!"

"Thanks," I muttered, swinging my backpack over my shoulders.

A metallic screech bolted through the hall. A hidden engine propelled forward. Lo and behold, the luggage carousel began to move in front of me. My hiking backpack led the way.

With all my belongings retrieved, I followed a stream of people toward the final checkpoint. "Welcome to the US," greeted the female voice originating from five flat screens on the walls of the passport control area. A picture of Mount Rushmore appeared on the monitors. Seconds later, a beach with a happy family replaced the stone sculptures. When Niagara Falls came, followed by the famous Las Vegas sign, the loop of pictures commenced again.

More travelers joined the line behind me in addition to the seven other passport control lines. In total, seven passport control desks let people pass the border. Yet not all control windows serviced international arrivals. Minutes turned into hours.

I worried about Guido, my husband. I couldn't call, text, or email to assure him that I stood only feet away from where he waited for me, inching forward in this painstakingly slow line.

Two Hours Later

"Your passport, please?" requested another uniformed woman behind a transparent plastic shield. I handed the double-chinned border employee my burgundy-red identification booklet.

"Where did you fly from?"

"Berlin."

"How long are you planning to stay here?"

"Six months."

The border control officer flipped through the green pages of my official document. She stopped at my J1 visa sticker.

"Who are you planning to stay with?"

"My husband."

"Place your right hand on the machine in front of you."

I did.

She stamped half on my sticker and half on the paper, saying, "Welcome to the US."

* * *

"Mareike, Mareike!" Guido's voice boomed through the crowd of waiting people. I zigzagged through travelers and flung myself into my husband's arms.

When we embraced, the overwhelming scent of Guido's aftershave exploded in my nose. The fragrance reminded me of my childhood. My grandmother used to wear a perfume that resembled my husband's aftershave. As a preteen, I loved the smell. Unfortunately, as a now-pregnant adult, the aroma repelled me like a mosquito.

I bit my tongue. After nearly three months apart, Guido probably wanted to put his best foot forward.

"What was going on back there? I waited for three hours," my husband moaned.

"I don't know. I probably waddled half a mile through the airport, then waited for my backpack forever, and stood in line to get my passport checked for an eternity."

"Anyway, you made it," declared Guido before shouldering my luggage.

My new home floated by through the windows of a taxi. The houses, people, and streets appeared all too familiar but also strangely alien. I wasn't sure what I had imagined. I had watched enough movies and documentaries to know that the USA wasn't much different from Germany. Yet I pictured everything more clean or shiny, perhaps futuristic.

However, a spirit of festivities to come sprung up in me as we drove through our neighborhood. Inflatables of kid-friendly horror movies were set up outside several houses. Spiders and skeletons decorated many outside walls. My brain rummaged through all possible occasions to provide my mind with reasons for those decorations.

Besides the decor for kids, I noticed some adult ones too. The word *Oktoberfest* popped up here and there. I had so many thoughts and so many questions. I had to admit that I had only once been to the Oktoberfest in Munich. Let's put it this way: the festivities weren't my jam. I'd instead go to our pub around the corner to hang out with our friends.

Guido squeezed my hand. "I'm so happy you're here."

"Me too," I concurred.

"Are you happy to be on leave?"

"Yes, but technically, I am on vacation. And I am a little scared that I will still be cc'd on most work emails." I had accumulated three weeks of unused vacation time to take before my maternity leave officially started.

"I am sure the lemonades will be made without you," teased Guido.

"Of course they will. I have nothing to do with the production."

Guido grinned at me. He knew that my position as a controller in a lemonade company only involved numbers.

"I can't believe I'm here," I repeated, kissing my husband on his cheek. Months ago, he'd convinced me that his stay abroad would only be a few months. *A couple of months*, echoed in my head. I rubbed my stomach. That was back when my tummy sat flat on my body.

When we first talked about Guido's stint in Boston, my hair stood up on my skin. The time period made the situation clear; if I'd stayed at home, Guido would miss the birth of his child.

"Why can't someone else go?" I had screeched at him.

"You know why. I am the lead software developer. I have to train these people to install, implement, and debug the software for the cashier machines," argued Guido.

I'd thrown up my hands, exasperated. "But why can't you train someone else to train the people in Boston?"

"There is not enough time. Listen, we'll talk about the options after I speak with my boss," Guido had soothed me.

Suddenly, I sat in my apartment, alone, pregnant, and trying to decide what was best for us. Either I had the baby with Guido or I didn't. Weeks went by, putting pros and cons on a list.

My sister, Ulrike, the world traveler, tipped the scale during my decision-making process, probably hoping to be able to swing by in Boston. But shortly before I flew to Guido, our cousin Annette told us all about her new *mom life*. All Ulrike heard was: babies cry during the night, no one can sleep, there is always a never-ending pile of food to be prepared, and nobody has time to deep clean the bathroom. Her excitement to visit us dimmed. On the other hand, I heard Ulrike could help with the baby, cook, and keep me company.

The cab stopped in front of a three-story gray house. Guido lifted my hiking backpack from the car trunk and carried my belongings to the house's main entrance. He pulled open a flimsy door with an oversized mesh window, and a spring on top of the frame pulled the door back in. He blocked it with his body and pushed the key into the main door.

"A door before the door?" I mused.

"Yeah," concurred Guido. "I believe they are called storm doors. But don't ask me why."

I had so many questions, but I swallowed them for now as we climbed up a narrow stairwell. How could anyone carry big or heavy items up? Of course my husband had rented an apartment on the highest level. My back was killing me when Guido unlocked the door to our nest.

It felt surreal to finally be standing in his apartment. Previously, I'd only gotten glimpses through my computer screen. A black floor cushion graced the otherwise empty living room. Instantly, I missed our cozy home.

Over the past several months, I had teased Guido about the emptiness within his apartment. Unfortunately, the living room hadn't become more inviting. Marks and stains on the off-white paint from a long line of previous occupants didn't help either.

Somehow, relief flushed my system at the sight of bare walls.

When we first moved into our current apartment back home, we'd spent a whole weekend tearing down the wallpaper. On another, the two of us painted the walls in a shade of cream. Here, half the work was done already.

The more significant issue was the apartment itself. The emptiness in each room glared at me. At least Guido had obtained a proper mattress with a frame; the inflatable one seemed gone.

On one level, I understood Guido's lack of furnishings. He basically only slept within these four walls. On the other hand, we had planned my stay far in advance. Disappointment bubbled up in my gut. Guido didn't step up to make our space more habitable. Now I had to. On the bright side, though, shopping for stuff I wanted to surround myself with would force me to explore my "new" hometown.

My sister had implored, *Only when you get lost do you discover new neighborhoods.*

Despite the visual unwelcomeness of Guido's apartment, a delicious fragrance layered the air. "What did you make?"

"Goulash."

"Yum." I took my shoes off to inspect the kitchen. Two empty blue bowls, different styles of spoons, and two mismatched chairs waited for us. Somehow, he had organized himself a proper kitchen. Go figure.

"Where did you get those?" I pointed at the dinnerware. I'd expected him to live on paper plates as a *Strohwitwer*.[1]

"I found the bowls in a box on the sidewalk," announced Guido. My smile slipped off my face. I couldn't believe he found unchipped, uncracked kitchenware on the street.

"I found the kitchen table and the chairs on a curb too," confessed my husband. No wonder they were mismatched. But Guido hadn't stopped there. "I stumbled upon an ironing board the other day as well."

Instead of questioning my husband if the

board came with an iron, I marveled aloud, "Is this wishing curb on your way to work?"

"Sometimes . . . and sometimes at random places when we go out for lunch or when I pick something up for dinner," Guido informed me.

"Ha," I huffed. My creep factor cranked up. "How about the bed and bedding?" I inquired. I imagined bugs hiding in the fabric only to crawl all over us as we slept.

"No, no," he assured me. "I bought it off Craigslist."

"Craigslist?"

"Yeah. It's like *eBay Kleinanzeigen.*"[2]

Guido poured the hot soup into my dish.

I nodded. "I can't believe I'm here," I sighed.

"Me neither," echoed Guido.

I gulped down the hot dinner. A sensation of home overcame me. "I have to call my mom to let her know I arrived in one piece."

My husband gave me a wry look. "Well, it's eleven thirty back at our parents'."

"Oh, I forgot."

"Just send her an email. I can enter the modem information into your computer while you shower," proposed Guido as a yawn escaped my mouth. "If you want, we can go to bed early today. I'm tired too." Guido smiled and finished his food.

"Sounds like a good idea," I agreed. I placed my dish in the sink after Guido and found my luggage in the bedroom.

My husband rinsed our dinnerware. "I made you space in the closet."

Two empty shelves above neatly stacked shirts, sweatshirts, socks, and underwear provided room for my clothes.

"Our appointment is at ten tomorrow."

This wasn't my first pregnancy visit, of course, but my first one in a new country with my husband—exciting stuff. Usually I either went by myself to appointments or with my mother or sister.

"I am already excited." I unclipped my backpack cover and pulled out my pajamas, cardigan, and toiletry bag.

"Me too," Guido said. "I have missed so much already."

"Well, yes and no, I guess. At times, though, it has been tough to be without you," I confessed.

"You are here now." Guido embraced me. I pushed my body against his. Beneath his new cologne, his natural scent filtered through. A sigh of relief relaxed my shoulders.

We were finally back together. Unfortunately, another smell disrupted our reunion. Sweat. My sweat. Self-conscious, I pulled away to sniff under my arms.

"I have to take a shower."

"I put out a fresh towel for you."

"Thanks."

I shuffled into the bathroom. Right in front of me sat the toilet. Next to it was the sink. Above the vanity was a hanging, mirrored cabinet, and under the sink was more storage. There was also a shower and bathtub in the corner of the bathroom; the entire room was barely wider than my wingspan.

I peeled my clothes off and turned on the water. From a short, stubby, pear-sized showerhead warm water drizzled over my head and shoulders. My lower back began to relax. The water rinsed off the journey—a clean start to a new chapter in my life that would launch after I dried off.

My *Aronal und Elmex* tubes of toothpaste pushed through the zipper of my toiletry bag. Underneath rolled my blue-and-white *Florena* cream. Abruptly, a memory sprang into my mind. A faint odor lingered in the air of Guido's aftershave: *Kölnisch Wasser.*

I had to devise a way to tell my husband that this one item in his self-care regimen caused me almost to puke.

I dried my skin, lathered my body in lotion, and put an extra dollop of Vaseline on my lower belly. Then I slipped into my soft, casual royal-blue pants and shimmied into my orange T-shirt with a green *Ampelmännchen,*[3] courtesy of my sister.

My hair dryer's cord tangled on the floor while I hunted down an outlet. None showed themselves to me. I wrapped my beige cardigan around my back, which my mother had knitted. I have always admired her craftsmanship, as well as her patience. The fluffy jacket turned out exactly how I hoped the knitwear would be. I loved the big pockets on the sides and the belt instead of buttons.

I scooted along, examining the walls of our bedroom. On my husband's bedside, I found a creamy-white plastic frame. I pushed the hair dryer plug in, but the end didn't budge. A barrier blocked the metal rods. I crouched down for a better look.

"No way," I wailed.

"What happened?" asked Guido.

"My hair dryer doesn't fit into the outlet."

"Are you serious?" Irony lined my husband's words.

I glowered at him. "I am not in the mood."

"You can't even travel to France and expect just

to plug in your electronic devices," Guido pointed out.

Of course he was right. I didn't know how often that irked me. Each country in the European Union had different outlets.

"How was the shower?" Guido asked, in an attempt to shift my annoyance.

"Nice, but why don't you have a long showerhead? It was such a pain to clean the tub."

"I don't know. There was none when I moved in."

"Oh. How have you cleaned the shower then? Moving the showerhead back and forth barely did anything to get rid of my hair on the sides of the walls."

My husband shrugged. He focused both his eyes on a YouTube video. Before snuggling up next to him with wet hair, I put the handful of clothes I'd brought with me in the wardrobe. To my surprise, all of Guido's hangers tilted upward.

"What's going on here?" I snorted.

Guido turned to me. "The space is too small for the hangers."

"Ha," I exhaled. Visually, the metal bar appeared to be mounted in the middle of the closet for the hangers, but the space to the wall proved insufficient to hang clothes properly. I smacked my forehead in my mind.

Unable to remedy the issue, I cuddled up to my husband instead. The moving pictures on the computer screen showed a guy hammering away on metal between dipping the silver material into roaring flames. The title under the video read, *Forging a Viking Axe*. *Hhhmmmm, this is new*, I thought.

"But if you want, we probably can get one," Guido continued, as if we were just discussing a specific topic.

I pushed my brows together, confused. "What do you mean?"

"I mean a showerhead. We can probably just buy one."

"That would be great. Bending over with my belly is no fun." I pulled up the thick white blanket, absorbing my husband's body heat as I drifted asleep.

<u>Thursday</u>

Luckily for me, Guido was by my side on our way to the gynecologist. My phone could display the directions, but the GPS took me on the least direct route without the Internet. I breathed in the air of my new temporary home. Like in the taxi, the houses and the people oozed little differences. Besides the language passersby spoke, the street signs were green and not blue. The ending of the street names was *Ave* or *St*, which I presumed stood for "street." I mused if all those *Ave*'s meant "*Allee*,"[4] but the road didn't look like one.

Another peculiar sight popped into view. Pairs of shoes hung with their laces tied from overhead wires along a busy street called Highland Ave.

"Do you think someone just dropped by with an extra pair and threw their shoes up there? Or did a dare leave a person to hobble home barefoot?" I guessed.

Guido followed my gaze. "I don't know." He shrugged. "Anyway, we're here." Guido opened the left of the double-sided doors for me in a five-story office building. Clean, sterile walls opened up in front of us in the entrance area.

"The ob-gyn is on the first floor. Do you want to walk or take the elevator?"

"Ob-gyn?" I probed. We lingered in front of the closed elevator doors. I figured *gyn* could mean "gynecologist," but *ob*?

"It means obstetrician and gynecologist," my husband explained.

"What's an obst—ob?" I blurted out loud.

He chuckled, "I am not sure what the difference is. If there is one."

"If there isn't a difference, why add it?" I really should start with a list of words and occurrences I wanted to check up on, I thought, instead of just accumulating them as mental bullet points.

The elevator doors opened up to a waiting area with four rows of six chairs each. A reception desk lined the left wall.

"Good morning," said a woman with a blonde bob. "Are you checking in?"

"Yes, my name is Mareike Korn."

The receptionist scanned her screen. "Well, yes. Please take a seat."

We did as we were told. We chose seats lined up on the wall, letting the quietness of the otherwise empty room sink in, yet my mind swirled with thoughts. My heart raced away. I had been to countless appointments before, but at home, with my gynecologist, whom I had known since I was fourteen.

"Mrs. Korn," called a female voice. A woman with bleached hair, about midtwenties, stared at me. Guido and I trailed the nurse into a medical examination room.

"My name is Joan. I will take your vitals," clarified the petite woman before me.

I nodded. She pumped up the round thing so

the cuff around my arms tightened and weighed and measured me.

Once she jotted the numbers down, she informed us, "You can go ahead and expose your stomach. Nurse Practitioner Johnson will be right with you."

"What's a nurse practitioner?" I quizzed Guido after the door closed behind her.

"I don't know. Maybe some type of doctor."

"But then why wouldn't she be called doctor?" I argued.

"We can ask her once she comes."

Minutes passed before the door opened again. A woman in a dark blue hospital uniform stepped in. "My name is Claire, and I am your nurse practitioner. If I understand correctly, you just changed to our practice."

"Yes," I answered with a nod.

"Okay, let's have a look."

Before pumping warm gel on my skin, she placed a thin, paperlike material on the edge of my trousers. Honestly, the person who'd conceived of the clever idea of a gel heater had earned my utmost respect. Gone were the times when the gooey, freezing mass just plopped onto the skin without warning.

"From the measurement, you are in week twenty-six. That means your son is due around January fourteenth. Have you decided yet how you would like to have the baby?"

I stared at her, then at Guido, who gave me the same stare back.

"Come again?" I requested.

"Are you planning to have the baby delivered with a midwife or a doctor?"

"What is a midwife?" I managed to ask.

"A midwife is a health-care professional who specializes in pregnancy, childbirth, and newborn care," summarized the nurse practitioner.

"Hhhhhhmmmmmm," I chirped. Many questions formed in my head, but I had problems articulating them. Wasn't this the reason I was at a gynecologist's office? I supposed a gynecologist wasn't just there for babies. I had seen one regularly since my first menstruation. However, she'd just described precisely my needs. Still, I wasn't aware of this option before.

My gynecologists hadn't told me of an alternative, but I remembered my mom mentioning that *Hebammen*[5] were used back in the day. I wondered if that was the same thing. I hadn't ever met anyone who had used one. Or had I just not listened?

"I think we'll have to think about it," I replied after an awkward pause.

"That's alright. If you decided to work with a midwife, you would also have the option of home birth."

"Definitely not," escaped my mouth without a second thought.

"In that case, your hospital will be Brigham and Women's. The hospital offers tours. You can see where everything is and how it all works. If you don't already, in addition to your pregnancy vitamins, you should take vitamin D. The over-the-counter ones are okay. Despite having only a few weeks to go, you can help your baby get in the right position if you walk as much as possible and use a yoga ball to sit on. Also, preparing your hospital bag now might be a good idea. From my experience, most parents-to-be think they still have time, but suddenly the baby arrives. Also, an anesthesiologist will be available to administer an epidural."

"Oh, that won't be necessary," I blurted out. I didn't want any painkillers. Women had given birth to children before any pain-suppressing medication existed.

"Okay," the nurse practitioner agreed with an expressionless face. "Your next appointment will be in four weeks. After you hit week thirty-four, you will have bi-weekly appointments. After week thirty-nine, we will change it to weekly or make a plan for when we should deliver the baby."

My husband and I both nodded. On our way out of the exam room, the nurse handed me a folder with several documents.

"Thanks," I said, and we both said goodbye.

Guido and I walked back home. My mind sorted through all of the information the nurse provided to us. Like an idiot, I'd just nodded. Well, I mean, why shouldn't I? I had just arrived. But still, I usually wasn't that taciturn. Even when the front desk lady proposed the next visit date to me, I just repeated my nodding, adding an awkward smile to make me stand out even more, but not in a good way.

"How about I give you a hundred dollars a week?" Guido interrupted, my thoughts replaying the doctor's office visit.

I side-eyed him. "Come again?"

"I know you make your own money, but this way you don't need to exchange any," he continued.

"Thanks." Slowly, I came back out of my headspace. "I thought we could check out one of those famous outlet malls. There are a couple not that far away," I proposed, egged on by the reminder to prepare for the baby.

"Oh," my hubby muttered.

He was surprised that I had planned to visit a store voluntarily. I was never a big shopper. Before explaining where we could find such a mall, Guido patted his coat down.

"Did you bring your keys?" he panted.

"My keys? You haven't given me any yet," I retorted, annoyed with myself.

"I think I forgot mine," Guido confessed.

"In the apartment?" I questioned stupidly.

He nodded, ashamed. "Yeah, I think so."

"Could you call your landlord?"

"Maybe," Guido answered. He pulled out his flip phone.

"How can it be that you still live like in the nineties but manage to survive in this century?" I remarked.

"As long as I can call someone, this device does exactly what it is supposed to do," Guido snarked back.

Who is calling anyone on their phone? I wanted to spout, but held my breath. Besides video-calling my friends, even my mom used text-messaging applications. Guido typed on the keyboard with his pointer finger.

The cold drifted into my inner layers. I shifted from my left foot to my right to help circulate my blood. My mouth opened but quickly closed again. I increased my movement. But I needed a nugget, a branch, something to lift my spirits. Even when I wasn't pregnant, coldness trumped hunger. Otherwise, I morphed into a bundle of spite.

I caged my emotions. Guido tried, but he only fumbled around without pressing his phone against his ear. Honestly, I could live if Guido left a message on an answering machine at this point. At least he would have reached out for help. Unfortunately, heat rose on his neck, and the frantic movements of his fingers gave his panic away.

"You don't have a number?"

My husband's face coloring faded out. "No," he squeaked out.

"Well, how about we buzz everyone in the house? Maybe they could call the landlord for us," I proposed.

"We could try it, but I've barely seen or spoken to the other people in the building."

"And?" I pushed.

"What if they think we want to break into their apartment?"

His question made me hold my finger right before pushing the first button. I completely understood what he meant. After all, "Opportunities make thieves," unfortunately.

"What do we do now?" At home, we could pluck plenty of options out of thin air. Each of our parents hid emergency keys. Here, now, a small dark hole opened up under my feet.

"I know!" Guido shouted with an idea, guiding me away from the entrance.

"Where are we going?" I asked as we marched along the street.

"To the back of the house," Guido said.

"The back of the house? But don't you need a key for the back door?"

"I am unsure about a back door, but there are fire escape stairs." We rounded the corner at the intersection.

I noticed a rustic platform—the metal stairs behind the kitchen window. I imagined this space to be an excellent spot in the summer.

We circled into the back alley behind two rows of houses. I marveled at the symmetry of the street. Three sets of metal stairs with three platforms linked together behind each building. Unfortunately, I hadn't paid attention and didn't count the houses. I didn't know which one was ours. Also, none of the bottom stairs touched the ground. Climbing had never been my strong suit, regardless of how fit I used to be . . . but pregnant?

"I think this is it," Guido said. We stopped at the fifth house from the corner. The stairs hung around two feet above my head. Guido reached for the end of the retractable metal construction, but his stretched-out arm missed by about a foot.

"How about you give me a lift?" I proposed.

"Sure," my husband agreed. Guido wrapped his arms around my thighs, boosting me up. Easily, my hand reached the lowest metal bar. After only two pulls, the stairs moved. They flipped downward, narrowly missing my face.

"Well, this wasn't too bad," Guido said.

"After you," I replied.

He climbed up one flight of stairs, with me close on his heels.

"What do you think are the chances that someone would call the police?" I huffed behind him.

"I don't want to think about it," Guido said.

"Me neither, but I just wanted to say that I feel very uncomfortable sneaking up in a dark alley to break into an apartment."

"Noted," Guido acknowledged, stopping any further uneasy discussion.

Without any hurdles, we managed to reach the third floor. Every time we passed a window, I fixed my eyes on the next stairs, hoping we wouldn't be seen.

Guido pushed the bottom window frame up, and to my surprise, the window snapped open with barely any resistance.

My mouth gaped open. "Was the window unlocked?"

"No." Guido's tone swam with incredulity.

My husband climbed into the kitchen first, and then he helped me come through. Guido relocked the window behind me before placing one fork, knife, and spoon on its frame. I wanted to protest—one-third of our silverware protected us. But if someone broke in, the metal clattering to the floor sounded the alarm.

"I am going to push the stairs back up," announced Guido. I nodded and watched him leave with the keys.

Tucked in the bed already, Guido joined me thirty minutes later, holding my hand.

"We have to leave. This is stressing me out," I declared matter-of-factly.

He nodded. "I understand how you feel. I will probably sleep with one eye open."

"We have to move," I concluded.

His eyes widened. "But where?"

"Home!"

"Home? I can't just leave," Guido protested, already shaking his head.

"Why not?" I asked, and Guido embraced me. "Can we just move, at least?"

"Sure, but I don't know how long it will take to find a place."

I frowned. "How did you find this place?"

"Craigslist. But do you remember how long I was looking for a place back home? It took me months to find this apartment."

"It's because you weren't here." I sighed. "Maybe you could ask your colleagues for leads?"

He laughed. "You mean all ten?"

"Why not? If only one person knows someone with a lead, that's more than what we know now."

Guido rubbed the back of his neck. "You are right. We can't stay here. But I can't promise how quickly we can find a new place."

<u>Friday</u>

I settled down in the beanbag in the living room. Sun rays warmed my face. The wind rustled the leaves on the trees outside the windows. Initially, I wanted to make a list of things we needed. And this place needed a lot to make it homely. Instead, anguish diminished my *I just arrived in a new country* glow. Instead of making bullet points of the best restaurants, what I should see before the baby comes, and perhaps trying to learn to cook, I dwelled over my journal to figure out what I wanted in our next apartment.

1)The place should have a good security system.

2)Minimum two rooms—I mean bedrooms.

3)Long showerhead.

4)Possibly a bathtub.

5)A kitchen.

6)I love this walk-in closet. I would be happy to have that

again if the hangers fit.

7)What else?

For the time being, this was it. A light bulb illuminated my thoughts. What would happen with this place? If Guido had a three-month termination period like our place back home, a move wouldn't make any sense.

That Night

A strange noise made my eyes go wide. Only one conclusion made sense. Someone was cutting down a tree—or so the noise made me believe. I looked at Guido. He didn't snore. The origin of the human-made noise was close by, though. Instinctively, I pressed my ear against the bedroom wall. *Aha!* Our neighbor was the culprit of the nightly disturbance. Rattled by this sleep interruption, I pulled my pillow around my head to block both my ears. The grumbling of the snoring from the other side of the wall did not subside.

A restlessness engulfed me, spurred by vivid imaginary pictures of someone breaking into the neighboring apartment. And I heard it all.

What would I do? *Could* I do anything? I tossed and turned, hoping to shake away the film in my head.

<u>Saturday</u>

Instead of dancing on cloud nine, a grayness colored any romanticizing thoughts of being in a foreign country. Thanks to Guido, the day started off with a hot brew of coffee. But we spent the rest of the day slugging around the apartment. The sleepless night brought out my laziness while Guido searched and posted to unearth a new option for us to live. I couldn't help him. I couldn't talk to my sister. I couldn't read any books. I only walked, napped, and ate whatever Guido gave me.

Of course, we had those times back home when days did not go as planned. When he'd decided to take the position to help implement the software in his employer's cashier system, I only presumed he could have backed out after learning that I was pregnant. But somehow, life lacked some sort of logic.

Instead, I gathered all the vacation time I had left before my maternity leave started and prepared a transitional document for my replacement as a controller in the lemonade company. Luckily, Nina had interned with me. Still, I turned my lists into a readable document, ensured that my Post-it system worked for her, and drilled into her that she would write down anything and everything if she changed the system. Despite all that, I wondered if I would recognize my place of work when I returned.

I had already received emails. I only put the work email access on my computer as a backup. But I regretted this idea after I received the first notification from work. Despite only being cc'd, I felt the urge to respond. On the plus side, Nina seemed to have survived her first week by herself. As the lemonade business was booming, I already knew that she would have a job alongside me once I returned to work.

The corners of my lips lifted. I was looking forward to returning already. I pushed my eyebrows together. I had just arrived for an adventure. This might be a real adventure and not a romanticized version of life. I took a deep breath, in and out. This was my life, and I would make the most out of it . . . after I had a nap. I was so tired.

<u>Sunday</u>

Haaaa! What a week it was! I had imagined going on a quest to explore Boston. Drinking and tasting our way through all the cafés my new neighborhood had to offer while gazing into the eyes of my long-"lost" husband.

Instead, I met our neighbor. Or more like the sounds the person emitted while sleeping. I should have been grateful that the snoring was the only sound filtering through the walls.

This drilled home again that I wanted to move. I did not want to wait for something serious to happen. This neighborhood looked and felt safe from the outside, but only until something happened to one of us. And I wanted to prevent that. Maybe the facade looked better than the interior. After all, I hadn't met anyone from this building or other apartments yet.

Oh, that reminded me . . . "Guido! Do we have to find a replacement for this place when we move out?" I inquired.

He turned his attention to me from the dirty water in the kitchen sink. "No. I called the landlord on Friday to explain to him that we want to move as soon as we find something new. And he told me that he's just about to send everybody an eviction notice anyway because he is selling the building."

"What?" I whispered. Elation, confusion, and disgust crisscrossed in my mind. That meant we *had* to move. We *had* to find something. The shift from *we wanted to move* to *we had to move* compressed my emotions into a pit in my stomach.

A Whole New World

OKTOBER

M	D	M	D	F	S	S
				1	2	③
4	5	6	7	8	9	10
11	12	13	14	15	16	17
18	19	20	21	22	23	24
25	26	27	28	29	30	㉛

To do

- new showerhead
- make list of what I need for the babe

monday 18

- Take a walk
- Drink more water
- Worry Less

tuesday 19

- walk, walk, walk

wednesday 20

- Pack up everything

thursday 21

We are moving

friday 22

- walk
- Find vitamins

saturday 23

sunday 24

- call Ulrike

Week 27

A Whole New World

<u>Tuesday</u>

Guido entered the living room with wide arms. "I found a place," he announced. "We'll move this week."

"What?!" I shrieked, caused by panic or euphoria—or both. "How?"

"I thought you'd be happy," Guido said with a frown.

"I am. I just thought that it would take a while. Not that we have a while, I guess, but after you said you looked for a long time to find a place,

I just thought that your search would take a while," I rambled.

"Well, I took your advice. I asked my colleagues for any leads, and Barret has a friend desperate for someone to take over his lease."

"Ha," I gulped, streamlining my thoughts. "Have you seen the place? Have you tried to break into the new apartment? How many square meters? What's the price? What's included in the rent? Can I see it?"

Guido took a deep breath. "I haven't seen it yet. It is near Union Square. The rent will be three thousand dollars. It's two bedrooms, but I don't know the exact size."

"This is a joke, right?" I exclaimed. Guido stared me down. "Three thousand dollars?" I barely earned that much after taxes. "How much are you making a month?" I choked out.

"Five and a half thousand," he replied nonchalantly.

My eyes widened, and my fingers touched my temples. Question after question flashed through my mind. But only one stormed out of my mouth. "Are we rich?"

"Hardly. Almost nothing is left after rent, bills, and groceries," he scoffed.

"Okay, I can't even. Are you saying this is what you are paying now?" I piped out air through my clenched teeth.

"Yep."

"Is the new place similar to this?" I choked out.

"I assume so." Guido shrugged his shoulders.

My jaw tightened. *He assumed so.* "You haven't seen the place? I don't understand. That doesn't make sense. I mean . . ." His words left me flabbergasted.

"Listen," Guido implored, "this is our opportunity to move. We have no choice anyway."

"But . . ." I let the word hang in the air. A repetition of my previous questions brought no new answers. And how could the rent be so high? We paid only $1,500 for seven hundred square feet back home. We split the rent in two.

There had to be a silver lining in this April Fools'–like situation.

"Is there anything included?" I pressed.

He shrugged. "Water."

"No electricity?" I moaned.

Guido shook his head from left to right. "No gas either."

"Gas?" I repeated. Deflated, I stumbled onto the floor cushion. Scanning our current place, I hoped the new apartment would be better. Or could the new place be even worse? But we had to hope for the best. It could be the same, maybe? But with more security.

"Do you know why the other person left the apartment?" I challenged Guido.

He answered, "Barret mentioned that he moved to California to start a new position there."

I backed off. After all, this opportunity had fallen into our lap. Guido promised he could shoulder the price tag. I just hoped Guido's colleague didn't set us up with a run-down hole.

. . .

Wednesday

We packed our belongings and filled up travel totes, backpacks, and trash bags within a day. Actually, within the morning, thanks to Guido's mere handful of furniture.

During the moving process, I came to an exciting conclusion. If the new place turned out to be a hellhole, I would just pack my stuff and return to my own four walls. There, my home, parents, sister, friends—a life—waited. But my decision could create tension between Guido and me. Anxious about telling him about my resolution, I tucked my thoughts into the darkest corner of my mind. The possible consequences of sharing my opinion scared me.

Would our marriage continue if I left? Probably. Maybe. Honestly, I wasn't sure. Over the course of the past twenty years, I have witnessed relationships shutter for less.

There it was. One of my biggest issues. Avoidance of confrontation. Even in times like these, a hurdle of doubt held me back from having an honest conversation with my husband about how I felt. Only to avoid inconvenient consequences.

Yet whose fault would it be if he missed the birth of our child? Guido had already declared his intentions to fulfill his employment obligations despite the special circumstances. Back home, however, a safe place and friendly faces surrounded me. There, I understood every word the doctor told me, and I didn't need to figure anything out. Having a baby in a foreign country was one thing, but traveling across the world only to move again so soon while pregnant was another. The stress caused by these thoughts unfocused my eyes. I took a deep breath in and a deep breath out. Everything would be alright. Guido was a good partner. I sighed and zipped up my backpack.

Thursday

Bags piled in front of our soon-to-be old home. I snapped a picture I planned to send my sister eventually to prove to her that we were moving and how little we had to move.

"I think that's Barret." Guido pointed at a white van. My eyes followed the vehicle until it stopped next to us.

"Good morning," a balding man greeted us. Wrinkles around his eyes and gray stubble on his chin placed him somewhere in his fifties.

"Good morning, Barret. Thanks for helping. This is Mareike," Guido said.

Barret had stepped out of a small truck with red letters spelling out *U-Haul*. I reread the word several times but didn't get why a company would name itself in a way that implied customers howled like a wolf.

"Good morning. Nice to meet you." Barret stretched out his hand. I mirrored his actions.

"Nice to meet you as well," I replied.

"My wife and I are redoing our house and thought you might have some use for these." Guido's colleague pointed inside the truck. A navy-blue sofa, a mahogany dining table, and a white coffee table with a glass mosaic were piled inside.

"Thank you," Guido and I declared in unison.

"You guys must have read my mind," I continued.

"Well, I asked Guido if he had more in the living room now than he did at his housewarming party. And his answer was no. So we figured you might be happy for some things," Barret explained.

"That's true. I already wondered where I could obtain more furniture for the apartment. So thank you," I repeated.

"Oh, I also have a yoga ball. Collette thought that you could possibly use it." Barret pulled a box out from the front of the truck.

"Thanks. That is very kind of you." I appreciated his generosity and took the unopened box.

With Barret's help, our stuff—my hiking backpack, Guido's hiking backpack, a blue rolling travel bag, a box with kitchen items, a bag full of personal hygiene products, toilet paper, towels, Guido's bike, the kitchen table and chairs, and the floor cushion—was loaded up within thirty minutes.

Barret drove, Guido sat in the middle, and I watched the world travel by out the passenger-side window. Bikes zipped past. Cars turned right without the light being green. Pedestrians crossed the street wherever they saw fit. My eyes tried to absorb all the details of the houses, stores, parks, and street names, but a disconnect to the outside world set in. An overwhelming feeling gripped my mind. I took a deep breath in and out. *I have enough time to discover all of this*, I promised myself.

"So, Mareike," Barret began.

I pulled my head out of my daydreams. "Yes?"

"We were just talking about the Halloween party next weekend. Nicole is organizing it. You are welcome to come."

"Thanks." My heart rate increased with excitement. I loved a good party. I loved to dress up. I loved to get to know people and maybe even make friends.

With a smile plastered on my face, we parked in front of our new apartment building. I could have sworn we were still in the old neighborhood.

The three-story houses resembled one another. Staring at my new temporary home, I pondered if Potsdam's picturesque architecture confused outsiders too. After all, most of the buildings twinned with each other. Perhaps the city imposed many rules on redoing houses to align with the historical appearance. To be honest, these rules brought a specific identity to my home. I kinda liked it. *Ha*, I'd never thought about my city in this way.

To my surprise, once again another door guarded the main house door of the building. The first frame snapped back with a bang every time we carried our belongings through. After the fifth time, Barret unhinged the spring. And of course the new apartment was also on the third floor.

Thanks to the steep stairs, the guys barely got the mattress, sofa, and table upstairs. I wondered why the architects of these houses never warmed to the idea of installing furniture cranes on the roof.

This apartment resembled the previous one, only with one tiny room more. I scratched my convex belly. Perhaps a baby room. The occupants before us left a flat-screen TV, but the display didn't work. "I can repair the television," Guido assured me.

A gasp of joy escaped my mouth when I walked into the bedroom. The walk-in closet provided enough space to let the hangers swing freely.

The kitchen was an actual kitchen. I'd tracked down fridges and hauled and installed counters and shelves more often than I had fingers in the last ten years. One feature in the kitchen intrigued me. I wasn't a big pantry person, but I loved the extra storage. When checking out said extra space, my eyes bulged at the stairs leading down. An unpleasant tingle in my tummy caused me to close the door instead. A button in the middle of the round doorknob stood out. I pushed the metal piece in, hoping I locked the door.

A little picture popped up in my mind. The previous apartment didn't have any door levers on either door. Maybe doorknobs were a standard feature here. I could not remember having seen a doorknob like this anywhere back home.

Another thing I'd noticed on our way from the airport to Guido's place was the windows. The two pieces opened from the top or the bottom. In front of most windows, a net protected the inside from insects. My mother would love this idea. How come these fly protectors hadn't yet pushed through on the German home-improvement market? Every summer, we worked on a fly-repellent solution. A couple of years ago, my parents had decked Ulrike and me out with sticky tape to hang around the house. The contraption worked somewhat. But the net in front of the window simply blocked the insects out. Ingenious.

Friday

I watched a squirrel race over the wires, jumping on a roof, then onto a tree, before the small animal vanished out of my sight. Cold air breezed through the living room. I tightened my cardigan. I opened my journal to scan my weekly schedule. Nothing was planned. No meetups with girlfriends after work, no festivals to look forward to, no birthday parties to attend, no family dinners to join in. A sense of freedom washed over me. But the emotion didn't feel real. I was a stranger, not just in a different town but in another country. I couldn't enjoy this no-strings-attached situation. My time here wasn't a vacation.

I reached for the doctor's note to remind myself what vitamins I needed and to pencil the next appointment into my calendar.

My eyes glanced over the date. October 11 stood there as my next appointment. I'd expected to read something like November 13. Confused, I reread the date again: 11/10.

The date printed on the paper was in the past and not four weeks in the future. Puzzled, I stared at the date. I got sucked into the fictitious world of time travel and was about to figure the plot twist out! Confused, I shook my head. I'd missed crucial information.

Instead of thinking the whole situation through, I wrapped Guido's comfy jacket over my arms. At least I could get the supplements. I pressed my feet into my boots, managing to tie my laces—barely. My growing bump made seemingly simple activities hard work. *Ding-dong*, alarmed the doorbell. I pulled myself up to open the door.

A woman of about thirty with a pixie haircut held a small child on her right hip and, behind her, twirled a toddler.

"Hey, I'm sorry. Mercer rang the bell by accident," the woman apologized. She followed my gaze. "This is Mercer. And this is Attila." The mother of two shifted her youngest to her other hip.

"No worries. What a nice name," I said. I made a mental note to research the name. Perhaps I had stumbled upon a good one for us to add to our list. We'd pored over baby name books and websites for hours, yet we hadn't found one we liked.

"Thanks. I am Henrietta," she replied.

"I am Mareike."

"We live right next door. I hope the kids haven't been too loud," she said with a smile.

I smiled back. "I haven't heard anything. But we just moved in."

"Well, it was nice meeting you. I have to get these kids down for a nap."

"Nice meeting you too!" I replied. Henrietta opened her white door, which was next to ours. I pushed my shoelaces into the shaft of my boots, zipped up Guido's jacket, and closed our door behind me to run my single errand.

I followed Guido's instructions on my quest to find a pharmacy. He'd even drawn me a little map last night. On my way, I turned on the wrong corner several times. I compared the street names on his map with the street corner where I paused. They didn't match up. On the bright side, I found a school that looked about twice the size of mine with the name of Argenziano, stumbled over several small shops, a cute little playground, and several small day cares. Unfortunately, I forgot my notebook at home to mark their locations.

Since my positive pregnancy test, I'd paid much more attention to kids' stuff. Not only did playgrounds and day cares pique my interest, but strollers, kids' toys, and baby carriers suddenly filtered through my consciousness.

I made quick decisions if I liked what I saw. I only wished my mother or sister were here. I never thought I would say that—I missed them. I was so used to having them around all the time that I felt a little bit of distance wouldn't *hurt* any of us. Well, true, the distance didn't hurt me. It showed me how much I missed them.

While marveling over everything baby, I stopped in my tracks, frozen to the ground. *D-R-U-G* spelled the first word above the entrance. My chin fell to the floor. I could not comprehend the words above the door—*Drug Store*.

I gawked from the sidewalk. The doors slid open and closed whenever someone rushed in or out. Everyone looked "normal." *Why wouldn't they? What did I expect?*

Actually, a vivid picture spun up in my head: If I went into the store, I would find small piles of powder, weed, pill collections, and crystallized drugs next to a scale and in front signs with the price per ounce lined up in rows seen through a glass window. Behind them, sales personnel in white lab coats ask: "What can I get you? We have everything from re-energizers, like Molly, to forget-me-nots, like weed, in twelve different flavors. We don't serve aerosols, glue, or gas. If you prefer sniffing, you should seek help."

Even though my uncomfortable emotions froze my feet to the ground, I decided to lead with my head after a "normal"-looking woman pushing a stroller came out of the store.

My logical reasoning propelled me forward. The glass door slid open. A wall of spice in the air hit my nostrils. My eyes only saw orange. Perhaps my pregnancy caused psychedelic sensations? Ever since my second trimester, smells did seem stronger. I even persuaded my hubby to stop bathing in his aftershave; moss or whatever made me gag. But would ginger layering the air infuriate me when I was not pregnant?

I moved toward the orange wall. These products were labeled "pumpkin spice." At the back of the store, bold red letters headlined: *Pharmacy.* My brain connected the dots. My veins pumped blood into my cheeks. I guessed the pharmacy sold medications, ergo . . . drugstore. *Huh.*

Several signs hung from the ceiling, grouping the products sold in different aisles like personal care, household, teeth, shaving, bathroom, and seasonal.

The air in my nostrils cleared up alright, but a new sensation crawled in. A faint scent lingered. A mix of different products caused an aromatic memory callback. Chocolates mixed with scents of deodorants. Aftershaves, sweets, and fruits intermingled with an overload of colors. With the unusual smells, the variety of products, and the packaging colors, the whole experience transported me to an *Intershop.*[1]

Unfortunately, we have yet to receive any D-mark to buy anything. If we managed, my mother would spend the money on After Eight, the delicious chocolate mint-flavored thin rectangular wafers. Excited, I tiptoed along the shelves like a little kid on Christmas Eve.

Back then no cash lined my wallet, but during this outing enough was contained in my purse to satisfy most of my needs in the pharmacy, thanks to my husband.

I loaded up a cart as if the world ended in seven days. I bought four fluffy baby blankets because the price tag buzzed with a "75% off" sticker, along with a new hair dryer with the correct plug. I sniffed through all the bodywash bottles and dropped Kiwi-Strawberry-Peach into my basket because why not? And I added some razor blades. Guido went through the blades in no time, along with snacks, mainly containing chocolate. I was pleased with my haul and lined up behind a woman draped in a flaming red coat.

"Do you have a rewards card with us?" inquired the customer's sales associate behind the counter. The shopper nodded. "You can type in your number right here." The cashier prompted the lady in front of me toward a credit card payment machine on the counter. The customer punched in her numbers on the keypad. On the other side of the counter, the sales associate scanned the items: diapers, shower gel, a fine liner, and a hairbrush.

"Your total is $45.99. Would you like to use your points?" the sales clerk asked.

"Well, I have those." The woman before me pushed a small pile of paper toward the cashier, who lifted one paper after another. She scanned each.

"And now I would like to use my rewards," the customer said.

The cashier busied herself on the computer display. "That brings your total down to forty-nine cents."

Wait, what? I wanted to shout out. *How could this be?* Didn't the store employee say the items' price tag was over forty dollars? *What just happened?* The questions hung on my lips, but I bit them back. Nothing in this interaction made any sense, likely including my questions.

The cashier bagged up all the items. The lady placed two silver coins on the counter. I rubbed my eyes. How could two coins pay for all her stuff?

"What's your phone number?" the cashier said, now addressing me. My eyes trailed the woman leaving the store. Still mind-blown, my attention slowly shifted to the store employee.

"I don't have a number," I mumbled.

"Do you have a rewards card with us?"

I shook my head no.

"Would you like to sign up for one?"

"No thanks."

The cashier scanned my items. "That's $89.57." A gasp escaped my lips. Ninety dollars? *How did this happen?* Well, actually, I knew how. During my state of euphoria, my inner calculator blacked out. And I completely forgot to buy what I came here for to begin with. I could quickly grab the vitamin D, but my feet didn't move.

The store employee waited for me to shell out the money. My cheeks burned. I opened my wallet to count the bills without a word, but I was completely stiff.

* * *

Broke, I poured out my hunting trophies on the kitchen table. Another pressing matter crystallized because of the diminished stash of cash in my purse. How much money would I actually need during my stay? I could have easily gotten by for a week or more with one hundred bucks back home. I mean, I could pretend that this was just a one-off, but what I bought wasn't so crazy.

Guido told me not to bother exchanging money despite my usual salary hitting my bank account. In the long run, I'd lose money with fees and the daily changing exchange rate. We hadn't really discussed how to manage our finances here, but he'd offered to give me as much money as I wanted. The invitation doubled as an opportunity to pull his leg, but I stayed tame and only asked for $100 a week. However, now the money sifted through my fingers like sand.

A discussion needed to happen. Technically, my expenses shouldn't be high. Guido paid all the bills. He went grocery shopping. Still, the lack of coziness in the house and missing baby stuff might present more of a dent in his bank account than he expected.

I swung myself onto the sofa in the living room. After only a couple of minutes, a slight shiver woke me up from my mini-nap. My body temperature had cooled off during my rest, along with the apartment.

I searched for the heater, but nothing caught my eye. No switch or dial stood out to increase the warmth in the room. Could there be none? *No way*. Perhaps the living room displayed a digital one on the wall. *Nope*. The apartment had apparently experienced its last renovation a couple of decades ago. But there had to be a switch, a thermostat, to heat our four walls. And there wasn't an alternative heating source either, like a fireplace. From what I remembered, Boston had proper winters, just like us.

On the other hand, perhaps this place didn't have a built-in heating system, and the landlord expected us to use room heaters. I had heard horror stories about crooked landlords from our side of the Atlantic. But for three thousand dollars a month, that would be an absolute scam.

I refocused my eyes, searching every inch of the walls from left to right. And just in case, from the bottom to the top too. Nothing, but my eyes lingered on a white metal box peeking out from behind the sofa, right under the window. My limbs warmed up by the sheer sight.

I pulled on the sofa. First on the left side, then on the right, until I could squeeze through the gap. I pushed the couch away from the wall, and on the flat surface, a long metal bar stretched across the bottom of the inside wall. The outer shell emitted iciness. I crawled along the metal bar, searching for the knob to turn on the heater. But nothing. I pressed on. My fingers slid along the bottom, just in case. There was nothing on either side of the metal bar, only dust: no knob, switch, or button. I searched again for a control panel on the walls, just in case. But my fruitless hunt only ended in more frustration and shivers.

Giving up, I shuffled into the bedroom. My cream cardigan hung behind the door, so I slipped the knitted arms over my skin and snuggled up in the bed.

My hand cradled my phone in an attempt to call Guido, but no ringing noise escaped from the internal speaker. I forgot I had canceled the contract three months ago. So, no roaming. For the time being, the electronic device was useless. *Oh no*. I just remembered. I'd forgotten to cancel our streaming services. I sighed. I hated monthly fees. Subscriptions were the worst.

Last year, my mother discovered that she still paid for our *Mickey Mouse* magazine, which I'd devoured until a decade ago—I loved to collect cards illustrating the world's natural wonders, like Niagara Falls. They'd stopped showing up at our doorstep years ago. We guessed where the paid magazines went during one of our afternoon café rounds. My father visibly turned red. He confessed he had been giving them to the neighbor's kids week after week. Yet he failed to mention his generosity to his wife.

Still frozen despite the sofa-pushing workout, I decided to do more physical activities to increase my body temperature. I pulled the yoga ball out of the box. The green ball unfolded on two sides: one left, one right. The opening contained one white peg. My heart sank. This wasn't a simple beach ball. I needed a pump.

Surely, we owned a pump . . . I hadn't seen one, but Guido rode his bike every day. He had to own a pump. But where was it? We didn't have a basement, at least none that I knew of. And he always kept his bike in the house. I couldn't fathom why he didn't leave his bicycle outside like everyone else.

If he had a pump, the manual air pressurizer had to be in the house. I searched every corner. The barely furnished two-bedroom apartment quickly revealed no pump of any kind.

However, the sparse look of our place grew on me. Even the contents of my hiking backpack didn't increase the volume by much. Of the fifty pounds I was allowed to bring on the airplane, seven would be eaten. Guido missed his Haribo gummy bears, Ritter Sport and Milky Way chocolates, and, of course, licorice.

He convinced me, "We can buy you more clothes here, but not German treats."

My mother had jumped at the opportunity. She loved to spoil her son-in-law, even though he was the reason one of her children was traveling to another country. But having Guido added to her family seemed to have fulfilled the desire for a third child she couldn't have.

Unfortunately, the German treats didn't help me solve the yoga ball issue besides eating my frustration away. Without a pump, though, I placed the flat yoga ball next to the table in the living room. I hesitated a bit. The coffee table displayed a sunrise above the sea through a glass mosaic.

I stared at the flat ball. Yoga wasn't on my mind, but the baby was. Rumor had it that if I sat on the fitness equipment, the baby's head would go down, moving it into the right place for the birth. I'd questioned my previous doctor if the baby's head was required to look down already. I imagined my own time in my mom's tummy, hanging upside down, and grew nauseous.

Deep breaths filled my lungs with fresh oxygen. I watched sparrows flying from one overhanging wire to the next. The show amused me until I spotted a lump. I rubbed my eyes. The item on the cable sharpened. The longer I stared, the more refined the form became. My mind formed an explanation out of the pictures my pupils provided. A squirrel hung with his arms on the black wire, only swinging with the cable's movement.

Somebody else noticed the squirrel too. A toddler pointed at the animal. The mother spoke on her phone. A truck stopped with a big stamp on the side of its vehicle only five minutes later: *The Works*. Two men got out. One of them stepped up on the back of the vehicle. He reached for the carcass with a pole but to no avail. After a short discussion, the men drove off.

A truck's engine rumbled by the house. I moved back to the window. A vehicle with a moving arm stopped under the squirrel. Two stabilizers moved out of the car on the street. A man got out to climb on the truck's back. A platform atop a metal arm elevated. With gloved hands, the city employee extended his arm with a small pole to reach the squirrel. After three pokes, the dead creature fell into a container.

I readjusted my cardigan again. The sun had begun to shade our apartment already. I checked my watch—5:00 p.m. Soon, Guido would be home.

I prepared dinner. I wasn't a decent cook. The kitchen scared me. This old kitchen didn't help to diminish my hesitancy either. After a few days, I finally realized what the kitchen reminded me of . . . the TV show *Mad Men*. The sight provided the sensation of just stepping onto the show's set. Honestly, the well-kept appliances had a retro-chic vibe to them, but I was scared of gas. The numbers displayed Fahrenheit. This information did not transfer into usable knowledge for cooking.

I'd twisted the stove's dials to turn on one hot burner in the morning to make myself a cup of tea, but the flames didn't spring on. Only one thing was for sure. The stove was not only baby-proofed already but mom-proofed as well.

At least we had some bread. I cut off six pieces and added a cube of butter, salami slices, cheese, cucumbers, and radishes to a wooden board. I arranged tomatoes and smoked salmon on separate plates. I hoped to dig out some minced meat from the fridge but only found potato salad to prepare our dinner table.

"Hi, honey," Guido called out.

Happy to see him, I swung myself into his arms. "Dinner is ready," I announced.

"Great. I'm starving."

I pulled my cardigan tighter. A light draft drifted over my neck.

"Are you cold?" Guido asked.

I nodded. "Did you notice that the heaters don't have a knob to turn them on?"

When Guido moved here in July, there was no need for artificially made heat. Guido widened his eyes. "Is that the reason the sofa is in the middle of the room?" Slightly ashamed, I didn't answer. The moment he finished his question, I sensed what would come next.

"We talked about this," my husband reminded me. "If you need a hand, just wait for me."

"But I was cold and wanted to turn on the heater. Besides, I pushed the sofa along the floor." Truth be told, I had always been independent. I hated to wait for someone when I thought I could do an activity myself.

Guido got up. He checked out the scratch marks from the sofa on the floor. My cheeks burned. I hadn't thought about the floor panels. I guess the cold froze my brain.

"Where would you like to have the sofa?"

"There." I pointed to the left wall, separating our neighbors from us. "This way, the heat, if the system works, could ventilate freely, and we have direct access to the window."

Guido lifted the sofa on each corner to place kitchen towels under its feet. He pushed the three-seater around, brushing against the metal shell of the heater. The top wobbled, and the movement dislodged the end cap.

I checked the opposite end out and detached the second cap. Now the top cover was easy to lift off. My nose tingled. Balls of dust cluttered up the aluminum fins.

"Good thing you didn't find the on switch." Guido's comments echoed my sentiments. Burned dust wasn't my ideal room-refreshing scent.

"Do we have a vacuum?" I gasped.

"Not yet," Guido responded.

"You think we could ask the neighbors?" I inquired.

My husband nodded. "Sure."

After only two knocks, the door next to ours opened. A male voice greeted Guido. He called to someone in his apartment. Another set of footsteps drew closer along with Guido's.

Still kneeling, my head turned around to see a pair of black ballet flats. Heat rose in my cheeks at the sight. I would have offered her slippers, but I didn't have any.

"Hello again," Henrietta said.

"Hey," I greeted her in return. In my new neighbor's hand hung a vacuum.

"Oh, what are you guys doing?" Henrietta shifted her eyes to the opened baseboard heater.

"We moved the sofa, and the heater fell apart."

"Do you know how to turn on the heater?" Guido asked.

"Of course, honey. It's right here." Henrietta proceeded back to the hallway. Opposite the entrance hung a dial, midair on the wall. "Here! You just turn it on." She twisted the dial. Immediately, pipes sprang into action in the walls. An audible flow moved through the air. "We usually leave it on seventy-five."

I turned to Guido. "What's seventy-five?"

"It's about twenty-five Celsius."

"You don't have heaters in Germany?"

Henrietta questioned. Her eyes stared at Guido. I bit my lips.

"We do, but you regulate the heat directly on the heater."

"How inconvenient," Henrietta replied.

"Hey," boomed a male voice. "A little help, please."

"I'm coming right over!" Henrietta hollered. She rolled her eyes. "There is just no break. But you'll see." Henrietta glanced at my growing belly. "We should get together sometime." She handed the vacuum to Guido.

Guido plugged the appliance into the wall outlet. The vacuum nozzle sucked on the outside of the heating unit. I checked out the apartment for other heaters. On this quest, I counted the outlets as well. Ten spread out in our space. Baby-proofing topped my baby to-do list. To my surprise, I found no outlet in the bathroom again. A sinister thought crept into my mind. Were there too many accidents?

The vacuum inhaled most of the dust. Once it was sort of clean, Guido reattached the caps.

We continued in the smaller room, kitchen, and bathroom. We fell on the sofa anticipating the heat to warm the rooms up.

"Is that the yoga ball?" Guido inquired.

"Yes, but I couldn't find a pump."

"I don't have one. If I need air, I just stop at a public bike station."

"Oh," I sighed, disappointed.

"Just buy one. There is a store called Target just down the street. We might get everything for the baby there. By the way, when is your next checkup again?"

"Actually . . ." I pulled out a sheet full of information. My name, current address, and the next appointment graced the top of the first form. "I think they made a mistake. They wrote the wrong date on here."

"Let me see," Guido said. I handed him the paper. The moment after he glanced over the document, he let out a sudden burst of laughter.

Heat rose in my cheeks. "What's so funny?"

"The date. The date is so funny," Guido explained.

I ripped the paper out of his hand. I double-checked the date again. Despite staring at the numbers, no hidden meaning, like 666, popped into my mind. "Don't you think something is wrong with the eleventh of October as a follow-up appointment?"

Guido held his belly in an attempt to tame his outburst. "The date is not the eleventh of October. The date is the tenth of November." Irritated, I double-checked the date once more. The handwritten numbers after the words "next appointment" clearly read 11/10.

"What?"

"They say and write the month first and then the day here," Guido explained.

"Oh," was all I could say. I was dumbfounded. I had nothing more to add.

<u>Sunday</u>

"Good morning!" I declared to my sister. Two whole weeks passed until we finally connected via video call. We'd exchanged texts through my computer's messenger app after Guido connected my computer to the Internet, but we hadn't managed to talk due to the time difference. At home, I spoke to her almost every day.

"What do you mean, good morning? It's a good afternoon. It's almost two," Ulrike scolded.

"I forgot," I admitted.

"I wanna hear everything. I miss our Sunday chitchat already. I can't believe you guys moved in your condition!" my sister exclaimed.

"Me neither, but we had to. You wouldn't believe how easy it was to open the back window from the outside. I just didn't feel safe. And the eviction thing is another topic."

My sister said, "I hear ya. Is the new place better?"

"I don't know. I already discovered a hidden door in the kitchen with stairs. I locked it."

Ulrike gasped. "How strange."

"Yep. I don't understand yet what that is all about."

"Well, you'll figure it out."

"This new apartment is almost even more empty. I feel like a squatter despite forking out a fortune. We don't even have blanket covers, and there is no long shower hose."

"What? But you know you can buy all the missing things," my sister proposed.

"Yeah, I know. It's just that I am a little bit pissed that I have to deal with these things."

She scolded from the screen, "Just make a list, and go get it."

"We'll see. You won't believe what else." I carried my computer to the window. "What do you see?"

"Oh no way, it looks just like in *The Town*, doesn't it?"

"My thoughts exactly—the house style, the overhead wires."

"You could rewatch it and see if you pass by any of the places in the movie."

"That's a great idea, but first I need to get used to my new environment. I wish you could be here," I whined.

"Well . . . regardless, this is still an adventure. You'll be happy you did it in a year," Ulrike promised.

The Fifth Season

Week 28

The Fifth Season

<u>Monday</u>

A cold breeze swept around my nose. Gray clouds shifted in the sky. Nevertheless, I managed to keep a skip in my step on the way to Target. After a thirty-minute march, a two-story building nestled in an intersection down the main road came into view—a red dot surrounded by two red rings towered over me. The store easily spanned a block. After the glass doors closed behind me, I almost fell back out again. Countless aisles containing piled-high products overwhelmed me.

I dug out the list from one of the many pockets sewn into Guido's spare winter jacket to limit the number of products on my receipt. Only four bullet points graced the paper: a shower extension, vitamin D, a blanket cover, and a ball pump.

Following the signs hanging from the ceiling, along the way I was tempted to stop by shelves offering tableware, kitchen items, and pillows. Despite my hands edging forward to inspect each product, I restrained myself with a firm grip on my list.

Bedding showed up first. Duvets lined a whole row. I browsed the shelves, searching for covers, but saw only linens piled up. Sheets with pillowcases in various colors and patterns waited to be purchased, but only one set contained a cover for our blanket. The brown dots on a white background reminded me of animal droppings. Despite my desire to feel the fabric of a cover at night, I just could not purchase this set.

Baffled by the limited selection, I pushed my cart along until the baby section opened up in front of me with rows of diapers, wipes, lotions, powders, milks, and toys.

My feet glided over the floor to check out each and every single item. Eventually, I stumbled upon my next must-have item: vitamin D. The container with the most gel caps landed in my cart. The first strike-through on my list—even if the pen moved only in my head.

I ventured along to secure another desperately needed item in the house: a shower hose. It was one thing to sleep without bedcovers but another to clean a bathtub with a barely turning showerhead.

Surprisingly, I discovered the object of my desire. Three showerheads with different hose lengths hung in one row, only two aisles down. Each head provided four different spray settings. I grabbed the one with the longest hose without knowing how long the water pipeline stretched. Only the inch symbol indicated the full extent of length, and the conversion rate from the imperial to metric systems still needed to be added to my knowledge base.

Guido had illustrated on his finger the length of an inch. But the distance from his first to his second finger joint measured longer than mine. Thinking of measurements, an inch increased to a foot, which my sister used in her work. Maybe I should ask her why there wasn't a mini-foot instead of an inch, just like a meter to centimeter. Perhaps the unit should be called inchy-foot to follow that logic.

I scoured more aisles just for fun. My heart skipped a beat. The stationery area displayed a whole section of washi tapes, notebooks, and pens. Automatically, my hands grabbed a set of fine liners, rolls of patterned tape, and a dotted notebook.

I piled a notebook, several washi tapes, markers, and scrap paper into my cart. Satisfied with my findings, I continued the hunt for a ball pump.

I found a yoga ball pump next to some blocks in the sports section. Only one remained, as if everyone needed a ball pump simultaneously.

I headed toward the checkout lane but stopped in my tracks. A rolled-up fluffy red blanket had my name embroidered on the fabric—only figuratively—stashed in an oversized shipping box right in the middle of a wide aisle. Naturally, I dropped the nap inducer on top of everything else in my cart.

I trotted over to the row of cashiers, focusing straight ahead to avoid more temptations. I estimated the price tag to prepare myself for the damage. The items added up to roughly $120. The spit in my mouth vanished. The hole in my wallet deepened. However, we needed everything. Well, not entirely true, but still, I desired to keep everything.

Pre-buyer's regret set in. Back home, stickers, pens, journals, rulers, tapes, hole punchers, scrap papers, pencils, and threads were neatly organized and decorated a wall from floor to ceiling. My heart grew heavy with every item of stationery that I returned to its designated shelf space before I lined up to pay. At least my total should be just under seventy dollars.

My feet rubbed against the soles of my sneakers. Only three checkout counters serviced shoppers. Ten other cashier machines slept, unused. The long lines almost braided together. The checkout line only decreased by a few inches within thirty minutes. The cashiers scanned items from patient customers. Thirteen people before me had lined up with their overflowing carts. Almost all of the baskets on wheels contained a mix of household items and groceries, along with black and orange Halloween decorations.

Moaning from behind me wore down my patience. An older woman rubbed her glasses, balancing a stack of aquamarine towels in her arms. My timid smile evaporated in thin air when the lady focused on the cashier.

"Can you at least open one other line?" the senior yelled loud enough for everyone around us to hear. I paled. I could never have imagined saying these words out loud. To my surprise, an announcement over the loudspeaker requested another store employee to open another checkout.

The light of the number 9 turned on. The woman behind me pushed me forward. "You should go first. Otherwise, the baby will be born here."

"Are you sure?" I mumbled; regardless of how simple, each word crawled out of my mouth.

"Absolutely," the lady's voice boomed into my face.

After hurrying to the cashier, I placed all my items on the black conveyor belt.

"How are ya?" asked the cashier.

"I am fine. Thank you," I responded with my best English. The young woman's eyes widened once I finished my response. My accent couldn't have been more different from hers.

In school, we learned Oxford English. Truth be told, I never knew what that precisely meant. No English teachers of mine originated from any English-speaking country.

"Are you French?" the cashier inquired as she scanned all four of my items.

"I am German," I replied.

The cashier nodded while bagging my purchases. "That makes $74.35. Would you like to sign up for a credit card? You would get ten percent off today," she announced.

"No. I have cash." I grabbed a bunch of bills and coins.

Secretly, the foreign money welled excitement in me despite the bills feeling like play money to my unaccustomed fingers. I'd totally forgotten what different money felt like. Before the euro rolled out to most European countries, an envelope with francs, lire, or Dutch guilders kicked off the anticipation of the summer vacation trip to come when D-mark still ruled our financial world. Yet with all the advantages the euro might have brought, the excitement of traveling to a foreign place with the same money we had at home took it away . . . just a little bit.

"Would you like to have your receipt in the bag?"

Guido's words rang in my ear, prompted by the cashier's question. Apparently, ink on receipts could be unhealthy for pregnant women. "Um, yes, please," I replied, despite the itch to double-check the narrow strip of paper, curious to learn where I'd miscalculated by three to four dollars.

The sliding doors in front of me opened up. A gust of wind created goose bumps on my skin. The air contained a hint of winter. Guido's coat barely stretched enough to cover my growing bump. With a paper bag in hand, I braved the cold air flying around my nose.

Back at Home

As I unpacked my treasures from the shopping trip, a sting of the left-behind washi tape still reverberated in my heart. Yet to save some money brought glee back into my veins. Sentences like "Do you really need it?" or "Sorry, we can't afford it," marked my childhood. These words crippled my spending habits to the point of going above and beyond conservative. With Guido's help, I'd unlearned self-imposed restrictions. A knock on the door interrupted my self-reflection.

"Hi, Henrietta," I greeted my neighbor.

"How are you doing?" she asked. Before I could answer Henrietta's question, the mom of two held up a book. "I did some spring-cleaning and found this." The title read: *What to Expect When You're Expecting.* "I thought you might be interested in it."

"Oh, thanks." I lifted the gift from her hands. An inaudible murmur through a speaker rustled through the hallway. Henrietta checked her phone.

"It's the babies waking up from a nap," she explained, before returning to her own apartment.

The door clicked into its frame. I wondered if her apartment contained more space than ours. Our small second bedroom could work for a tiny child. The next-door apartment, however, housed four people.

The two kids may have shared a room. Ulrike and I only got separate areas when I turned ten. In the beginning, I missed her so much, only to not want her to come into my room ever again six months later—sibling's love.

Wednesday

I stretched out on the sofa. Henrietta's book rested in my hands. A mountain of pressure piled up on my shoulders. Since arriving here, I hadn't done much baby preparation. Heck, three weeks had passed before I bought my vitamins. Despite the ample amount of time on my hands, my enthusiasm for doing something useful displayed a minus on the scale.

Frankly, my brain was jumbled up. I lived in a different country for the first time. Plus, my limited mobility and muted energy levels made it difficult to complete any activity despite a whole list spelling every item out.

Henrietta's book lined up behind a stack I'd already consumed. During my breaks back home, newsletters posted about parents-to-be landed in my mailbox periodically. I bought books or borrowed them from the library. Naturally, I jotted down a list of things I thought we needed based on the information I'd gathered thus far. My focus shifted with my husband's absence and the birthing place up in the air.

Weeks whisked by with my head in the sand. Eventually, my mom cornered me.

"Listen, if you leave before the baby's born, you don't need clothes for the baby. So less luggage. Your maternity leave starts when? Third of December?" she probed. I nodded. "You will have to be back at work on the eighteenth of March?" Again, I nodded like a good little girl.

"I will probably fly back by myself," I responded. "Well, plus the baby. Guido should return in April and start his paternity leave then." Why didn't important things just simply fall in line smoothly?

"So the baby will be roughly six weeks old," my mother said.

"Yes, I think so," I replied.

Naturally, after our conversation, my mother stocked her house with six-week-old boy clothes. She even obtained a crib from her elementary school friend's daughter's best friend . . . or something along those lines.

I pulled out my journal. Only two crossed-off items on my never-ending list highlighted my underachievement. Why did someone who came out of my body need a room full of stuff?

Unfortunately, crying about my lack of preparedness didn't help. But days, weeks, and even months of room to work with still allowed me to check the main points off my list.

My eyes crisscrossed over the lines. After placing a couple of stars on some of the must-have baby items, my mashed brain revolted against the idea of absorbing any more offspring-related words.

Thursday

Another half-baked day floated by, filled with walks, checking social media for my friends' activities, and daydreaming. My eyes fluttered to the big-screen TV hanging on the wall. Conveniently, the remote control lay under the sofa. With one swing, I pulled it out.

Oh man, relief had flooded my heart when I noticed that I forgot to terminate my subscriptions to the various streaming services. But on the other hand, I paid more now. Back in the day, I cut down on my monthly cable payments, but suddenly streaming services had popped up, and we got subscriptions to most of them. Now I paid double what I used to. Unfortunately, the desire to watch a show whenever I wanted trumped my urge to save. And at this moment, these services rescued me from my thoughts and my worries.

After turning the television on, a reel of films lined the screen, all in English. The shows I had started a couple of weeks ago had vanished. So I returned to the suggestions, which included *The Town*, *The Social Network*, *Good Will Hunting*, *Black Mass*, *Gone Baby Gone*, and *Mystic River*.

A loose thought tugged at me. My left pointer finger bounced up and down in quick intervals. *Didn't all those flicks take place in Boston?*

Despite the proposed selections, nothing piqued my interest. I craved a light, fun movie and pulled up the old standby: *27 Dresses*. I laughed. I swooned. I cried—and I didn't know why.

The door suddenly unlocked, and Guido stepped in. "You're home already?" I called.

Darkness already dimmed our living room. I pulled my new blanket up.

"What happened?" Guido asked.

"Nothing." My broken voice, pale face, and red eyes told a different story. "I couldn't hold my tears back when I watched the movie," I confessed.

"What drama did you watch?" Concern layered my husband's voice.

"*27 Dresses*." Even before the title left my mouth, Guido rolled his eyes. After roughly thirty views, my husband was done with the movie. Every time I needed a lift, the film never disappointed me, but tears kept flooding my eyes this time. "I'm sorry, I can't stop crying. I don't know why." I rubbed my eyes.

Guido pulled me in. "How about we blame it on the hormones." His confidence stabilized me.

"I like that thought." My breathing steadied.

"Maybe the party tomorrow will cheer you up," Guido suggested.

"Party?"

"The Halloween party my coworker invited us to."

I pushed my eyebrows together. Despite rummaging through my brain, I had no memory of Guido informing me about a party.

"I mean the party where you dress up, like for *Fasching*,"[1] Guido explained.

"I know what Halloween is, but . . ." The sentence hung in the air. Perhaps he had told me, but I only pretended to listen.

Instead of arguing with my hubby to figure out exactly when he'd told me, I speculated, "Maybe I have baby brain already. But what are we going to wear?"

"We could swing by a costume store tomorrow."

"Or we could first brainstorm what we want to dress up as. Maybe we could make a costume ourselves," I proposed, but hit myself on the head before I finished the sentence. We weren't at home. In this apartment, we didn't have any resources.

Fasching brought out my creative side. A lot of excited energy created our costumes. However, somehow Ash Wednesday crept up on me every single year. Two weeks before the parties, my sister and I would realize our lateness. Year after year, we pulled through, though. For the past decade we'd come up with unique costumes under pressure, if I said so myself. One year we went as Greek goddesses, and for another we put Pikachu together only to do Super Mario the following year. At the beginning of my pregnancy, Ulrike jokingly proposed that I dress up as a kangaroo. The baby could rest in the pouch.

Sadly, though, I would miss Fasching, but there was the chance to dress up for Halloween. My memory flashed back to women carrying around a DIY oven or doll arms sticking out of a white shirt with bloodstains on them. Neither idea appealed to me. The bigger question still hung in the air. Did I want to bring attention to my growing bump or not?

Hmm. On second thought, I could dress up like a Greek goddess again. Wrapping a bedsheet around my body would cover up my baby bump. We only owned one, though. Even if I went draped in a white sheet, could we sleep without a sheet for the night, or would we have time to wash it? Would it dry before we crashed on the mattress? Perhaps . . . Maybe?

What could Guido be? Usually, he only dressed up because Ulrike and I made an outfit for him. He only wore it to humor us.

This year, though, Guido aspired to dress to impress. Why else did he propose to visit a costume store? These "party people" weren't his longtime friends or colleagues. He had just started a new job. Well, technically, he didn't, but this position placed him in a new office with people he didn't know, in a town he wasn't from, and a country he wasn't accustomed to.

I scanned our place, wandered into the bedroom, and checked out our closet. Guido's five white non-iron dress shirts were lined up on hangers. His ten polo shirts towered, color-coordinated, on a shelf below the hangers. Three pairs of jeans covered the lowest shelf.

My pile of clothes lay below his. Even though my mess bothered him, my hubby stopped remarking on my sloppiness after I spent months training him to clean the apartment with me every Saturday, along with countless weeks educating him that cooking and washing the dishes was a two-person job.

Suddenly, an idea sprung into my mind. I lingered on his gray polo shirt. My gears shifted. Two white stripes broke up the gray. The costume lay right in front of me—grayscale.

Sunday

My eyes scanned my weekly overview. My mouth gaped: Reformation Day. Usually, we commemorated this day, besides other festivities, with delicious raisin buns. Instead, I put the final touches on my husband's costume.

"I don't think anybody will get it," Guido complained.

I pushed my lips together. "I have an idea." I taped six black strips of my precious washi tape over Guido's right chest and wrote over two strips of R G B vertically with my white gel pen to indicate that grayscale is a variation of Red, Green, and Blue of screen's color models.

Pleased with myself, we put on our jackets to find our first stop before the party: the liquor store. We trotted along Mass Ave. I tightened my jacket to prevent the chilly air from cooling me down. Dressed-up kids chaperoned by adults crowded the sidewalks. Most of the children already carried a big loot of sweet treats. And most of the kids' costumes showed little protection from the frosty fall air. The children's orange plastic pumpkins overflowed with sweets despite the chill factor. It was freezing.

Perhaps because winter crept up, the atmosphere caused Fasching butterflies in my tummy. Come to think of it, 11/11 was also just around the corner, which initiated the fifth season. Oh, I loved me a great *Schnapszahl.*[2]

A scary thought formed in my head while we trailed behind a group of kids with a chaperone dressed as a unicorn. *What if they don't celebrate the beginning of the fifth season here?* That would mean no Berliner, not even an accidental one filled with mustard. I doubted Guido would like me cutting off his tie just because the clock turned eleven minutes past eleven at the beginning of the carnival season. Come to think of it, I hadn't even seen him wearing a tie since I got here.

"I was thinking we could take a trip to *the* Niagara Falls next weekend or the weekend after?" Guido proposed, pulling me out of my thoughts.

"What? The Niagara Falls are so close?"

My fingers shook. My feet trembled. I pinched myself. One of the world's most famous natural attractions existed just a short driving distance away? Niagara Falls used to be an unattainable destination. Ever since the waterfalls were featured on a collection card from one of my old *Mickey Mouse* magazines, I dreamed of visiting them. Not just them, though, but the Grand Canyon, the Great Barrier Reef, and the Northern Lights too. I never imagined I'd be able to visit one of them.

"This might be our only chance to see the waterfalls for real," Guido pointed out.

I nodded. Another thought tugged at me. A trip would give us some much-needed couple time. For the past few months, his absence had opened up an empty canyon in my life. Besides my family, no replacement for an excellent partner to hang with had materialized.

"It's a seven-hour trip," Guido said.

"Seven hours? For the weekend? That's like going from Bremen to Munich," I cried.

"We could leave Friday, stay in Albany for the night, and drive up on Saturday. I was just thinking that it is closer from here than from Potsdam."

He checkmated me. Any counter-argument I'd formed dissolved on the tip of my tongue.

Despite Guido putting this absolutely logical reasoning on the table, I didn't feel like going on a road trip just yet. Seven hours was still far. "I don't know. I just arrived. I haven't even really been to Boston yet."

"Maybe we could explore Boston this weekend and Niagara Falls the next," Guido proposed.

"That sounds like a plan," I said with a nod.

Guido opened the store's door. Rows of shelves with liquor opened up in front of us. My eyes scanned each label I passed carefully, yet none of the names rang a bell.

So my old habits set in. I chose two bottles with the label designs I liked best. My right hand held a blue bottle. Golden tree branches framed the maker's name, and the variety, Riesling, was my favorite. After years of slurping my favorite grape, I'd discovered an extensive flavor spectrum from sweet to dry.

My left hand held a dark brown bottle. The green label displayed a messy slated house on a patch of green grass. Below, in bold maroon letters, stood *Merlot*.

Guido scanned fridges filled with beer, which lined an entire wall. I grew up on *Wernesgrüner*.[3] That's what I drank. However, I joined my husband on his quest, just for kicks. My eyes lingered on Pumpkin Spice, Flannel Friday, hazel-, pecan-, and maple-infused beers. *Mmm.*

I continued to browse along the shelves to see what else the store carried. Shockingly, no *Paulaner*[4] dominated any prime viewing spot despite the advertised Oktoberfests on every corner. One row stocked different beer brands, and the aisle marker spelled out: *Craft Beer.* Instantaneously, paper supplies, scissors, glue, and rulers popped into my inner eye. I had so many questions.

Ten minutes later, Guido carried a mixed-flavor box of ghost-decorated Sam Adams six-packs toward the counter. In front of us stood two men. One of them wore a ninja costume. The other sported a red Lego piece.

"The ninja costume is a good idea," I marveled.

"I prefer the Lego," Guido replied.

"Do you want to be a brick?" I teased.

He snorted. "A Lego brick."

"Why would you voluntarily be called a brick?"

"Because it's a Lego."

"I wouldn't want to tell anyone that you dressed up like a brick," I said, before the man behind the counter turned his attention to us.

"ID, please," he requested.

ID? That meant identification, right? I pushed my eyebrows together. For the first time ever, I was asked to show proof of my age. I rummaged through every pocket of my jacket. Of course the last one I searched contained my blue wallet. I pulled out my ID and showed the card to the cashier.

"What is this?" he asked. My heart rate increased because of the skepticism in his voice.

"That's my identification card," I stammered.

"I don't know what it is. That means it could be a fake. I can't accept it." He pushed my ID back to me. My mind exploded. Yet there I stood, schooled by a random stranger in a foreign country.

Miraculously, though, Guido produced his passport out of the depths of his green backpack. To my surprise, the material hadn't fallen apart years ago. Quite the opposite— even without Guido tending to his backpack, the almost pristine fabric only showed a few black marks from his army year.

"How about this?" Guido held his international travel identification booklet up. Wide-eyed, I watched. The seller checked my husband's birthday.

A howl of protest developed in my throat. My ID contained translations in English and French in addition to German lines. Also, both of us also displayed signs of aging. A couple of gray hairs had grown on Guido's head, and we both had a few wrinkles. Well, that thought wasn't my proudest, though. Usually, I attempted to cheat time with concealers and hair dye, but today I wanted to play every card only to buy the liquor, despite not consuming a single drop.

The cashier accepted my husband's document and scanned the beer-carrying boxes and the two wine bottles. After Guido paid a small fortune for the alcoholic beverages, we returned to the street to be surrounded again by the Halloween spirit.

I cradled my belly. My face lit up. Groups of kids accompanying their parents still roamed the street to fill their plastic hollowed-out pumpkins. They knocked on doors. Once they opened, the children called out: "Trick or treat?" A bowl with sweet treats answered their question. I wondered, though, if anyone would pull a trick.

We not only passed several costumed groups of little ones but several decorated houses too. Some of these houses went all out, decorating the outside of their homes with spiderwebs on bushes, skeletons, and gravestones or blown-up monsters in their front yards. This sight increased the feeling of festivity by a thousandfold.

Guido guided me toward a row of the same house style. Three stories followed double garages on the ground level. All five houses displayed the exact same lined green facade. My husband rang the bell on the second home. I touched the outside of the house. The siding gave off an artificial feel, like vinyl. The scarlet-red door opened, and a female mummy greeted us. "Hi, Guido, come on in. You must be Mareike."

We stepped inside, and Guido closed the door behind us. "Yes, I am Mareike." My name came out sharper than I'd meant it. The crowded living room squeezed anxiety into me. Inside the house, strangers conversed with each other.

"Nice to finally meet you. I'm Nicole." Her big brown eyes twinkled.

My voice quivered. "I have heard about you as well."

She worked in the same office as Guido and kept the office running smoothly while also organizing social outings for the team. If Guido had a question, she was the one who answered it. Thanks to Nicole, our health insurance listed me alongside my husband. She'd even helped line up the gynecologist appointment before I ever set foot at the arrival gate.

"Guido, are you grayscale?" Nicole asked, scanning his outfit.

"Yes!" my husband exclaimed.

"What a great idea," Nicole said.

My husband gave me a proud look. "It's all on Mareike."

"That's awesome. You look amazing too," Nicole told me.

"Thanks," I whispered.

She asked, "How is everything going so far?"

"I am still getting used to my new surroundings." My weak tone barely resonated over the loud music.

"Hold on a sec." Nicole marched through costumed people in her living room. My head followed her through the crowd until she vanished behind Frankenstein.

Guido introduced me to various people whose names I forgot immediately. I wandered off to give Guido space to have fun instead of strangling his hand. Protecting my belly from the people around me, I made my way through monsters, witches, fairies, and movie characters. Timid smiles whooshed by my face. Unsteady eye contact flickered over my pupils until I found great company: the buffet.

Sliders, carrots, cucumber-filled sushi rolls, salsa, guacamole bowls, and chips decorated the marble island in the middle of the kitchen. My hand balanced a paper plate with one of each food item only seconds later. Leaning on the counter, I nibbled on a tomato-less mini-burger.

Crumbs of bread tumbled back onto my plate when I tried stuffing the whole thing into my mouth. The party in front of me could have taken place behind a wall. Back home, I wouldn't have hesitated to jump right in to converse with everyone. But here, my rusty English hindered me from diving in despite surviving doctor's appointments and shopping trips.

Instead, I stuffed the pieces of baked wheat into my mouth rather than using this perfect opportunity to break out of my shell. Having to use a second language brought my prickly side out. Instead of getting over my antisocial attitude, I munched on the food all evening.

* * *

After the party, Guido and I made our way down the quiet street. "Did you have fun?" he asked.

I shrugged my shoulders. I was unsure how I should explain to my husband that I had difficulty socializing, so I only answered, "I am feeling tired."

His hand warmed mine during the cool last night of October. Only a few other pedestrians headed to their destinations. The dressed-up kids from earlier already dreamed in their beds. Still, I expected the sidewalks to be filled with people. After all, a day of celebration of some sort had just passed. We'd attended a party, not filling our bodies with liquor only because of our special circumstances. Back home on a night like this, the pavement would be filled with people staggering, barely holding in their overflowing stomach contents or excessive liquid.

I probably would have been one of them. Yikes. But this year, no alcohol. I kinda liked the feeling.

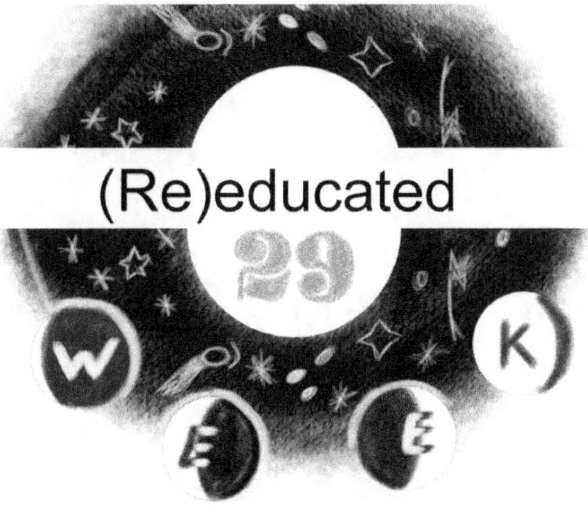

1
· walking
· prep dinner

monday

2
· look for a cooking class?
· walk

tuesday

3
· send bday e-mail to Doreen?
· walk

wednesday

4
· walk
· organize computer

thursday

5
· walk
· get organized

friday

6
Boston!!

saturday

7

sunday

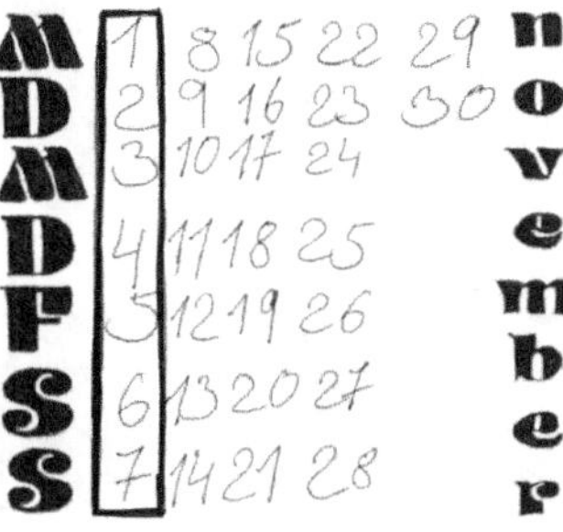

TO DO
· Walk every day
· Review Baby List
· Clear out e-mails

Week 29

(Re)educated

The Week

Somehow, the week passed. The days melted together. Nothing exciting happened besides my daily walks and a couple of texts with friends. No one popped over, zero run-ins in the kitchen, and I had no motivation. An emotion blossomed. Loneliness rooted itself in my heart. Unfortunately, Guido showered the growing sensation with his unreachability.

My thoughts piled on. Most days, I sat alone in the apartment, which I didn't choose. I never realized how much stimulation I drew from other people's energy. At one point every day, we looped around the same interaction, initiated by a call from me.

"Good morning," Guido said.

"Good morning," I replied.

"How are you doing?"

"Good, I just wanted to talk," I admitted.

He sighed. "Well, that's nice, but I have to work."

"Okay. See you for dinner," I murmured.

The black display on my phone reflected my frown. To lift my spirits, I woke my phone again to waste time checking out pretty pictures of my friends on social media.

Night Adventures

Sweat coated my skin. Guido cuddled up to me, but I pushed him to his side. I opened a window. At first, the frigid cold air had pushed us to sleep with socks, but now the room was a sauna without the relaxing benefits. When we slept, the window stood ajar. So we paid for the outside to be warmed up. Oh, hello, global warming.

I snuggled back on the mattress, pushing my pillow under my back. The back pain subsided a little bit, but an uncomfortable pressure remained. I switched positions but didn't find the right one. My eyelids stayed open.

I tiptoed into the living room, and a cold breeze froze me in my tracks. I ventured to the thermostat with my cardigan hugging my upper body. The thermostat read sixty-five degrees. I presumed Fahrenheit. Otherwise, that temperature would be heatstroke hot in Celsius. To help me out, Guido explained, "Thirty degrees Fahrenheit equals winter cold, sixty amounts to pleasant early summer days, and ninety is desert hot."

The conflicting temperatures in our apartment failed to instill in me the feeling of early summer. The cause for this issue hung right before me: the central heat adjuster. I don't think that I'd ever seen a central heating system, even before the Wall came down. How could I not remember how annoyed my mom used to be every winter to adjust every single heater in each room in our first house?

I threw the fluffy beige blanket over myself after resting for a little longer on the sofa, defeated by a built-in system. Unfortunately, my hot-water bottle still lay in bed with cold water. My trusty friend had increased my body heat since college. Guido used to make fun of me for bringing the transportable heater everywhere. Sometimes, though, his body heat just didn't cut it. However, I could position the hot-water bottle wherever I pleased . . . like on my neck, back, arms, or tummy. My hubby wasn't that flexible. He moaned, groaned, or complained when I tried.

<u>Saturday</u>

"Good morning," Guido said, rubbing his hand on my back.

"Good morning," I yawned.

"Why did you sleep out here?" he asked.

"It was so warm in the bedroom," I mumbled.

"Apparently, the sofa made you sleepy."

I stretched my arms in the air. "I could use a coffee today."

"It's coming right up," my husband offered as he busied himself in the kitchen. "What would you like to do today?"

"I don't know. I am oscillating between hanging out and being somewhat productive," I mused.

"How about you get dressed? I am making coffee, and after your hot energizer, we can go discover Boston?" Guido proposed.

My thumbs rose. "Sounds good to me. But we have to do something about the heating situation. It's so cold in here but too hot in the bedroom," I said, before stumbling back into the heat zone to grab my clothes.

When I returned to the living room, Guido dumped out his backpack on the sofa. I gasped. Crumbs of dirt and food tumbled out, along with socks, underwear, bike lights, a computer cable, pencils, and a fountain pen.

"What are you doing?" I wondered out loud.

"I am looking for my tape measure," Guido answered.

"Why? And why would you own one? You don't even own a complete set of cutlery," I complained with way too much irritation in my voice.

My husband peered at me. "I thought that we could switch rooms. I wanted to measure where to put the bed here in the living room."

"That's sweet of you." He was right. Swapping the rooms solved the problem. "But if we do this now, we'll waste half a day rearranging the apartment. Let's go. I need a change of scenery."

I slipped into my winter footwear, and the shaft hung loose around my ankles. "Would you mind tightening my boots?" I implored my hubby. "I can't reach them anymore."

"Absolutely." My husband kneeled to help me, and my irritation grew. I physically wasn't able to put my shoes on myself anymore.

Unfortunately, other changes accompanied my shoe-tying inability. I'd shelled out a fortune two years ago for properly fitted, adorable bras, and of course, eventually, my breasts spilled out above the hem or squeezed out below. Dressing myself appropriately increased in difficulty by the week. My new clothes reflected the changing circumstances. My standard had changed to pull-up-able and zip-able. Period.

Nobody prepares you for all the reshaping, though. My friend Maria had tried, but her words failed to penetrate my knowledge bank. To be fair, I thought she was just complaining about her body, about her clothes not fitting, about food she now hated, about being tired. I gladly lent her an ear. Only now did I understand her lamentation.

Dusky water-heavy clouds moved westward. This strange yet oddly familiar world was just as cold as my own home. Boston twinned with Potsdam's weather. It would have been such a treat if Guido could have been transferred to a year-round summer location like Hawaii. Unfortunately, would-haves and could-haves did not change the fact that his company built up an office here in Boston.

We piled into the underground. The public transportation rumbled through a tunnel but rode up to street level.

"That's our stop." Guido pointed at the display: *MGH*. We jumped out of the train. I hooked my hand into my husband's. Escalators carried us down, and a busy intersection greeted us. Guido guided us away from the hustle and bustle of the city. Redbrick buildings surrounded us with barely any traffic.

"Where are we going?"

"Discovering history," Guido replied.

"History? I didn't know that you were a historian," I teased.

He laughed. "I meant the history of the city."

"Okay, tell me something about the houses on our left," I challenged him.

"Thank you for asking. I have been waiting for this moment."

"I am all ears," I chirped.

"So, the houses on our left are part of the Beacon Hill neighborhood, which was built before and during the nineteenth century. The streetlights are powered by gas and never turned off."

"Not even during the daylight?"

Guido gave me a slight push to cross the street. "No, as it would be more expensive to pay someone to turn them on and off daily." He pointed at the redbrick buildings again. "Also, if you ever consider buying one of these houses right here, you will not only be asked to shell out a six-figure amount, but you would also be forced not to change a thing, as they are historic."

"Even not inside?" I snorted.

"Not even inside."

"Ha, and I thought the rules my parents had to follow for their timber-frame home were strict."

"And this is the State House." Guido pointed at a prominent building with red bricks, arches, white pillars, and a golden dome. "The dome is covered in real gold. Can you imagine?"

"No." Whenever I learned facts about the past, I imagined how people's lives must have been. Suppose they knew that history would remember them, their inventions, or circumstances. Unfortunately, my memory didn't comply with my desire to keep this information in my brain. Imagine my history teacher's disappointment when I blanked on Friedrich's burial date at his famous summer palace despite having observed the ceremonies. To be fair, I was only eight at the time, but still. Instead, my brain retained useless gossip about famous people, which was oh-so irrelevant to my life.

"This is Boston Common." A vast green area opened up in the middle of the town. "It's the first city park in the USA. Do you see the dried-out area?" he asked.

I swung my head to the right, seeing an empty, shallow pool filled with brown, mottled leaves.

"This is the Frog Pond. In the summer, people can wade in the pool. The water will be turned into a skating rink in the winter, or so my colleagues told me."

"Nice, but I doubt I will be skating soon. Besides, we both suck at it," I pointed out.

"Well, it could be worth a try. We could practice. There is a ring right around the corner from our house."

"Really? But I am still pregnant. Imagine I do a belly flop," I said.

"You're probably as graceful as a ballerina," he teased with a twinkle in his eyes.

I pointed to the birds on my right. "Do you see what I see?"

"You mean the geese?" he asked.

"Yes, the geese. Have you ever seen a goose in November? During winter?" At least twenty birds grazed on frostbitten grass and pooped everywhere they stalked.

Guido confessed, "I am not sure."

"Aren't they supposed to fly south?" I asked, trying to recall any snippets of long-past biology lessons. Most nature science subjects fared only marginally better than my memory of history eleven years after graduating high school.

"I suppose so. Maybe some of their ancestors got lost and also lost the knowledge of direction."

"Huh," I said. "I always assumed that birds just know. Apparently not!" This flock of geese right beside us proved me wrong.

"But we are here," my husband announced. He averted my attention to the spot we stood on.

"And here is . . . ?" I asked. We stood at the edge of the park. Houses lined up on the other side of a busy street.

"Look down." Beneath our feet lay a round plaque with leaves decorating its edges. The words under the decoration read: *Freedom Trail Boston*—an imprinted golden weather vane centered in the middle of the shield-like shape. Concrete surrounded the gold-coated metal.

Red bricks formed a line leading away from the place we stood.

"This is the ultimate Boston historic check-off route," Guido informed me. My husband grinned at me proudly. I tilted my head in question. Guido pointed at the red bricks on the ground. "This red line connects lots of major historic sites in the city. It's a good place to start discovering your new home." *Temporary home,* yelled my inner voice. "And it guides us through interesting neighborhoods," Guido added.

"You haven't done that yet?"

"No, I haven't had time, but now we can discover it together."

"So, let's go," I proposed, barely containing my excitement for this little adventure.

"Hold on a sec. I just want to check if there is a guided tour." Guido vanished in the building before me, only to come out shortly after with a leaflet in his hand.

"We missed it, but we can self-guide our way through." Guido unfolded the map, and a red line sprawled along the glossy paper. The names of the historic sites appeared on the left and right of the mapped-out route.

"That sounds like a plan," I agreed.

"Right this way." Guido drew a line with his hand in the air right above the brick line on the ground. I hooked my arm in his again. However, the red brick line led the way instead of ticking off the first checkpoint.

Despite churches always providing a calm place for me, my father used to drag us to every church in every town and country we went to on vacation. I never understood why. My mom insisted that he just wanted to appreciate the architecture. As preteens and teens, however, my sister and I never understood his enthusiasm. As a grown-up, I was churched out.

We went into the Granary Burying Ground, admired the statue of Benjamin Franklin, and almost missed the Old Meeting House, which blended into the street view. Next, we trotted toward the Old Corner Bookstore. Today, a restaurant dished out food at this location.

Secretly, I wanted to snag a book that I already owned but with an American cover. Only because of my sister did I discover that books translated into other languages received a new eye-catching cover design.

Frankly, the concept was lost on me. Supposedly, people in different countries had different tastes, like how Ikea built different furniture in France than in Germany to target each cultural style, flavor, and unique taste buds. I understood that, but I didn't get the change in visual representation of the content with books. Despite my irritation, I secretly hoped to start a collection of *Grimms' Fairy Tales* printed in the same year but in different countries. The icing on the cake would be if my collection were bedazzled with sprayed edges. One day, I promised myself, one day.

We wandered to the Old State House. "The Declaration of Independence was proclaimed here," continued Guido, my tour guide.

Impressed, my ears pricked up. Despite my flailing knowledge about the past, Nicolas Cage's *National Treasure* movies increased my hunger to gather interesting facts. I rummaged through scenes still imprinted in my memory to determine if this building had appeared in the films. Nothing sprung up.

My eyes scanned the house in the hopes of jogging my memory. Stairs to the basement led to an underground stop. But why? The question vanished in thin air the moment we dipped into Faneuil Hall. There, a ranger educated visitors about the historical aspects of the location. Unfortunately, most information got lost in translation, except one: the building was still in use. I loved it when historic sites still served their intended purpose if it was ethical.

My tummy rumbled. "What time is it? I'm hungry."

Guido checked his wristwatch. "It's two o'clock. And it's perfect timing. There are food stands in Quincy Market, and then we can have dessert in the North End before the Paul Revere House."

Right behind Faneuil Hall, an ample space opened up with a long, prominent building in the center. Golden letters above the entrance read: *Quincy Market*. Four-story-high houses squared the building in. Stores on the ground floor invited shoppers. Most peculiar, there were Dutch flags with the word *OPEN* spelled out on them.

History-wise, this area used to be dominated by the British. However, the city of New York once belonged to the Kingdom of the Netherlands. If my memory served me right, the town was called New Amsterdam back then. So, perhaps somehow, the Dutch flag installed in stores wormed itself through time—one more thing to research.

Between a pillared entrance, stairs led into the market. I expected vendors to sell fresh fruit, vegetables, and bread under the sky. Instead, fast-food sellers with take-out counters lined the hallway. However, crowds swarmed the food stands, so the food offered here had to be delicious. We squeezed through the maze of people. The dishes ranged from burgers and ice cream to steaks and Chinese food. But my eyes landed on a white soup served in a hand-sized bread bowl. Every other person we passed carried one of these.

I loved soup. I had to have one. After only a couple of minutes, we located the seller. *Boston Clam Chowder*, read a banner above the stall. Even though I was pregnant and hungry, we ordered one to share.

One of the first pregnancy myths I busted was "eating for two." At first, I put twice as much food on my plate the moment my belly showed a curve. Guido finished my leftovers whenever I said, "I can't finish it."

He ate the food but demanded, "Next time, take less. I am not the house pig." To be fair, I didn't want him to finish my food either. My pregnant friends' husbands grew their bellies, too, but didn't lose the extra weight after nine months.

The soup, bread, and much-needed water bottles revived our energy to continue on our quest to discover the historic landmarks sprinkled through downtown. After we crossed a highly congested street with a park in the middle, we entered another neighborhood with many restaurants. All seemed to have Italian names.

"Oh my, there is a bakery." I could barely contain my excitement. I missed mine so much. Who knew that the lack of bakeshops would be one of my biggest takeaways from moving to a different country?

"It sounds like you've never seen a bakery before," Guido teased.

"No, the opposite. I've barely seen a bakery here, but I just realized that there is one on almost every corner in our neighborhood in Potsdam."

"No, there isn't," Guido argued.

"Do you want to bet?"

"Sure, how about I'll get you a slice of cake daily for your afternoon coffee?" Guido suggested.

"And if I lose, I'll get you a class with a master bladesmith," I said. Guido's eyes nearly popped out of their sockets. If he lost, I would definitely jot this idea down for his birthday or next year's Christmas present. My map app searched and searched for Chopin Strasse,

Potsdam, but nothing happened. "I need to do something with this phone."

"Maybe a new SIM card or a phone just like mine," he proposed. "But first, let's check out the pastries."

"And I have to use the bathroom." My eyes flickered past the shops' windows. They glided over a long line of people. "Wait? Are they standing in line for the bakery?"

"I think so."

"I am not waiting half an hour in this weather to get something sweet between my teeth and then waiting in line behind a bunch of other women to use the facilities too." My standoffish tone made my attitude clear. I'd rather get nothing. I never stood in line for pastries, not even back in the day when people would wait in a line that wrapped around the neighborhood to get a watermelon from Cuba.

"There might be another option off the beaten path. Even if we can't find a dessert, perhaps we might stumble upon a bathroom," Guido said, trying to soothe me.

Only a couple of minutes later, we passed another bakery. Different cookies, tubelike stuffed treats, biscotti, and macarons made our mouths water through the display window. The smell of freshly brewed coffee enveloped my senses. The warmth of oven-baked goodies wafted through the heated air in the store.

"What can I get you?" the bakery employee asked.

"I'll take one of these." My finger pointed at the roll containing quark[1]. Or pudding? Who cared? My eyes inhaled the stuffed baked goodies. "And a hot chocolate, please," I added, to satisfy my need for a beverage.

My eyes scanned the shop to no avail. No bathroom sign signaled for a spot to relieve oneself.

"And I'll take the raspberry tart and a coffee, please," Guido requested.

The woman behind the sales counter scooped up the treats. She placed the desserts in a white box. We opened the container immediately after sliding onto chairs at a window table.

After I took a hungry bite into the afternoon treat, the white cream decorated my mouth. My tongue cleaned every layer of dairy product up. I eyed my husband's baked good. "How is yours?"

"Good. Do you want to try it?" he offered.

We exchanged our goodies. Guido's fruit tart exuded just the right amount of tartness to the raspberry flavor.

"So Gill has offered to organize a baby shower for us," Guido mentioned.

"A baby shower?"

"Yeah, it's like where people celebrate the baby's birth before the baby comes and bring gifts for the soon-to-be-born baby."

"Like in the movies?"

"Yes. It sounds like a tradition around here," Guido replied.

"But I don't know anyone," I protested.

"That's why Gill proposed organizing the shower. She would invite a couple of people from work and their partners. This way you could meet some people and a couple of my colleagues."

"I guess that would be nice." I shifted in my seat.

"Why don't you use the bathroom?" Guido suggested after he noticed me rubbing back and forth on the chair.

"I haven't seen a bathroom sign or any possible door that could lead to a bathroom."

My husband craned his neck. "I don't see anything either," he said. He went to the counter. "Excuse me, do you have a bathroom?" he asked.

"No, we don't," the lady responded.

As if on cue by the word *no*, I suddenly really, really needed to pee. My mouth gaped. My upper leg muscles tightened. I squeezed all of my lower muscles together.

"Let's pack up," I prompted Guido.

I searched the street up and down, trying to guess where a bathroom could be. Nothing on this street screamed, *bathroom available*. I disregarded all eateries. They would want me to buy something to use their facilities. I jumped from one leg to the next.

"I need to go. But I don't know where," I let out through gritted teeth.

"You know what? Let's go back to Quincy Market. I bet there is a public bathroom."

"I don't know if I can make it that far," I said, my voice quivering.

"It's either that or wet pants for you on our search for a loo," Guido said nonchalantly.

Convinced by his words, I joined him in turning back westward. I hobbled along the pavement, holding the excess water in just barely. I pulled myself together. I took longer strides until a drop moistened my underwear. I wished I had panty liners hidden in my pockets. Unfortunately, when my menstruation vanished after getting pregnant, those liners stopped being part of my daily just-in-case bag anymore. And I had ditched my just-in-case collection since I came here. Besides blood-drop barriers, my emergency pack contained tampons, used to hold condoms—which I forgot about—painkillers for the unexpected migraine at the worst moment, tissues, allergy drops, and a small tub of *Florena* cream for dry lips.

I cramped up my lower belly muscles to prevent further leakage. The walk back seemed longer now with my shorter strides. I tried to keep up with Guido's pace, who pulled me forward to move just a little bit faster about every ten steps. The embarrassment of his wife wetting herself in the middle of the street would be far greater than pushing me along, which I usually hated. My mouth sealed in fear that the spring in me might burst open.

We paused on the main street at the red "don't walk" signal. Cars drove by. My hopping on the spot increased. *Turn green, turn green, turn green!* I yelled in my mind. I almost joined people who chose to cross the street during small pockets of no cars driving through.

Finally, the color of the sign changed to white. I sped across the street. My knees weakened. The bodily fluid pushed on the release valve.

We reentered the crowded area where gold letters on the big building in front of us read, *Quincy Market.* Shivering, I followed Guido's lead. My brain functions slowed to redirect all the energy to the muscles keeping the collecting water in my bladder. Although I almost reached a state where I stopped caring. I just wanted the pressure to stop. If I made a puddle right now, who cared? I didn't know anyone around me.

Sweat pearled on my forehead. Guido conversed with a guy from the first food stall. "Okay, so the bathrooms are in the middle of this building, and the stairs are from the outside."

My feet frantically lunged forward while keeping my hip movements to a minimum. Moisture collected between my thighs. Pee or sweat, or perhaps both combined. But who cared? Nothing trailed down the inside of my leg just yet.

Lo and behold, I finally saw the sign: *Bathroom.* A drop dislodged from within me, wetting the cloth above my jeans when my brain registered my target. Yet I braced myself.

A scary thought entered my fragile state of mind. Vivid memories of me in line for the girls' bathroom, pretty much anywhere growing up, popped into my head. Women's bathrooms always had a long line. There had to be a cosmic collision. Women either needed to use the bathroom simultaneously, or there was a conspiracy to keep women suffering through limited toilet space. Regardless, I prepared myself to hold in the extra water a smidge longer.

I tiptoed toward the relief. The stairs led downward. My eyes scanned the hallway. The under-crossing led to another set of stairs on the opposite end. Two gaps in the wall signaled entrances. The closest one displayed a black square with an *M*. The same gaps split the wall on the left side, this white sign with the black letter *W*. I jumped into the opening, and an empty, clean bathroom opened up in front of me. Only one flush from another stall reached my ears. Without hesitation, I approached the closest bathroom door. I pushed the separator in, but the pressed wood pushed back.

"Oh, I'm sorry." A woman straightened up.

Behind her sat a young girl on the toilet, grinning at me.

"I'm sorry," I offered. The mom closed the door in front of me. I skipped over two doors. The urge to go almost brought me to my knees. I barely closed the lock behind me. I pushed down my pants, ripped off a couple of sections of toilet paper, and placed them on the seat before plopping down to finally let the water flow.

A river flowed out of my body. I relished the feeling: relief.

* * *

"And how was it?" The grin layered in Guido's tone made me smile.

"Unbelievable. I could swear I just set a new record," I said.

"Well, I would almost bet that other pregnant women might be happy to challenge you," my husband countered with a smile.

"You are probably right, but you have no idea how light I feel right now."

"Do you want to look around a bit more?" my husband asked.

"Sure. Now that I feel better, I can look around a little longer." We passed several stalls selling items such as scarves, dresses, hats, and miniature cars outside of the market space.

Several brick-and-mortar shops lined the side of the square. One, in particular, caught my eye —a cell phone store. I pulled my husband's hand toward the electronics shop.

"Good afternoon. Can I help you?" A young woman in her midtwenties approached us.

"Sure, I am looking for a SIM card." I showed her my phone.

"We don't sell SIM cards here. Only phones with or without contracts."

"Oh," I gasped.

"But since you already have a phone, some providers offer a rebate when you switch. You can keep your phone and your number."

"That's a German phone with a German number."

"Oh, I don't think that works then," the young woman informed me.

"So, do you have a contract for three or six months? And how much would it be?"

"Most contracts are for two years, and the average price is forty-nine dollars plus tax per month."

"Two years," I echoed.

"Well, you can buy the phone. Your monthly payment would be lower. Also, there is currently a discount on the activation fee."

My breath caught in my throat. We should have left when she informed me they didn't sell SIM cards. I was determined to keep my phone until the software was no longer updated. My phone had cost an arm and a leg.

But, hooked by the information given to me, I heard the woman out.

"So, what do you think?" the sales rep asked, interrupting my train of thought.

"Could you write down what the costs are for me? I just have a hard time following," I said.

"Sure, how much data do you use?"

"I don't know." I shrugged my shoulders.

"Are you streaming music or movies on your device or browsing the Internet?"

"I am just browsing," I confirmed.

"Okay." The young woman pulled a glossy sales brochure out. On the cover, she jotted down: *Monthly payment for the phone: $40, and $80 for one line*. "That means you would pay a hundred and twenty dollars per month, plus an activation fee today of forty dollars. I could quickly run your credit score, and then you can choose your phone." The woman smiled warmly at me.

"I don't think I have a credit history here. I just arrived."

She sighed. "Very well. That might mean you need to leave a deposit."

"A deposit? What kind of deposit?" I asked.

"This would be three monthly payments upfront," she replied.

"On top of everything else?" I stuttered. The woman nodded. "I think that I have to think about it. Thank you for your time," I said, before dragging Guido out of the store.

Our feet, flat like pancakes, carried us from one phone store to another. All four big cell phone service providers caused me a massive headache. Each store provided me with similar numbers to the first one.

Why couldn't this be simple? Why didn't my phone just work here? I totally understood that I needed a new number, but forging out a pile of gold wasn't an option.

"I think we'll go back to the landline. I buy the phone, pay a small monthly fee, and can talk," I said.

"I wouldn't mind that, actually," my husband agreed.

"Did you hear how expensive a cell phone would be?" I asked, continuing my tirade.

"Nope, but I think we can probably live the way it currently is."

"Maybe," I sighed. "I just want to call you whenever I want."

Guido peered at me. "Even though I love you, I have to work. And every time you call me on my mobile, I pay as well."

"But the baby," I whined.

"You can call me when the baby comes; if not, just send me an email."

My shoulders hung. The attempt to successfully connect better to my husband had failed.

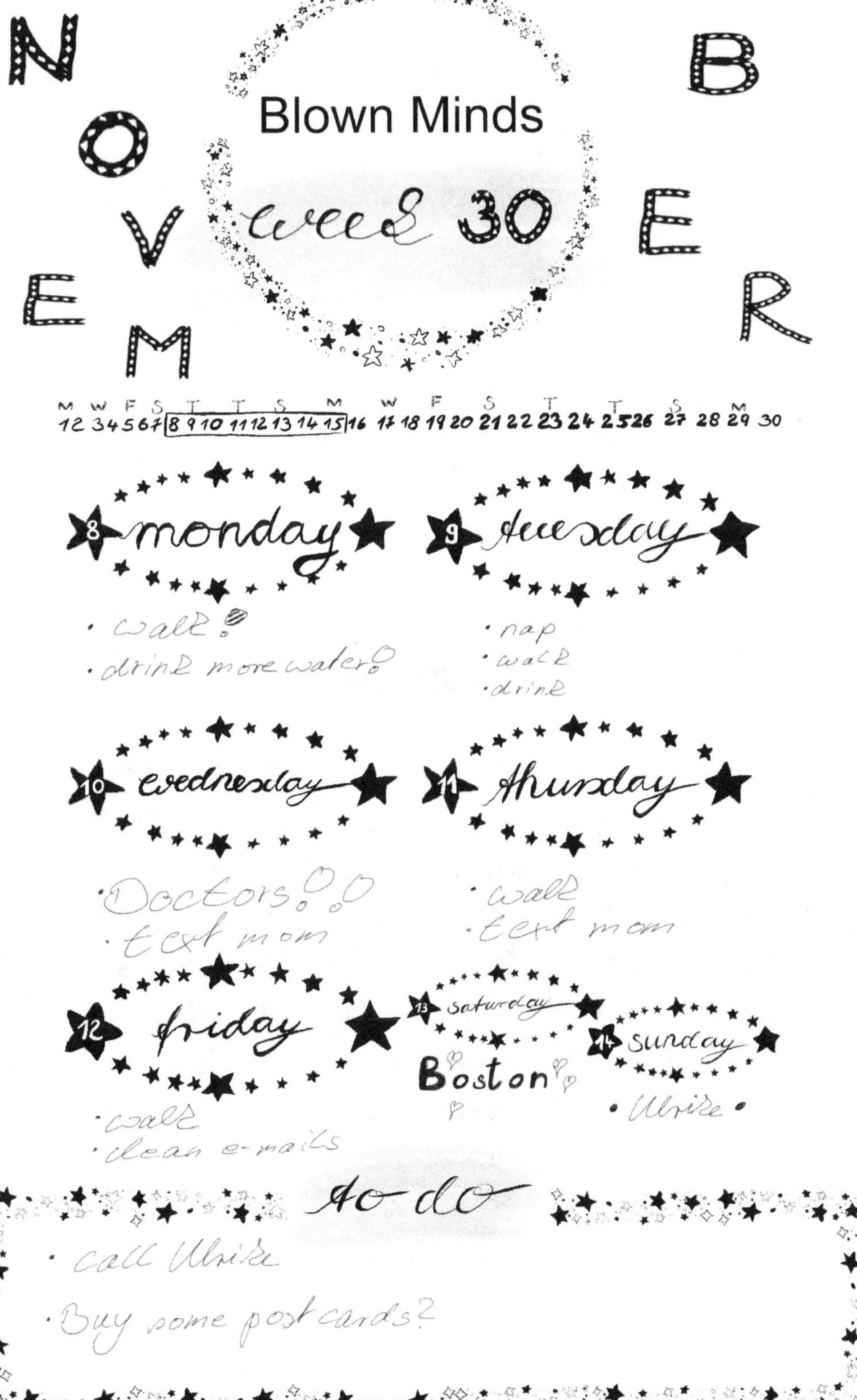

N O V E M B E R
Blown Minds
week 30
M W F S T T S M W F S T T S M
1 2 3 4 5 6 7 8 9 10 11 12 13 14 15 16 17 18 19 20 21 22 23 24 25 26 27 28 29 30
8 monday
· walk?
· drink more water
9 tuesday
· nap
· walk
· drink
10 wednesday
· Doctors
· text mom
11 thursday
· walk
· text mom
12 friday
· walk
· clean e-mails
13 saturday
Boston
14 sunday
· Ulrike
to do
· call Ulrike
· Buy some postcards?

Week 30

Blown Minds

<u>Wednesday</u>

I tossed and turned. My body failed to find a comfortable position to rest in. Eventually, I dragged myself into the kitchen, poured Choco Pops into a bowl, and pulled the red blanket over me on the sofa. Fistfuls of the cereals toppled into my mouth. My other hand doodled baby clothes in my journal. The baby's arrival approached with giant leaps. The prenatal visit in the morning reinforced the looming reality. Slight panic gripped the speed of my pen. We still lacked many items in our baby prep arsenal. A stroller, diapers, and baby clothes still topped my list.

Alas, the baby shower was happening on Saturday. I'd warmed up to the idea of celebrating the baby before he came along instead of trying to meet everyone once the doll-sized human joined us outside of my womb.

My mother, of all people, thought this American tradition was blasphemy, which would bring bad luck to the baby. I rolled my eyes at her attitude. Every year, my mom gave me the evil eye when I mentioned that my friend Susie celebrated her birthday on the Saturday before her actual birthday. Yet my mother had no issue celebrating her birthday every year in June, as she hated celebrating her actual birthday in November. Go figure.

Eventually, my brain shut off. Guido had already gone to work when I woke up again. I wrapped a wool cardigan over my chilled body. On the nightstand hung green calf-high socks, courtesy of Guido's army days. I considered reading a book but had momentarily forgotten where I was. At home, I had many choices. A bookshelf covered one whole bedroom wall.

My eyes wandered over the kitchen counter; an unfolded letter lay under an envelope. I drew the paper closer. My eyes skimmed over the contents. My heart raced.

The unfolded paper contained a bill addressed to Guido. The sender was a gas company. My eyes scanned each line again. My sudden air intake cramped up my lungs. Every value I read exceeded my expectations, and not in a positive manner. Our usual energy bill averaged around fifty dollars for a two-bedroom apartment. The square footage of this apartment was about the same. Yet this bill displayed twice the amount of what I was used to. Even accounting for conversion, this bill exceeded my experience. Yikes. My heartbeat increased again. We could not pay a hundred dollars just for energy. Perhaps I misunderstood the numbers displayed in black ink on the white sheet. Our bill back home included water as well. This bill may have included every additional cost?

My hand shot forward to grab my phone. I called Guido on his office line to avoid charges on his cell phone.

"Good morning, sleeping beauty." Guido's optimistic tone lifted my spirits.

"Good morning. I am calling because I just saw our energy bill." My shocked tone bombarded him.

"I opened the invoice this morning. I was talking about it with my colleagues; it seems to be the norm."

"*The norm?* I almost had a heart attack." My head spun—the norm. Every month, a hundred dollars? For how many months? The cold season had just begun.

"That's just the gas bill," Guido explained.

"What? The gas bill? What does that mean?"

"We'll also get an electricity bill, but let's talk about it tonight, okay? I have a lot to do."

"Okay," I agreed reluctantly. What was there to talk about, anyway? We couldn't change the bill. Well . . . Every month, I always double-checked all our bills: electricity, water, phones, Internet, insurance, rent, and any subscriptions for mistakes on each invoice. Additionally, energy-preserving measures busied our household periodically. From fridge replacements to no-draft windows, extending to simple light bulb changes, all decreasing our monthly amounts to utility providers.

I marched to the thermostat in the hallway. The former shoebox-sized bedroom was always too hot. The former living room resembled an icebox.

The central heater still stood at seventy-five. I turned the thermostat down to sixty-five. But I wasn't done there. Next stop: the kitchen. Every time I worked at the counter, a breeze caused my arm hair to stand up.

My palm glided over the walls. The coldness of the surface chilled my skin. A soft draft from closer to the ceiling pushed against my face. I climbed onto a dining chair. A bone-chilling draft above the cupboards hit me like a cold shower—an idea sprung up. Two blue blankets courtesy of the airplane were piled up in the walk-in closet. I stuffed the knitted material into the gaps between the ceiling and kitchen shelves. The draft lessened.

My arm brushed against the kitchen window frame when I stepped down—another draft. My fingers hovered around the window. Air filtered through the entirety of the wood. No quick fix came to my mind.

My eyes wandered around our former living room. A bag full of kids' safety items lay on the floor. Thanks to a coworker of Guido's, we were all set with plug protectors, doorknob covers, cabinet locks, and drawer latches. All the items had landed on the floor. I scooped up a handful of outlet covers.

Two double plugs were installed on the outside walls left and right from the baseboard heater. I held my hand against one. Sure enough, a noticeable draft pushed through. I pushed the plug covers in.

Several holes around the outlets let air in. Not just holes—the space between the apartment wall and the outside wall was empty. I considered stuffing the hollow space with something. Anything! A couple of advertisement booklets, our sheets, and our blanket fell into my view. Quickly, I dismissed these options. I saw the headline: *Stupid German woman sets house on fire to keep warm*. Instead, I left the wall alone to prepare for my bi-weekly gel fix from the baby doctor.

* * *

"Mrs. Korn!"

I followed a woman dressed in a lilac nurse's uniform. A question lingered on the tip of my tongue, but I caged the words in my mouth. Did she wear her uniform from her home to her job? So far I'd noticed several people working in medical offices and hospitals on the street in their attire. The color palette rivaled Tropifrutti.[1] However, I'd barely seen a nurse back home with their uniforms on the street. Perhaps I paid more attention now since I had to visit a doctor's office more often.

"Hi, I am Judy." A woman with an instrument on wheels came into my room.

"Hi," I answered without offering anything else.

"Please give me your arm."

I followed her prompt. Then she left me so that my provider could come see me. However, I had no clue if my provider was a specific person or a position, as I had seen several people so far. Most of the time, the person who came to see me was a nurse practitioner, not a doctor. Another option opened up in my mind. The words might be synonyms to one another.

"Good afternoon. I am Skylar," a woman with a gray streak in her otherwise mahogany-brown hair introduced herself.

"Hi, I am Mareike," I heard myself say, even though the woman in front of me held a patient folder with my name in her hand.

I lay back on the cushioned medical bed, my head on the elevated headrest, and my shirt pulled up and pants unbuttoned. The warm gel on my skin, along with the ultrasound scanner's motion, surprised me every time. The sensation soothed my mood. Admittedly, the warm gel calmed my senses.

I could clearly remember the first time gel was slapped on my skin in preparation for an ultrasound scan because I had a stomachache that wouldn't go away. The iciness pulled every fiber together like the instant dehydration of a fresh, juicy grape to a dried-out raisin. The scan revealed an inflamed appendix. The doctor promised me a bikini cut, which left me sleeping in the fetal position for two weeks.

The gel cooled, and the nurse slid the cursor from one end of the white baby shadow to another on the computer screen.

"Do you want to hear the heartbeat?" The nurse's eyes surveyed mine.

"Sure," I agreed.

A rhythmic sound filled the space. My baby! That was my baby. As the pulsating heartbeat continued, something dislodged in me. Something deep within me. Tears rolled down my cheeks. We were going to have a baby.

A new person was growing inside me. Soon, we would be a family of three. Guido and I would be responsible for a helpless person 24/7, and we still didn't have everything we needed yet.

"Would you like to have ultrasound scans to take home?" the nurse asked.

"Sure," I automatically answered, as if I didn't know any other words. Of course I had learned more words in English, but evolving from my school English into usable everyday English was much more challenging than I initially thought. After all, I had studied English from the third grade until the end of school, except that I almost failed my A-level examination.

I cleaned up the rest of the gel the nurse had missed from my skin and pulled my sweater down. A strip of paper inched out of the computer station. The nurse ripped the paper off. She folded the unborn baby pictures and placed the paper in an envelope before handing me my baby's first photo.

"Please make your next appointment at the reception desk."

"Sure," I repeated myself. Honestly, I found myself more and more punch-able with the repetitiveness of my singular answers.

After the nurse proposed my next appointment

for December 8, I zipped up and tightened my scarf.

Once outside, I turned left, then right, leaving the medical building behind me. My feet edged a little down the road on the fastest route home. But honestly, nothing waited there for me. The walls created a safe space but lacked the warmth to be called a home.

My gaze zoomed down the opposite way. The spirit of adventure gleamed in my eyes. I changed my direction and trotted along the streets to absorb every detail.

Unlike me, Ulrike religiously planned short trips every other month and two long trips a year. Sometimes jealousy overcame me, and a snarky comment slipped out. She always rebuked me, "You can travel too. You just have to plan it," or "You are always welcome to join me." Which I never did.

I took in the different-shaped houses. I realized why my sister traveled the world whenever she could. My new temporary home was so similar, yet so strange.

My eyes scanned the opposite sidewalk, and I stopped. The roads in this country had yellow stripes in the middle of the pavements instead of white ones. This street had three lines in three colors: green, white, and red. A flag? Or just the colors of a flag? Like the ones in stores? But this was on the street. My brain crunched geographical information. A couple of explanations wormed themselves through the mix of confusion. The most likely one was that this street was, or used to be, mainly inhabited by Italians. This was an exciting way of honoring one's origin.

I continued my promenade. More impressions of my new home filtered through me. My feet stopped in their tracks . . . I backpedaled. A big sign with four capital letters, *YMCA*, interrupted my thoughts. My mouth fell open. I repeated the letters in my head. Again, I repeated them, but this time with my mouth and vocal cords as I sang, "*YMCA, da da da, YMCA*," which I had to accompany with the band's gestural body lettering. I just couldn't stop myself.

But what did it all mean? Were the song and the nondescript building in front of me connected? I tried to remember more of the lyrics. Nothing came to me. I hesitated to go inside, but the desire to boast to my sister that I had been to the YMCA trumped my fear of initiating a conversation with a stranger.

"Good morning. How can I help you?" a woman with curly red hair greeted me.

"Good morning. I was wondering what this place is." The words bubbled out of me.

"Well, it's a YMCA," the woman answered.

Really? I thought to myself. I shifted my gaze to look around. "I don't understand," I said, bridging the awkward silence, hoping to get a better explanation from her.

"The Y is like a gymnasium, a community space," the woman behind the desk explained.

"Oh, okay," I replied, not really knowing what to make of the information. My gymnasium provided anyone who attended a university entrance diploma at the end. But alas, I was in a different country. Yet the lack of kids roaming these halls punctured my assumption.

"Would you like to join?" The woman placed a form with a pen in front of me.

"No, thanks." Her action proved my point that this building wasn't a school. I made my way out of there. On the beige wall next to the exit door hung a white sign. The words read, *Young Men's Christian Association*. A gasp escaped me, and my jaw dropped to the floor.

All the way to our apartment, I puzzled over the acronym and the word *gymnasium*. One of the few English lessons in the back of my mind was that of false friends.

Even Guido had recently fallen into this trap. Every time Guido stated his family situation, people in his office chuckled. I encouraged him to ask why his colleagues stifled their laughter. Initially, he didn't have the nerve to do so. I could only imagine how he felt. My husband was in a new office, working in a country with a language that wasn't his mother tongue.

However, after one particular incident during a group meeting, Nicole took Guido aside. Guido repeated, "We are getting a baby," instead of

"We are having a baby." Poor Guido. Now he says, "We are expecting a baby." So maybe the gymnasium fell into the same word category. A word that sounds the same or is spelled the same as a German word but has a different meaning.

Saturday

I stretched out on the sofa. My back ached again. Darkness spread outside the window. A yawn escaped my mouth while I opened my laptop. Heat rose in my face—the computer clock displayed two in the morning. Ugh. Guido slept in the bed. I cuddled up behind him and listened to his rhythmic breathing. My brain drifted off again.

"Good morning," Guido whispered into my ear sometime after sunrise. The freshly brewed coffee smell lingered in the air. He pushed a mug in front of me. "Did you sleep well?"

"I don't know. The sofa isn't that comfy."

"I didn't want to wake you up," he said. "You seemed tired."

"Thanks, but I actually still had to work a little."

"Don't worry about work anymore . . . You are officially on maternity leave."

True, but my inbox filled up with emails from Nina, my maternity replacement, and Katharina, our financial advisor. I guess my handover documentation wasn't as good as I thought it was. But the company would move along, even without me.

"So, we have to leave in thirty minutes." Guido put on a lilac V-neck sweater. A white collar from the dress shirt below rimmed his neck. I sipped on the black liquid to get my spirits going.

"Leave?" I echoed.

"For the baby shower."

"What time is it?"

Guido checked his watch. "It's eleven thirty."

"Eleven thirty. Eleven thirty? I slept thirteen— no, fourteen hours? And I don't feel rested."

"Well, it's good then that we are going to see

other people. Maybe that will wake you up," he suggested.

Twenty minutes later, we stepped outside of our apartment building. "What is that smell?" I gagged.

"Probably a skunk," Guido guessed.

"A skunk? In the city?"

"Yeah. There are a lot of them. Sometimes when I came home late from work, I saw one shuffling around each block or so," Guido marveled.

"Wow. I think I have only seen real skunks in a zoo."

* * *

The bus ride to Fresh Pond increased my liveliness. Once we got off the bus, a residential area surrounded us. Tri-level, single-family stone houses lined the streets. Most of the buildings had fenced-in green front yards. Bushes pushed through the metal weaves. Trash cans lined the edges of the sidewalks, and cars lined up along the side of the street.

"Did you see that?" I pointed at the third trash can in front of us. Guido shook his head. "The lid of the container bounced up." The moment the words left my mouth, the cover moved up again. We drew closer. The lid pushed up again. A bean-sized black nose poked out for a moment.

"What is it?" I wondered.

"Let's see." Guido brought his right hand forward but held his body back. He jumped back when the lid moved up again. But Guido dared himself to look once more. I moved closer and pushed the cover open. A squirrel lunged out on the edge of the plastic trash container, jumped to the closest tree, climbed the trunk, and vanished behind clusters of fall leaves.

"Hey, you did a good deed." I congratulated Guido with a kiss on his cheek as we continued on our way to our destination.

Three houses down, bound to a black gate, a dozen metallic pink and blue balloons reached for the sky. White letters on the latex promised: *About to Pop.*

"Oh no. Shouldn't we have brought something?" I showed Guido my empty hands.

"Gill repeatedly told me to not bring anything."

"Still," I protested. This was my first baby shower. Not only that, this was *my* baby shower. We should have brought something. Fear crept up in me. I bit my lips.

Guido squeezed his own hands. "It will be fun." The self-encouragement helped him push the doorbell. Seconds later, the beige door swung inward, and the storm door swung outward.

A woman with a gray pixie cut in a reindeer sweater stood in the frame with a warm smile. "You must be Mareike." She pulled me into a hug. "I'm Gill. Please, come in."

We followed our host to the second floor. One of two doors stood ajar. Murmurs, laughter, and light jazz music streamed from the space behind the open door. The music in itself put me at ease.

I started to pull one foot out of my boot before Gill entered her apartment.

"Don't worry about it. You can leave them on," she told me.

"Umm," I started to protest, scanning my and Guido's footwear. Dirt and water encrusted the lower part of our shoes. Guido's footprints lined up behind him. "Are you sure?" I questioned timidly. There was no way anyone would enter our apartment at home with shoes in this state. I didn't know anyone who would let me in without giving me an evil stare if I dared go ahead, regardless of what season we were in.

"Of course," Gill responded. With a big smile, she pushed us both over the threshold. Before I looked at anyone's face, I noticed that everyone I could see still wore their street shoes. I had so many questions.

"The guests of honor are here," Gill announced when she closed the door behind us. My cheeks burned. Two men and two women conversed behind a white leather sofa. One of the women wore her black hair in a ponytail. She held the hand of a man whose broad shoulders implied a former swimming career.

The other woman had long, highlighted blonde hair. Barret, the only one I knew, stood very close to her.

A chunk of distress tightened my neck. Four sets of eyes zeroed in on me. Drilled to the floor, I wished I could recede into a shell. Instead of rushing to me all at once, the two couples waved at me, smiling and nodding. I loosened my jaw, relieved that the other guests didn't bombard me with their attention.

Steps from behind drew closer. I turned around. A balding man in another Christmas sweater carried a plate covered with a sheet of aluminum foil. "Hi, I'm Greg, Gill's husband."

"Nice to meet you," Guido and I greeted him simultaneously.

"Here is some alcohol-free bubbly." Gill offered me a flute with pinkish liquid in the glass. The carbonated beverage tasted like raspberries. Come to think of bubblies, this was my first carbonated beverage here. We usually bought a case of *Apfelschorle*,[2] sparkling lemonades, and sparkling water. For some reason, Guido hadn't gotten any since I got here. However, what I really missed was *Waldmeister*[3] lemonade to quench my thirst.

I fidgeted with the glass, sipping periodically while glancing at the other guests.

"It's good to see you again," Barret greeted us as he shook our hands. "I'm glad you guys found the place okay. Originally, we were thinking of offering you a ride, but we had to drop the boys off at Collette's parents'—of course, only after Charlie threw his milkshake across the car. In addition to cleaning the interior, we had to go back home to change our clothes."

My eyes widened at the declaration of their kid's behavior. For the most part, I had pushed away the kids' tantrums I'd witnessed so far, hoping our child would be quiet and timid like me when I was little. According to my mom, I was only like that outside the house.

"But we're happy to bring you home after the party ends," he offered.

Before I could protest, a woman in a black knee-length dress wrapped her arm around

Barret. "Hi, I'm Collette. Nice to meet you," she greeted me while stretching out her left hand.

"I am Mareike, Guido's wife.”

"Have you seen the food yet?” Collette asked. “Gill made those amazing cupcakes."

Her prompt made my head swing around. Under a window, bright sun rays illuminated a buffet flanked by more balloons with the text *Let's Pop*. But something draped over the window caught my eye.

"What's on the window?" I probed.

"That's cling film," Barret explained.

"But they forgot to use the hair dryer to tighten the plastic," Collette added.

"Hmm. I don't understand," I said. Guido raised his eyebrows.

"It's to prevent drafts from coming through the window," Collette replied.

"Oh, I think we need that."

"Look, Mareike." Guido pointed at a second table, pushed against a wall to our right side.

Onesies were lined up on a thread hung up by clothespins. A turquoise chalkboard in an 8x6 frame read in black chalk, *Onesie-Making Station*.

Next to the arts and crafts hung a sign—*Gift Drop-Off*. Below, a tower of gifts were piled up. I paled, and a layer of sweat cooled down my skin.

"Look at those cookies." Guido picked a round one up. A baby drinking from a bottle was drawn on the flat shape with frosting. Besides sliders, pizza, and fruit skewers, additional edible baby feet cookies decorated the wooden table. I pushed one of the tiny burgers into my mouth. Gill lifted a napkin decorated with baby bottles from the table. She offered it, and I wiped the grease off my mouth's edges.

"Thanks," I mumbled.

"Congratulations. Is it a boy or a girl?" she asked.

"A boy."

"Don't forget to cover his penis, or you'll get hosed."

An awkward chuckle escaped my mouth. "Do you have children as well?" I inquired.

"Yes, four. Four boys," Gill replied.

My eyes widened. "Four?"

"Yes, but they are all in college now." She paused before continuing, "So, I hear you are on maternity leave already."

"Yes, I am. Just started," I explained.

"Do you know that the insurance covers birth preparation classes?"

"No, but thanks," I responded.

"What do you do when you aren't on leave?" Gill's husband, Greg, joined us.

"I am a controller."

"Oh, excuse me," Gill interjected suddenly, darting toward the kitchen.

"A controller? As in, you are controlling something in particular?" Greg asked.

"Well, I guess I am controlling the bottom line, I would say."

His eyebrows pinched together. "I don't understand."

"Well, I am working for a small lemonade company," I said. "In a nutshell, I am making sure that the numbers add up and that the company runs a profit. Often they need to cut some costs as ingredients increase in price. So I check all options to decrease production costs, from finding new suppliers to proposing different packaging options—like changing materials and leaving material that might not be necessary for the main product. What do you do?"

"I am the tech guy in the office," Greg explained. "I will take over for Guido once he leaves."

"How is the new apartment?" Collette inquired.

"So far, so good."

"Do you have enough freezer space?" she asked.

"Hmmm. What do you mean?" I had never purposely checked my freezer and thought, *Guido, let's roll and get a bigger fridge.*

"You'll want to prep as much food as possible and freeze it, so you don't need to cook as often. Trust me, honey, once the baby is here, you will be exhausted and glad to have something ready to just be heated up."

My eyes widened as I slowly nodded in agreement. That made perfect sense. I just never saw myself doing that, especially not with my cooking skills. I side-glanced at my hubby, who was in a deep conversation with a man I hadn't met yet.

"Hi, I am Paula," the black-haired woman introduced herself to me when she came to join our conversation.

"Nice to meet you. I am Mareike," I replied.

"How have you been settling in?" she asked.

"Well, so far. I guess. Everything is still pretty new to me."

"Which day cares have you applied to so far?"

"Day cares? Applied?"

"Yes, the moment we knew we were expecting, I

put us on the list for four day cares," Paula explained.

"Where did you get in?" Collette asked.

"None. We ended up with a nanny share till preschool," Paula replied.

"Okay, everyone," Gill's voice boomed. "Let's all gather together. I prepared some games."

Oh no! Games? What kind of games? "In this bag are several items," she began, holding a stone-gray bag big enough to challenge a briefcase. Three zippers in different lengths offered access to pockets from the front to the middle of the bag.

"Without looking inside, you have to write down what you think each item is just by how it feels." In her other hand, Gill held up a wooden board with papers and pens lying on it. She handed the stationery to her husband, who took a piece of paper and a pen before passing both items on to me.

I followed his lead, taking a paper and a pen and passing the rest on. Greg had already felt the items in the bag and was jotting down ideas of what they could be. Once done, he passed the bag to me. I reached inside. Five items of different sizes tumbled in the confined space. Four of them were wrapped in plastic. Woven fibers created the fifth one. Maybe a washcloth? But the dimensions were off. Perhaps a towel. But the thin material made me doubt my conclusion. Maybe it was some sort of onesie. Despite being clueless, I jotted the onesie down. One out of five, hurray.

Feeling good about myself, I gave the bag to Guido. Four more people waited for their turn after my hubby.

Everyone else reached into the bag, guessed, and wrote down their thoughts. The company of others was very nice. At home, Guido, our friends, our family, and colleagues surrounded me daily. I chatted with my sister throughout our days apart too.

With all this change, I hadn't noticed how lonely I'd felt in the past couple of weeks. I had pushed this acknowledgment away every time I had missed my sister's phone call because we were still in bed. And when I tried to reach her, she was working. This time difference really took its toll.

"Alright. As everyone had a turn already, let's find out how many items you guessed correctly." Gill turned the bag upside down. The contents tumbled out in a pile. Now, seeing the items, I rolled my eyes at myself. A pack of baby wipes, a wrapped-up pacifier, a small pack of diapers, nipple cream, and a swaddling blanket. I got zero right.

"And this is for you." Gill pushed the bag in my direction.

My eyes widened in surprise. "Pardon me?"

"We heard that you didn't have a diaper bag yet, so here you go," she explained.

Before I could protest, Gill had already set up another game: guessing baby food—blindfolded. Oh, man. Some of the spooned-up mash was horrible. Were the taste buds of babies so different from adult ones? I was a total sucker for any type of applesauce, sweetened or not, but I could barely swallow some of these samples. Note to self: Try everything before giving the food to the baby.

"Okay, how about opening some gifts?" Gill proposed after we wrapped up the food guessing game.

She sat me on the sofa and gave me one gift-wrapped item after another. I opened a big box of diapers, a mobile, a baby bouncer, and a baby footprint kit. This felt like my birthday and Christmas came on the same day. Overwhelmed by the generosity of Guido's colleagues, I could only say thanks. I was not prepared for so many gifts.

Shortly after I finished unwrapping, the party dissolved, with every guest receiving bagged cupcakes. Barret carried the box of diapers and mobile. Collette brought the bagged cupcakes downstairs for us.

"Are you sure this isn't inconvenient?" I said.

"Don't worry. We have a big car."

Soothed by her words, I swung the diaper bag around my shoulder. Guido carried the bouncer with the onesies from the arts and crafts station and the footprint maker.

"Thank you very much for taking us home," I told the couple.

"It's honestly not a problem at all. We have the evening free anyway; the boys will sleep over at Collette's mom's," Barret replied.

"You don't know how much we needed this," Collette added. "We can eat what we want. We can watch what we want." Relief was evident in her voice.

Collette and Barret guided us along the walkway. Suddenly, he stopped next to a red car. Not just a car but an enormous pickup truck. I mean, ginormous. The hood of the vehicle was as high as my head. I wasn't tiny, more so average, I would say, for a woman. But how could a car be allowed to be above five and a half feet?

The vehicle's body hung at least a foot above the wide wheels. I hoped a ladder to help climb into the seat was attached somewhere.

"Thank you so much for helping us out." Guido placed the bouncy chair in the back of the pickup truck.

"It's no problem at all," Barret repeated.

Collette opened the back door for me. Simultaneously, a step extended downward. With the help of the metal railing, I hauled myself into the truck's back seat. A roomy interior dwarfed me. From the outside, already the truck rivaled the length of a van. Our little Peugeot would fit in the entire passenger area. The truck hummed through the city. Despite it not even being five, darkness blanketed the town. The faux leather seats made me feel like a toddler just about to ask, "Are we there yet?"

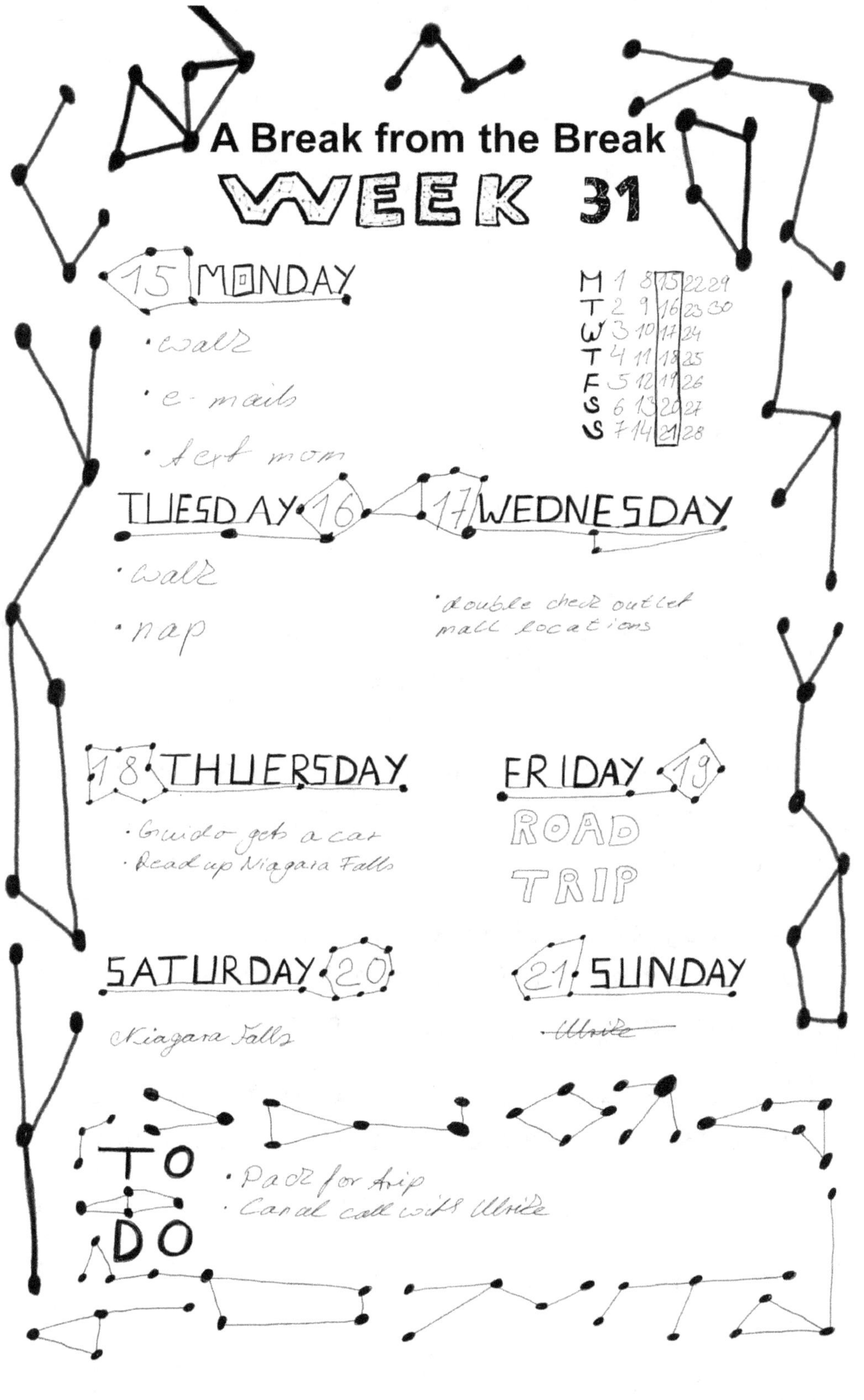

A Break from the Break
WEEK 31

15 MONDAY
· walk
· e-mails
· text mom

M 1 8 15 22 29
T 2 9 16 23 30
W 3 10 17 24
T 4 11 18 25
F 5 12 19 26
S 6 13 20 27
S 7 14 21 28

TUESDAY 16   17 WEDNESDAY
· walk
· nap
· double check outlet mall locations

18 THUERSDAY   FRIDAY 19
· Guido gets a car   ROAD
· Read up Niagara Falls TRIP

SATURDAY 20   21 SUNDAY
Niagara Falls   Ulrike

TO · Pack for trip
    · Canal call with Ulrike
DO

Week 31

A Break from the Break

<u>Thursday</u>

There would be no chitchat with my sister this Sunday. We were going to Niagara Falls. I texted Ulrike.

I am so jealous, she replied. *I want to see them too one day. Until then, I am looking forward to hearing all about them.*

I wrote back, *There's still time to visit us. They are closer to here than they are to Potsdam.*

Well, you're right, but I can't make it.

"What are you doing?" Guido asked.

"Texting my sister. How is the car?"

"The car is nice. It feels brand-new, and the automatic is so easy to drive. Plus, I found a map. I will just put the visitor parking pass in the car and then study the map."

"Okay. Have you packed a bag already?" I said.

"No. I'll do it before going to bed."

"Okay." I turned my attention back to my sister.

I just realized that it's late for you, I texted. *Why aren't you sleeping?*

Inspiration struck me. Anyway, I'll go to bed in a couple minutes once I finish something. I wish you guys a nice trip. Talk to you next week.

Yes, thanks. Have a lovely weekend yourself.

Friday

My eyelids inched open but soon plunged down again. Black rubber brushed against the asphalt. The white noise increased my desire to drool. Yet my conscience overruled my eyelids. Instead of surrendering to my napping mode, I stretched out my limbs in the contained space of the rental car. The bright sun hung low in the west. Yet our trip to Niagara Falls had just started.

Twice a day, I marveled at the quick sunrise and sunset. Dawn and dusk lasted much longer back home. Was the difference noticeable in the summer as well? One of the best parts of July and August was hanging out with friends; for hours, the twilight drew out late into the night. Now the intensity of the lightness had increased just enough to be noticeable as well.

But with my limited knowledge of nature sciences, no proper explanation volunteered in my head. Maybe, just like the quick change of day and night, the brightness correlated with my new geographical location. After all, the East Coast mirrored Germany's seasons. I consulted my phone, painfully aware of no Internet availability, but still pulled up the general map of the world. Unfortunately, a pixelated resolution was displayed on my screen. I zoomed in and out to compare our current location to home ineffectively.

Fortunately, a paper version of the world stretched out on printed pages bound by rings within my arm's reach. Glee poured from Guido's pores when he studied the map. I couldn't even remember when I had last used a paper map.

"What are you doing?" Guido asked.

"Finding out if Boston lies on the same level as Potsdam." The colorful overview mainly showed visuals of streets and towns in Massachusetts. At the end, the world was illustrated in black ink. My right index finger hovered over Boston. The tip drew a line toward Europe. "Aha," I exhaled. "The geographical location of Boston does not align with Berlin," I informed my husband.

"Oh, that's surprising."

"Yes, it is. Boston sits much closer to the equator."

"Maybe that's the reason the light here seems brighter," Guido wondered aloud.

"I've noticed that too, but if a country is closer to the equator, doesn't the climate increase in its tropical-ness?" I asked. A picture of the rainforest drifted into my mind, but no water droplets layered the air.

"Perhaps the reason for your confusion is the map itself," Guido said.

"What do you mean?"

"Well, the countries on a world map do not reflect their sizes proportionally. The Mercator projection provides a visual 2D explanation of the world but distorts countries' sizes compared to reality."

Heat rose in my cheeks. "Mmmmhhh, what?" Discovering gaps in my knowledge always smacked me in the face, especially in the presence of my husband. "So what does that mean?" I gulped, painfully aware that my husband had already figured out that I missed crucial information.

"Germany roughly fits into California," Guido explained.

"Huh." Despite this amazing information, this nugget of knowledge didn't answer my question at all. Or did it? I mean, what if, in reality, Boston lined up with Potsdam and not Barcelona. From what I had seen so far, even the flora could be compared to the one at home, along with the seasonal changes.

The trees passed by faster as Guido accelerated. "What are you doing?" I squinted at my husband. Guido overtook a car on his left side.

"Passing him," offered my husband.

"I saw that, but in the right lane!" I exclaimed, dumbfounded by his nonchalant attitude.

Guido wasn't a bad driver, but he wasn't well-versed either. To be fair, neither was I. We barely drove anywhere, even though we owned a Peugeot 103. We used the car once a month for hiking in the Harz or Elbe Sandstone Mountains. Yet we both had received our driver's license at eighteen. We'd accumulated plenty of experience. Passing in the right lane, however, could be punished with a fine and result in a point in Flensburg, where the German motor vehicle authority is headquartered.

Before I voiced my objections, several cars in the right lane overtook drivers in the middle, and middle drivers overtook vehicles in the left lane. What was going on?

"It looks like passing in the right lane is allowed around here," Guido said to justify his actions. Cars drifted by left and right.

"Maybe," I caved. Signs on the interstate floated by. The green displays instead of blue ones triggered unexpected chuckles from me.

"What's so funny?" Guido asked.

"Have you noticed that we are driving through the world or better parts of Europe?"

"What do you mean?"

"I've seen exits for Amsterdam, Rotterdam, and Verona, as well as Rome," I explained.

"I guess whoever settled here first originated from those towns," Guido speculated.

"You're probably right. But why?" If I remembered correctly, the first official settlers ended up in Plymouth for less than desirable reasons. Oh, we did need to visit that town.

Anyway, I pondered over why those people settled here back then. Exploring, treasure hunting, escaping dire circumstances? I made a mental note to research this history later.

I stifled a yawn. The interstate stretched out into an endless drive of boringness.

"Why don't we just get off here and see if we can find somewhere to stay overnight?" I suggested.

"I was just thinking the same thing." Guido exited the interstate and drove north on a random street. At the beginning of our trip, several signs indicated gas stations, restaurants, and accommodations. But for the past two hours, nothing. Even exit signs had vanished. My eyes scanned the gas tank indicator. Only a few millimeters remained before the red block signaled the need for an energizing liquid.

My right pinky finger bounced up and down on the roof handle. My shoulders tensed. My eyes scanned the sides of the interstate, and then a click forced my head to spin. The gas refill light turned orange. The air in the car grew heavy, and my eyes squinted. I searched for a refill station.

My husband indicated to the right. The exit street circled outward onto a smaller road. The forest grew denser. No gas station, no restaurant, no hotel, no bed-and-breakfast appeared.

The sun had set in the west. Guido snailed over the road. Any slower, and I would have bet he was trying to mimic every horror movie. Already in my mind, someone creepy would pop out from behind the tree trunks any minute. To underline the eeriness, mist covered the street. Layers of colors ranging from blue to yellow to orange and pink faded into the black of the night. Guido slowed down even more.

"What are you doing?" I shrieked.

"Look." He pointed at a ten-foot-tall sign: *Black Forest Motel*. I rubbed my eyes. Sure enough, a blank space graced the sign before the word of the night: *Vacancy*. The announcement stood smack in the middle of nowhere. No, not nowhere. Right in the middle of a darkening forest. We continued on. After ten minutes, which felt like an hour, a one-story building came into our view. Paint peeled off the window frames. Wood chipped away from pillars that held the roof over the walkway into the individual rooms. An artificial light source lit up one room. Three cars were parked in front of the structure.

The office door creaked as we entered the main door, and simultaneously, a bell rang above us. A perky young woman with pink cotton lips and extra-blonde hair gave us a warm grin. "Welcome to the Black Forest Motel. Would you like a room?" Taken aback by her appearance, neither of us reacted to her question. The young woman's smile faltered. Her eyes flickered back and forth between us. "Do you need anything else?" she continued, unsure what to do with us.

Guido cleared his throat. "We do need a room." His voice quivered slightly. I froze in the middle of a "Bates Motel" hotel, questioning my reality once more. *The Twilight Zone* used to be my go-to show. Now I appeared in one. My heart rate increased. Excited, fearful, and timid, yet full of glee, I absorbed my experience abroad.

Guido received a key from the woman after he paid for the night. "What time will breakfast be served?"

"We don't offer breakfast. We are a motel."

"Okay, thanks," Guido sighed.

This place is called a motel because it has no breakfast? sat on my tongue.

"Is there a place nearby where we could find some breakfast?" Guido asked.

I feared her answer: six more miles south.

"Just follow the street for maybe two miles, and you'll see a diner on your right side." Her words lifted my spirits. A diner! Ecstasy filled my being, just like in an American movie.

We shuffled along the row of doors and stopped before what should have been number nine. Only one metal pin remained on the end tip, flipping the nine over to look like a six.

I unlocked the door while Guido got our bags out of the car. Of course, our rental was parked conveniently right in front of room number one. The motel door swung open, and I switched on the light. Guido gasped. I laughed. After all, we had entered our very own personal twilight zone. Every shade of icky brown competed for space in our one-night accommodation. Between the carpet, bedcover, wallpaper, window curtains, dresser, nightstand, and reading lamps, I couldn't decide which room item got the worst shade of brown. Unfortunately, the color scheme also competed against a smell. A familiar smell, yet I had trouble believing we'd find the source of the scent in this room.

The stale perfume of cigarette smoke hung between the fabric's threads. Ashtrays with dark shadows waited to be used on the nightstands, even though "no smoking" signs had been plastered in the reception area. A white sticker next to the door to our room spelled out the same message.

I glanced through the window curtains. Darkness enveloped the trees. Running into the forest wasn't a good idea. This strategy didn't bode well in horror movies, and neither did it appeal to me in real life.

I eyed our rental car. Guido followed my gaze to the automobile. "The back seat is too small. Besides, it will be freezing." I pursed my lips. No other feasible option came to me. Defeated, I closed the curtains.

"Did you ask for the Internet password?" Toothpaste was splashed on the cappuccino wood-framed mirror. Guido shrugged his shoulders. I pushed the brownish shower curtain aside. And I just couldn't. The brown plastic-wrapped shower showed off blackened scratches on the sides.

Unshowered, I changed into my pajamas and peeled the faded chocolate-mousse bed comforter back, only to discover a thin beige mattress cover tucked in so tightly that I barely managed to press my aching body between it and the thin linen sheet. I pulled on the fabric's sides, hoping my hubby would hurry up. I shivered and forgot my urge to check my messages on my phone.

Guido snuggled up next to me. I pressed my cold feet onto his warm skin. At least the mattress invited a slumber when combined with my hot hubby.

"Do you hear that?" Guido whispered.

I pricked up my ears. A rhythmic squeak, with a soft moan weaving in, filtered through the air. Guido grinned expectantly. Periodic banging against our wall really made the actions of our neighbors obvious.

"How about we try that?" Guido asked.

"We already made a baby," I yawned.

Saturday

No cars passed us on the single-lane street. Low-hanging clouds grayed out a farm-like landscape. Only pictures of basketballs with names and numbers pinned to the overhead wire poles provided a touch of color.

"Do you know what that means?" I pointed at the signs on the side of the road, which clearly weren't street signs.

"Maybe they're for kids on a school team?" he proposed.

I pulled out my notebook.

1) Why do shoes hang from overhead wires?

2) Why are there two doors?

3) What do the signs on the side of the street mean?

And I almost forgot . . .

4) Why does the sun set so fast?

What else . . . ? My fingers drummed my pen's tip periodically on the page. My eyes zeroed in on the horizon. Two houses on the left and right of the street came into view. Once we passed them, several more houses sprung up. These homes created a townish sort of feel.

"I think this is it." Guido parked in front of a building with a storefront and tall windows—the diner. Guido pointed at a snoozing cargo deliverer. We both sized up the transporter. Massive was the only word to describe the vehicle. When I say massive, I mean enormous. The hood easily spanned four fridges in a single line.

We'd passed several commercial vehicles on the interstate. These long-distance trucks mustered way more horsepower under their hood than German ones. Come to think of my past experiences, I'd never been overtaken by a truck on the Autobahn, the German interstate. My husband positioned our car in front of the beast of the street—dwarfed in front of the grill. I snapped a picture to prove its massiveness just when my tummy growled like an angry dog.

We stepped inside, and I pinched myself. Six tables with four metallic chairs occupied the space in front of us. Six booths lined the walls, with guests on both sides of the aisle.

An older woman in a baby-blue dress and a pearl-white, black-stained apron approached us. My smile widened like a little girl who had just received a treat. Actually, this was a treat. I was in the middle of my very own American experience.

The server led us to a booth and cleaned up the used dishes on the table. Then she wiped the table down before placing a one-page menu, two porcelain cups, and two glasses full of ice in front of us. She filled the plastic cup with water and poured coffee into Guido's cup. Before she filled up mine, I covered the opening with my hand. A drip of the brown liquid burned my skin.

"I'm sorry, hun," she apologized.

Instead of arguing over my own stupidity, I asked, "Do you have hot chocolate?"

"Sure, hun."

The waitress left us studying the printed paper with the dishes they offered. However, she returned only moments later with a big ceramic cup topped with whipped cream, marshmallows, powdered chocolate, and green sprinkles. She placed the cup in front of me.

"Are you ready to order?"

"I think so," we said together.

"I'll take the hash browns with egg and ham, please," Guido stated.

The woman scribbled on her notepad before turning her attention to me.

"I would like to have the pancakes with strawberries, please."

"You've got it. "

Guido reached for my hands. "So, I think the outlet mall is maybe ten minutes from here. I can't believe you want to go shopping now," Guido complained.

"It's not that I only want to go shopping. I want to shop in an outlet center for our child, for whom we still have almost nothing."

"Watch out! The plate is hot," the server warned. She put sizzling dark brown and beige food in front of Guido. A tower of pancakes topped with whipped cream and strawberries ringing the plate's rim landed in front of me. Not just the food landed on our table, but our bill as well. "Whenever you're ready," she added before turning her attention to other customers.

Even though I was starving when we entered the restaurant, I barely finished my breakfast. Guido finished his, though, and eyed my leftover strawberries. "You know, once the baby is born, my weight will go back down again," I teased.

"Do you want to let the food go to waste?" he countered.

* * *

Guido pushed the gas pedal. The car roared. "Next up, gas station," he announced.

"And then some baby shopping," I added.

"And then visiting one of the world's wonders," Guido said.

"I am so excited. We traveled for hours, driving around the world, staying in a motel, and eating in a diner. We hope to buy some well-priced baby clothes and see some impressive nature."

"Yep," Guido managed. He indicated left to drive into the gas station.

"Have you seen the prices?" Three different lines indicated three different types of gasoline sold, with the cheapest being $3.20. My heart rate increased its speed. "Perhaps we should start talking about finances more. I feel like money is running through our fingers like sand," I whimpered.

"The prices are per gallon, not liter," Guido reminded me as he drove into the gas station.

"Oh."

"So, it's actually cheap," he added.

The moment he stopped next to a gasoline pump, a man approached us.

"Which lead do you want?" the man asked after he picked up the pump nozzle.

"I'm sorry, what?" Guido gasped.

"This is a serviced gas station," the man replied.

"Excuse me?" Guido's bewilderment reflected mine.

"I put the gas in the car. You stay in your car. I will pay for you if you give me your credit card," the man explained.

My skin crawled with every word. His last statement made me hold my breath.

"No thanks," Guido answered. "That is not necessary."

The man pointed to a sign above the gas prices—*Serviced Station*. Guido turned to the indicated spot. "Ugh," escaped his lips. "How about I give you twenty bucks, and you fill up the car for that much." A relieved sigh slipped out of my lips. Guido pulled a twenty-dollar bill out of his wallet. The man filled up the car.

"That is strange," I said, exhaling.

"I have heard about this before. Apparently, it is a common practice in some areas," Guido replied.

"It is? I don't feel comfortable handing over my card while we're sitting in the car," I said.

"Me neither. That is why we're paying cash."

"Should we tip him?" I asked my hubby.

"I don't know. Maybe?" He pulled out five dollars in single bills. "What do you think?" he asked, unsure.

I shrugged. Guido handed the man the money when he leaned over the open driver's-side window.

"Thanks. You're all set," the gas station attendant said after the transaction.

* * *

Somehow, Guido remembered where to drive without a GPS voice telling him what to do or where to go. In awe of his ability to remember the map, I watched as he drove on a country road until we rolled along a newly paved two-lane street. We both saw the sign: *NY Highland Outlet Mall.* Arrows pointed left and right. Guido drove left. He crossed over into the parking lot of the mall. I clapped my hubby on the back for his accomplishment.

Guido parked the car in an empty parking lot. I counted sixty free spaces. However, more parking wrapped around the entire one-level mall, with overflow areas nestled deeper in the forest.

I stretched my limbs. Water hung low in the air between the surrounding evergreen trees. Only a tiny patch of light shimmered through the densely covered morning sky.

Freshly packed black mulch between bushes edging the car park area spiked the air with farm fumes. People dressed in green clothes power-washed the sidewalks with high-pressure water.

We strolled by bag, shoe, and women's and men's clothing shops. Every store's sign displayed the same: *CLOSED*. This circumstance shouldn't have been a surprise. The vacant parking lot already told us.

"When do they open?" Guido asked.

"I don't know."

"Ten thirty," he said.

"No. It's nine thirty."

"They open at ten thirty. It's written right here on the door," Guido pointed out.

"Oh," I coughed out. I suppressed the urge to slap my forehead.

"Shall we see if we can find a coffee?" I asked. Guido nodded. I threaded my arm through his and pulled him forward onto the quest of wasting an hour.

* * *

At 10:29 sharp, we stood in front of the baby store. A woman unlocked the sliding doors. Red signs boasting "75% off" hung from the ceiling.

"Good morning. Can I help you find anything?" The young girl with the keys in her hands gazed at us expectantly.

"We are looking for newborn clothes." My voice echoed in the store.

"Boy or girl?" the sales rep inquired.

"Boy," Guido said.

"You'll find all newborn sizes over there." Our heads turned in the indicated direction. "I can show you as well. Just follow me." We trailed the young woman. "Here you'll find zero to three months, four to six months, and seven to twelve months—from here lined up to the wall," she explained.

"Thanks," I replied with a smile.

"If you need anything else, please let me know." She headed back to the front of the store while we browsed the selections.

"Oh, look at this." Guido held up a doll-size onesie. The green sitting frogs were so cute on the baby outfit.

"Do you think it would fit?" The romper could fit a baby doll.

Guido checked the size. "It says newborn, " he said, holding the dress against my belly.

"Really?" I rolled my eyes to the piled-up sales tables next to us.

Every onesie, every two-part outfit, increased in adorability. From elephant prints to duckies, monkeys, and lions. We purchased them all. One of each. But who could have predicted that Guido would top my pile of baby clothes? He fell in love with the ducky prints, buying four in consecutive sizes.

We both had satisfied grins plastered on our faces. Our baby would have at least thirty outfits to choose from when he was born. And one more item ticked off my list. Hurray!

* * *

We wound our way through the fall landscape. On one side, a big lake appeared. A wall with a building attached ran along the water. In the distance, a tower with a needle reached into the sky. "Is that Toronto?"

"I can't imagine that you can see Toronto from here."

"What is it?" I inquired.

"I don't know," Guido replied.

We passed our first sign for Niagara Falls. Only two more miles. I sat up straighter.

I noticed the "Welcome to Niagara Falls" sign with excitement. A couple of high-rises marked the skyline.

We drove up to a sky-high hotel. The name of the building contained the word *casino*. Only a few existed in Germany. Neither Guido nor I had ever been to one.

We checked into a room. Food and the urge to finally see the reason for our long drive shrugged off our tiredness.

After a short promenade, we found a sandwich shop. Bundled in our winter jackets, we hit parklike trails. Lights illuminated the stone path. Water drops vibrated through the air. A gazebo opened up to a gap between the river's edges. Niagara Falls. Well, we sort of saw them. We leaned forward. Blue, yellow, and pink lights dyed the water mass into giant cotton candy balls.

I squeezed Guido's shoulder. "Can we come back tomorrow?" I asked. Guido opened his mouth to respond, but I quickly added, "I'm freezing."

We reached the entrance of the hotel with swift steps on empty streets. The flickering of the fireplace right off the reception area instantly caught my eye. The gas fireplace heated my back. I turned to defrost my front. A poster informed guests of a planned hotel and casino renovation to commence within the coming weeks.

Guido's eyes trailed every single person who vanished behind three sets of double doors.

"How about we each take fifty bucks and call it a day when they're gone?" Guido grinned at me, and I added, "I only have five twenties. Here's sixty. I'll take forty."

"Are you sure?" Guido asked with one hand on the door.

"Yes, I am," I confirmed as the casino entrance closed behind us. A hue of soft yellow illuminated a hall filled with gambling tables and machines. We strolled along the carpeted floor and passed a poker table with two people playing. So far, the guests averaged around sixty years old. I always pictured hotheaded young men losing their lives in a gambling hall.

We watched. But the money of the players vanished within minutes. I pulled Guido toward the row of slot machines at the back wall of the casino. We both pushed in the requested amounts of bills and pulled the lever. Pictures on three reels whooshed by. My hope to get a triple match increased.

Ding, ding, ding, ding, ding. We turned to the left. An older woman, accompanied by another, screamed. We gasped. The woman had won. A casino employee approached the winner. "In what currency would you like the fifty thousand dollars cashed out? We have everything: dollars, Canadian dollars, euros, yens . . ."

"Can I have more?" Guido asked.

I bit my lip. He could spend as much money as he saw fit, but we weren't losing peanuts here. With the edges of my lips pulled up, I purred, "You know, with another hundred dollars, you could buy me a gift card for a foot massage."

A sharp exhale reached my ears. Guido got up. With the money gone, we returned to our room. Before bed, I received my foot massage and drifted off to sleep.

Other Countries, Other Customs

Week 32

Other Countries, Other
Customs

<u>Monday</u>

Week 32! Only . . . or suddenly? For me, the pregnancy stretched out like gum. Not only that, in horror I discovered that the first Advent happened yesterday. How could that be? Even though December came at the same time every year, I felt so unprepared this year. I wasn't much of a Christmas decoration person, but we didn't have a single Christmas calendar. Ugh. Most years, we had at least seven displayed in our home.

Guido always got three, and so did I. We each received two chocolate calendars courtesy of our parents. One came from work with lemonade samples—which my sister always tried to pre-empty on the Second Advent when we devoured our first *Stollen*[1] of the season. And we would get several courtesy of promotional advertisements in our mailbox every year. But this year, zilch. My chest tightened. We had to have at least one Advent calendar, even if I had to make one myself, as my mother used to when Ulrike and I were little.

In proper mom form, she would sew one; on top of the black background, the girl from *Sternentaller*[2] smiled, and coins rained. She'd attach twenty-four pockets at the bottom of the canvas, where she put in knickknacks every year. My sister's Christmas calendar represented Goldmarie[3] receiving her gold from Frau Holle.[4] Of course, jealousy of each other's calendar caused sisterly fights. We still owned our kiddie ones. In fact, my mother decorated with both every year.

I rummaged through my brain to find an idea, scanning the living room simultaneously for some inspiration for a quick DIY version. My eyes landed on the pile of bills from the previous apartment. Paper boxes came to my mind. One or two boxes would have been perfectly fine, but twenty-four . . .

Every time I folded paper, an uneven mess came out. I searched for envelopes, but we didn't have those either. What else? A gray paper tube sprawled out on the bathroom floor. Hmm. Perhaps "candy" rolls?

I marched into the bathroom. One tube lay on the floor, and two were in the trash. Yikes! Twenty-four unused rolls were stacked under the sink. Would Guido mind unfolding toilet paper from a tangled mess for the next few months? Probably not.

My mind drifted back to the idea of making paper boxes. I pulled out some old bills and letters asking Guido to sign up for credit cards.

Every day, a promotional letter landed in our mailbox with offers like, *Spend $1,000, get $200 back*. To get my first credit card approved, I moved mountains. The bank denied me a credit card due to my lack of credit history. I was granted one after showing the bank my employee statements with regular income from my part-time gigs since I was sixteen.

I folded one paper after another into a box. Hours later, forty-eight halves were scattered on the ground. I put them together to get twenty-four boxes. The text and numbers on the paid invoices added an unexpected texture to the calendar. I didn't mind the print. Only one issue persisted: I couldn't write on the folded box.

I glanced at my stationery stuff. Three washi rolls lay in my pencil case. I pulled out the black one with gold stars, cut two pieces off, and stuck the two strips on a folded gift box to form the number "1." I repeated the process with the other twenty-three boxes. The result was a complete Advent calendar. The boxes turned out to be adorable, if I did say so myself.

<u>Tuesday</u>

Propelled by the sheer cuteness of my DIY Advent calendar, I scraped together more paper to make one for our neighbors. Henrietta and her husband, Tanner, had invited us for Thanksgiving dinner. Warmth heated up my body. My first American holiday with an American family. As this calendar doubled as a gift, the printed paper wouldn't cut it. In the name of craftiness, my mind wandered back to my washi tapes.

I folded, flattened, refolded, and straightened out folded lines. My fingers itched. My hand muscles burned. After the forty-eight lay in front of me, I plastered my striped washi tape over every visible corner of ink on the boxes, inside and out; instead of folded bills, patterned black-and-white origami boxes piled up. I admired my craftiness, but one snag remained. The calendars needed surprises inside.

I rummaged through my memories. My mom always stuffed Advent calendars herself every year. Instead of sweets, she put pens, hair clips, bouncy balls, matchbox cars, bobby pins, and hair ties into the pockets. One year, she put paper and instructions for origami shapes inside, which I hated. I only managed to successfully make the box-folding one. The others I screwed up.

I could not think of any filler, so I prepared for a stroll. The cold air hit my face. I usually stretched out my daily walks, but chilliness slithered into my jacket. A quick, fast-paced walk would be enough for today.

Instead of working up a sweat, I stopped in my tracks. On the other side of the street strutted five birds. If I was standing in front of them, their heads would almost reach my kneecaps. One of the birds spread its wings. Brownish-black feathers rivaled the wingspan of a swan. The birds didn't mind the people on the sidewalk.

I was impressed by how much wildlife coexisted with humans in this town. Zeroing in on the pharmacy, I opened the glass doors.

Instead of pumpkin spice, a new scent greeted me. I couldn't put my finger on the airborne perfume, but the fragrance touched my memories. The spice was ginger. When my mom put the spice in any dish, I could taste the seasoning before the fork landed in my mouth. Weirdly enough, ginger in ginger ale and gingerbread was delicious.

The flavor stuck in my nose, and my tummy rumbled. I moved from one aisle to the next on the gingerbread hunt, wondering if they carried *Nürnberger*[5] here.

I turned onto the sweet treat aisle and stopped before red strings. The letters on the packaging spelled out *Twizzlers*. My eyes scanned the candy in front of me. Perfect. I scooped up one red package of the stretched-out candy. My arms overflowed with Skittles, Reese's, Hershey's, and Mike and Ikes. In short, any candy I didn't know.

Close to a minor accident involving tumbling sweets, I balanced my bounty between my arms and upper body until I found a shopping basket. Nonchalantly, I dropped them all in the cart.

I continued my quest for the Christmasy baked goods, ambling along the heads of the aisles. And lo and behold, Speculoos cookies lined up in the seasonal section. I scooped a bag up. The packaging read: *ginger cookies*. They didn't look like Speculoos at all. Besides feeling soft, the baked goods didn't display any pictures. A hint of false promise annoyed me. The scent tricked me into thinking I'd found a piece of home. I twisted the packaging around. When did I become so stuck-up? Who cared about the pictures on the package? I popped a bag in my basket.

As I pushed the cart along with the Christmas stuff, I added chocolate Santas to my growing pile. But I worried about whether Henrietta would be so keen on me giving her son sweets for twenty-four days. My eyes landed on a bag of marbles. I had fond memories of building marble tracks with my sister. But would the boy keep the tiny glass balls from his younger sibling?

My head spun. Who knew finding nice presents for a child would be so hard? I hoped it would be easier when I had my own child to consider. When I was about to give up, I noticed a display of matchbox cars stood before me. Two sets fell onto my growing shopping mountain.

Pleased with having sorted out the Advent calendar issues, I trotted to the checkout counter. A display of cards blocked my path. A sigh relaxed my shoulders. Christmas cards were lined up on a cardboard stand. I grabbed two sets of ten cards. While the young employee scanned one item after another, I relished the store's heat, dreading the cold outside after paying for my bounty.

At Home

Bundled up on the sofa, I scanned my inbox. Emails from work trickled in, which I may or may not answer. After all, I was out of the office. Years ago I stopped responding to work calls or emails during my vacation. Yet this time around, guilt dripped into my boundaries. While I contemplated why my attitude toward my rules had weakened, I heard the door to our apartment open.

"Hey, honey," my husband greeted me.

"Hey. How was your day?" I asked him.

"Good. I just bumped into Henrietta."

"Did you ask her what we could bring for Thanksgiving? I don't want to feel useless again, like at the baby shower."

"She asked us to bring something German."

"Something German?" I whispered.

"Yeah, some typical German food."

"What? Like sauerkraut or Thüringer?"[6]

"I guess so," he replied with a shrug.

My head spun. What did we usually make for lunch or dinner back home? I had yet to see any sauerkraut or Thüringer here. On the other hand, I hadn't looked for it either. I was in a foreign country and was excited to try the local food.

"Any ideas?" Guido pushed.

"No. Not really. You?"

"Me neither." Guido typed on his keyboard. "So, typical German food is Currywurst," Guido read out loud.

"Have you ever made those?" I didn't know anyone who made Currywurst[7] themselves. One just buys it, just like Broiler,[8] Wiener,[9] and, of course, Döner.[10] I licked my lips.

"What do you think of Stollen? With Christmas and all," Guido said, yanking me out of my food dreams.

"How many people do you know who bake Stollen?"

"Have you seen any in the grocery store?" Guido countered.

"Or perhaps Quarkkeulchen.[11] Do you think we can buy quark here?"

Guido shook his head. "I haven't seen many familiar products around here. I hadn't really looked for them, but maybe quark and Rollmops[12] are available."

I grinned at the idea. "Mmm, yum."

"They definitely have potatoes. So potato salad should be possible," Guido added.

"That's a good idea," I said.

"Potato salad is easy to make, and maybe we can make a Quarkkeulchen for dessert."

I nodded eagerly. "Sounds like a plan."

"I'll go shopping." Guido wrapped his coat around his shoulders.

"Okay," I replied as he left for the grocery store to get the ingredients.

Just after I cleaned the kitchen, Guido popped back home with fewer groceries than I'd expected.

"I think we need to rethink what we're going to make. They didn't have quark or Rollmops. While I searched, I kept my eyes peeled for Rote Grütze[13] and pudding powder."

"You are so sweet. But what are we going to do?" I groaned.

Guido shrugged. He unpacked a bag of potatoes, one onion, a jar of pickles, and a package of bacon.

"At least the potato salad looks promising," I noted.

"Yeah," Guido agreed, peeling the potatoes in the kitchen.

"If we have flour, sugar, and butter, I might be able to make Mürbeteigplätzchen,"[14] I proposed. My screen gave me several hundred recipe options. With Guido by my side, I might actually not burn the oven-baked cookies.

"That's awesome. If you need anything we don't have, I can get it," Guido offered.

"Let's see. I need flour, sugar, butter, eggs, vanilla sugar, and baking powder," I read off the recipe with the title: *The easiest cookies you'll ever bake.*

Guido rummaged through the cabinets. One ingredient after another lined up on the counter.

"Nice," I thanked my husband. "Who knew we owned baking powder and vanilla sugar?"

I hunted for a bowl. No such luck. Oh well, our soup pot would do the job just fine. I read through all the ingredients, my pointer finger drumming on the counter.

"How many grams are in a bag of baking powder?" I asked. Guido wrinkled his forehead.

"The recipe calls for a bag, but we only have this 8.1 ounce container."

"I don't know? Just search for it!" Guido said.

"Okay, so I need seventeen grams." I checked the other ingredients. "Do we have a scale? The recipe is in grams and liters."

"I don't think so," he replied.

"How do I measure all the ingredients?" I whined.

"I think we have cups."

"Cups? I think we have two. But how is this supposed to help me?"

"These are cups for measurement. You just have to convert the units." Guido popped different-sized cooking cups with handles next to the flour. The sizes were imprinted on the handles: 1 cup, ¾ cup, ½ cup, ⅓ cup, ¼ cup. Teaspoons and tablespoons repeated the same numbers.

I popped all the components into the pot, then mixed, shaped, and baked the cookies to the best of my ability. "How about we add some sugar-lemon glaze with sprinkles?" I proposed.

"Sure, but we have no lemons or sprinkles. But I could get both tomorrow morning," Guido said.

"But isn't tomorrow a bank holiday?"

"Yes," Guido confirmed. He poured the potato halves into the pot with water.

Confused, I raised a brow. "So won't the store be closed?"

"I would say not. Most stores are open on Sundays. Not just that, I had to work on Independence Day, Labor Day, Indigenous Peoples' Day, and just two weeks ago on Veterans Day," he explained, slicing the pickles.

This surprised me. "So, do you have to work tomorrow?"

"No." My husband pressed his lips together.

"Okay, well, we'll manage without glazing. How about I start doing the dishes?" I offered. Guido nodded in agreement and cut the bacon into small pieces. I reached for the over-sink light switch. A mowing sound froze me on the spot. "What is this?" I yelled.

"That's the grinder! A food grinder," he explained. Wide-eyed, I fixed my eyes on the switch. Guido turned the chopper off. "Don't ever put your hands in the drain."

I stared at the opening in the sink and back to the on/off button. The light switch was installed exactly next to the grinder switch. They both had the same design, size, width, and color. No label or other marker screamed: *Watch out, next stop hospital!*

Thursday

With the potato salad in a pot, cookies piled up on a plate, and a bag with the Christmas calendar under our arms, we waited for the neighbors' door to open.

"Come in, come in," Henrietta called.

The smell of seared meat sizzling in oil mixed with glazed vegetables in a frying pan made my mouth water.

"Oh, you know a mulled wine would be nice right now," I said.

"Next year," Guido replied, glancing at my protruding belly.

Three sunflower-yellow ukuleles hung on the wall above a moss-green, child-size guitar flanked by two walnut adult guitars. Pushed to the side in the living room was a pile of colorful kids' toys. In the middle of the mass sat a dining table covered with a pearl-white tablecloth. Six porcelain plates ringed around the edges were accompanied by silverware and wine glasses. A crimson mousse, which could double as a grown-up version of Rote Grütze, gave the table a splash of color. Bread rolls towered on another plate.

"Who plays?" Guido asked.

"Tanner. He's teaching percussion at Berklee," Henrietta replied.

Tanner placed our potato salad, now in an off-white ceramic bowl, next to the red dessert-like dish.

"What is Berklee?" I asked.

"It's a college to study music," Tanner said. Henrietta followed with a plate of green beans and some sort of cake.

"So what's the difference between a university and a college?" Guido asked.

"Colleges offer only undergraduate degrees, and universities offer both undergrad and grad studies," Henrietta educated us.

Tanner returned with an enormous bird—a chicken on steroids. I glanced over the food on the table. The entire meal could feed at least ten people.

"Please sit," Henrietta said. "Do you want water, lemonade, cranberry juice, or cider?"

I squinted. Hmm. "But cider has alcohol."

"Well, no. This isn't a hard cider," Henrietta explained. She handed me the bottle.

The white label on the green bottle lacked alcohol per volume information.

Tanner's forehead wrinkled up. "You don't have cider in Germany?"

I pressed my lips together. Guido chuckled. "We do, but it is always with alcohol."

Henrietta's eyes widened. "What do you call it without alcohol then?"

"Sparkling or non-sparkling apple juice," I stated with a smile.

"That's so interesting," Tanner said with a nod.

"Anyway, in that case, I'll have the cider, please." I held my glass up, and Henrietta poured the brownish liquid into the goblet.

Tanner hurried back into the kitchen. Henrietta called Mercer to the table and buckled Attila, Mercer's baby brother, in a high chair. Guido sat down next to me, and Tanner poured wine into their glasses.

"Thank you so much for having us." I raised my bubbly juice. Guido, Henrietta, and Tanner lifted their glasses as well.

"Thanks for coming," our hosts pronounced. The four glasses reverberated off each other.

"And thank you for the Christmas calendar,"

Henrietta added, glancing at the pile of boxes on a bookshelf behind us.

"You're welcome. I hope the kids like it," I offered with a timid smile. Guido rubbed my back to boost my confidence.

"So, do you start on the twenty-fifth or the first?" Henrietta asked after taking a sip from her glass.

I copied her. The sweetness, paired with the bubbles, created a pleasing mixture in my mouth. "Twenty-fifth? There's only a twenty-fourth," I explained in surprise.

"No twenty-fifth? When does Santa come?" Mercer cried from his chair.

"Well, Santa comes to Germany on the evening of the twenty-fourth. When I was little, I had to sing him a song or recite a poem."

"You saw Santa?" Mercer screamed in our faces.

Instinctively, I knew the wrong words had left my mouth. I clenched my jaw to gate the next damaging slip-up. My grandpa had always dressed up with a fake white beard, a red coat, and two cleaned-up, sewn-together coal bags. Truthfully, at least eight years passed until I realized the man in the red suit was a family member.

"None of us ever see him," Mercer explained.

"But we put out milk and cookies to get a glimpse of him," Henrietta added.

"I always miss him. But he drinks the milk and eats the cookies." The boy's gaze fixed on me.

My head swiveled between one white-faced adult to the next until I ended back with the boy. "You know," I began, buying myself more time to think about how to get my head out of the hole I'd dug and not crush a kid's fantasy about the man in the red coat. Suddenly, an idea came to me. "You know, I think I only saw him because he had to come so early to us so that he can manage to be here during the night while you sleep." I searched again for help in the room.

"I don't understand. Why can't he come to us on the twenty-fourth and let us see him?" Mercer protested.

Why did he come on two different dates in different countries? Did he come on different days in other countries too? If I remembered correctly, Russia celebrated Christmas in January. And what was with Nicholas, anyway?

"So is Nicholas coming to you?" I asked.

"Nicholas?" Mercer repeated. Henrietta's and Tanner's faces bared blank stares.

"On the evening of December fifth, we clean our winter boots, put them in front of our doors, and the next morning, chocolate and some small gifts are in them, which Nicholas has put there," I explained.

"I want that too," Mercer cried.

"Well, we hang our 'boots' above the mantelpiece," Tanner said.

"You hang boots on what?" Guido asked.

"Well, it's not really boots, more booties, and we call them stockings. Traditionally, they are hung above a fireplace. But as we don't have one, we'll put them on the doorframe," Henrietta explained.

"Oh, I see," I said. Henrietta nudged her husband. Tanner got up to cut the big bird on the table.

"What kind of stuffing is in the turkey?" Guido asked curiously.

"It's a chicken in a duck in a turkey," Tanner explained.

"It's a Turducken," Henrietta added.

I scratched my forehead. Never had I ever seen anything like this dish.

"We got it especially for you," Tanner said at the exact moment a three-meat chunk dropped on my plate. My eyes scanned the pile, and my brain tried to explain the food before me. This pile contained just meat stacked on top of one another.

"Here, have some cranberry sauce," Henrietta offered. A blob of the jelly-like crimson mass landed on my plate. Guido placed a roll on his plate, along with a spoonful of beans. I pulled the meat apart, cut everything into bite-size pieces, and shoved a mix of each item onto my fork.

"So, have you figured out a name yet?" Henrietta asked.

"No, not really," Guido answered.

"I find it very hard to name a child," I said.

Tanner looked between the two of us with a smile. "I thought it was very easy."

"Well, we want the kid's name to be universal, so to speak," I explained.

"What do you mean?" Henrietta asked.

"Guido's grandparents are French, plus he still has other family living there, so we want the name to be easily pronounced in French and, of course, in German too."

"Also, Germany has stricter naming laws, I suppose," Guido added.

"How so?" Tanner asked.

"Well, the name should be easily identifiable as a person's name and should be non-offensive and prevent being made fun of, I guess," I explained.

Tanner and Henrietta displayed no expression on their faces.

"For example, we can't name the child VW because the letters are associated with a car and not with a person," Guido described.

"So, what if you really like a name and want to give it to your child?" Tanner inquired.

"Well, you can sue the state and fight for it if you want. Every couple of years, I read that people are doing that," I informed our hosts.

"I didn't know that," Guido admitted.

Henrietta changed the topic. "So, what's your first impression of Boston?"

I shrugged. "People seem really nice so far. Not that I know many."

"And what's the biggest difference between Germany and the US?" Tanner asked.

"The size. You can drive from north to south in Germany within twelve hours and west to east in six, maybe seven."

"That's so interesting," Henrietta remarked.

"That's true. Once, we drove from Fredericksburg to Indianapolis for the weekend because my parents had tickets for the Indy 500, and that was a fourteen-hour car ride," Tanner mused.

"Wow," Guido said.

"I think driving fourteen hours south would bring us maybe to Rome." Guido nodded in agreement with me after I calculated my estimate in my head.

"When is Mercer going to school?" I asked, taking a bite of my food.

"He'll start kindergarten next year," Henrietta replied.

"But isn't he already in kindergarten?" Guido asked.

"He's in preschool now," Tanner explained.

"But . . ." I began, not sure how to ask the question. "But preschool is after kindergarten, isn't it?"

"No, kindergarten is the first year of school."

"But isn't first grade the first year of school?" Confused, I gazed at Guido.

"Kindergarten is. Isn't it like that in Germany?" Tanner asked.

"Not really, as kindergarten is the place where kids go before school, and preschool isn't that common at all. Even if it were, the order would be kindergarten, preschool, first grade."

"Oh," Henrietta, said, looking as confused as Guido and I felt.

"So, are you going to get some good deals tomorrow?" Tanner changed the subject again.

"What's tomorrow?" I asked in curiosity.

"Tomorrow is Black Friday," Henrietta explained.

I'd heard of Black Friday before. All the stores back home started advertising sales with this headline, but I needed to understand the campaign. Now I knew where it came from.

"I don't blame you if you don't go shopping," Henrietta said.

"We actually still have to get a couple of high-priced items, like a stroller."

"Maybe we should look into it. Perhaps we can get a good deal?" Guido suggested.

"Do you already know which one you want?" Henrietta inquired.

"Unfortunately not. The one I had my eye on isn't sold here, so I feel like I need to start my research from scratch." I scooped up the last pieces of food on my plate.

"This was delicious," I said. The meal was rather good after I got over the meat with meat stuffed meat.

Once we cleared the table, Henrietta returned smaller plates to the living room, followed by her husband with dessert.

"What kind of cake are we having?" I contemplated how to fit more food into my belly.

"It's a pie—apple pie," Henrietta informed us.

"From Petsi's," Tanner added.

My eyebrows raised in surprise as I looked over the dish. "What's the difference between a cake and a pie?"

"A pie usually contains some sort of fruit," Henrietta explained.

Hmm, was such a distinction also made in Germany? I never thought of cakes, pies, and tortes[15] as being different at all.

Tanner dished out pieces of the apple pie.

"What does a traditional Christmas dinner look like for you?" Henrietta asked us.

"Well, we have potato salad and wieners on the twenty-fourth," Guido replied.

"And usually chicken with a stuffed apple on the twenty-fifth, and duck with potato dumplings and red cabbage on the second Christmas holiday," I added.

"The second Christmas holiday?" Tanner asked.

"Yeah, the twenty-sixth," I confirmed.

Guido took a bite of pie. "They don't have that here."

"Oh," I gasped, feeling slightly awkward.

"We usually return to work on the twenty-sixth," Tanner explained.

"Could I use the bathroom?" I asked.

"Sure. It's the door next to the front door," Henrietta said.

I got up to find the restroom. "Ouch!" I yelled out.

"Are you okay?" Tanner asked.

"I stepped on something sharp," I explained. Due to my tummy, I reached down unsuccessfully. Guido reached down instead. Between his fingers stuck out a thorn.

"What is it?"

"I am not sure. It is sharp, but it's not a needle," Guido said.

"Is it a hedgehog spike?" Tanner asked.

"A hedgehog spike?" Guido and I questioned in unison.

"Yeah, it's our pet," Henrietta explained.

"You're saying you have a real hedgehog as a pet?" I repeated.

"Yes, and we let it out every night in the living room," Henrietta said.

"So, you have a hedgehog, which is not hibernating," I began.

"That's correct. It is an African pygmy hedgehog and is not supposed to hibernate. She would die if she tried," Tanner explained.

I had so many questions. I knew people who would take in hedgehog babies from time to time. If they appeared to have lost their parents, they would hibernate in a box somewhere in their rescuer's house, but only to be released back into nature in the spring.

"You can keep the spike if you want?" Tanner offered.

"Oh, no, thank you. Maybe Mercer would like to keep it in his collection." As if on cue, the boy rushed toward Guido to collect the finding.

Hmm, maybe he would be a good parent, and I would always find the wrong words. Okay, okay, bad thinking, bad thinking. Perhaps I could learn from him how to talk to kids. At least my Santa misstep seemed to be forgotten.

* * *

We lay in bed, phasing into our nightly routine. With a belly rub, I soothed my tummy. Guido watched some more muscly men hammering on semi-molten metal on his computer screen. My mind drifted back to the dinner and the awkward Santa discussion. With that, I remembered the cards I'd bought.

"Have you signed the Christmas card to your brother and parents?" I asked.

"No, I didn't."

I extended my hand to a pile of cards with a note on them: *Please sign, M.* "If you do it now, I can send them tomorrow. I don't know how long it will take for them to arrive."

Guido checked his watch and then looked at the pile of cards again. I could totally guess his answer. "How about I look through them over the weekend? Maybe I am going to write a couple as well."

"Sure," I agreed, before dozing off.

Advent, Advent...
Week 33
december
M T W T F S S
29 30 1 2 3 4 5
6 7 8 9 10 11 12
13 14 15 16 17 18 19
20 21 22 23 24 25 26
27 28 29 30 31 1 2
29 Monday
· walk
TUESDAY 30
Let's go shopping
WEDNESDAY 1
· walk
THURSDAY 02
· walk
FRIDAY 03
· walk
SATURDAY 04
· walk
· naps
· eats
SUNDAY 05
2nd advent
· Ulrike
· Guido at Taunus
TODO
· Hang calendar
· Grit stroller

Week 33

Advent, Advent . . .

<u>Tuesday Night</u>

My alarm sounded. I pushed the snooze button and cuddled up to Guido. His body heat lulled my consciousness back into dreamland. Seconds later, my phone vibrated under my pillow again. I stopped the alarm. 2:00 a.m. My eyes peeled open. My arms stretched out, and I dragged myself out of the warm bed.

"What time is it?" Guido yawned.

"I have to pee," I whispered.

"Okay," Guido murmured. I froze. His breathing slowed. I dislodged a brown cloth bag from under my side of the bed and tiptoed to the former living room doorframe.

Quietly, I pulled out my December decorations. I tightened each individual box for the Advent calendar out of order with white Christmas lights courtesy of Henrietta. Guido's breathing echoed off the walls as my fingers sorted out the string. I pinned the lights on the doorframe and hooked our calendar to the bulbs.

A warm feeling of Christmas sprung up in my belly. I loved the season, not so much for Christmas itself but for everything that came with the holidays. Gingerbread hearts, mulled wine, *Stollen* on Sundays, and at every possibility, Secret Santa, Christmas markets, tree buying and decorating, game nights, and of course, the ample amounts of chocolate from calendars.

If we had been home, a tree would have already spread cedar perfume throughout the apartment. On the first Advent, we would pull out our nutcrackers, light the first candle on the Christmas pyramid, place two or three *Schwibbögen* [1] in our windows, decorate our Christmas tree, and, of course, we would have kicked off the season with our friends with a mulled wine and gingerbread heart tasting around every stall of any Christmas market available to us. We would hit a different Christmas market every weekend. Excited about the thought, I couldn't wait to check out the Christmas markets around here. Minus the mulled wine, of course.

Wednesday Morning

With a grin, I fell back into my bed only to be awoken by an obnoxious smell just minutes after dozing off, which reminded me of . . . of . . . I couldn't put my finger on the scent. I could almost grab the hint in the air. The smell vaguely reminded me of peanuts. My tummy turned. I pinned my nose to close my nostrils. My already ready-to-go hubby chewed on something. I should have tasted the sweets beforehand.

"Isn't it too early for sweets?" I teased.

"Well, not after such a nice surprise. When did you do all this?"

"Here and there . . . and last night," I offered. "How is it?"

"Delicious. So, what are you planning for today?"

"I decided to get some groceries."

"You don't need to if you don't want to. I am happy to pick them up after work," Guido said.

"Honestly, it is completely embarrassing that I haven't been already," I admitted.

"Well, the store is conveniently located on my way home. But go for it. Just nothing heavy," Guido reminded me.

After he left, I drank my coffee, put a slice of bread with jam into my tummy, and trotted toward the store.

The grocery store towered over me. The building alone promised more products than I could ever need. A second entrance caught my attention—*BOTTLE RETURN* was plastered over the sliding doors. The sides of my lips swung up high.

Prepared, I entered with my bag of returnable items in my hand. Three six-foot-tall moss-green machines greeted me. Plastic bags, caps, squashed plastic bottles, labels, and beverage cans littered the space. *Not very inviting*, I thought, but I entered anyway. I wanted to get my deposit back.

I skimmed over the display. The machine was similar to the ones I knew. I pushed the first container into the receiving hole, but the bottle didn't fit. I tried a different one.

The machine rolled the bottle in, rolled the container around, and then popped it back out. The display read: *Bottle not accepted*. The bottle was intact, the cap was on, and the barcode was readable. I went over the label to find any indication of the deposit amount. The black ink at the bottom of the paper read: *Deposit 5c in VA and NH*. Five cents in VA and NH? As in *VA* for "Virginia" and *NH* for "New Hampshire"? I didn't understand. I had never seen only one or two states listed. In this small space, trying to figure out why the machine in front of me didn't accept the bottles— frustration set in. I checked all my other bottles. None were returnable. I shook out my bag. The bottles landed in a bin with a sign that read, *RECYCLABLES*, and I marched into the store.

I grabbed a shopping cart—the volume of the four-wheeler made the ones I was used to look like dollhouse toys. My feet carried me into the rows of food. My hunch was correct. The interior of the grocery store could house three Aldi's.

A thrill came over me. I knew that I was abroad—hello, language—but once I got over the feeling of being overwhelmed in this shop, I was able to absorb a large number of unfamiliar foods. Most products, like milk and juices, were easily identifiable, but the fruit and vegetable section blew my mind.

At first, I pushed the cart behind a row of busy cashiers. Near collisions with mountain-high groceries in shopping carts kept me on my toes until I reached the beginning of stocked-up shelves. The refrigerated section opened up on my right side. I scanned every product. There were so many things there: cheeses, yogurts, milks, and juices.

The biggest milk container was 1 gallon—that's a lot of milk. I also checked out the smaller containers—1 quart and ½ gallon. Guido and I usually only needed half a liter of milk a week. The penny-pincher in me made the call. I placed the 1-gallon container in the shopping cart, promising myself that I would simply make buttermilk if the liquid soured. Easy-peasy.

Conveniently next to the dairy items, the juice section began. My heart skipped a beat. There was a 1.5-liter bottle of aloe vera juice. I chucked the bottle next to the milk in my basket without thinking.

The endcap of the aisle held cornflakes, but Guido had bought the store's brand of Choco Pops. When I first saw the size of the bag, I couldn't stop laughing. That bag could have fit me like a minidress. I expected the breakfast food to last us for weeks on end, but to my surprise, Guido finished the contents within two weeks—with help from me, of course.

My eyes scanned the items in my cart, estimating how much more I could carry home. So far, my two items left a lot of space in my metal basket. However, I still needed some chicken, fresh veggies, and fruits to replenish our stock of healthy foods for potential hot meals.

I roamed the aisles to gather the remaining items on my list and checked out every other product just because. All the flavors to choose from in the chip, coffee, and yogurt sections, and everything in between. On top of my new discoveries, the volume of items captivated me.

I skipped the dry household items to check out the veggies and fruits. The area seemed normal enough from afar, but my giddiness grew once I set foot in the produce aisle. Roots were lined up, and *real* aloe and prickly cactus leaves rounded out one of the displays. On the other side lay freshly watered green leaves, including something with a white bulb. I moved closer. The sign read: *fennel*. I had never seen a fennel plant before, even though I was raised on fennel tea.

I rounded the corner and landed in the fruit section. The red strawberries enticed my eyes. I chuckled at the word *strawberry*, though. A picture of berries made out of straw popped up. The German word translated to "soil berries," which sounded less taste bud pleasing. Regardless, I held them against my nose. I sniffed its flesh. Nothing. That wasn't a good sign. The two-inch delicious-looking red fruit wouldn't contain any flavor. I returned them with an itch of disappointment.

In the end, only familiar foods landed in my cart—bananas, apples, spinach, lettuce, and mandarins made the cut. My cart had no aloe leaves, corn husks, or random roots.

I got in line behind a woman who had just paid when I finished placing all my stuff on the rolling band. The cashier greeted me with a "How are you?" I only nodded, unsure of how to reply.

She scanned every item. An older gentleman bagged them for me—and when I say old, I mean old. His bones poked out of his paper-thin skin. Age spots covered most of his wrinkled face. I offered to help, but he brushed me off.

Five plastic bags in my left hand and another five in my right swung back and forth. My arms tensed quickly from the weight. Even before the pregnancy, my arm muscles bordered on being underdeveloped.

My hands wrangled with the bags. A sensation of moisture crept up from my inner thighs. I convinced myself that the liquid was just sweat. I carried a heavy load. But I knew better. A drop escaped me—I couldn't believe this was happening. The pressure on my bladder mounted.

I scanned the street. A cute little cupcake bakery on the corner of the next intersection signaled to enter with an "Open" sign. My waddling legs carried me toward the pastry shop.

The bags wrung my wrists. The weight pulled me down, and the water accumulated in my lower tummy. I girded my loins. Sweat bubbles ringed my upper lip hair. I increased my speed. The bakery drew closer. My heartbeat and breathing increased. My vision tunneled. My lower body strength weakened. But I couldn't. I was in the middle of the street. People frequently passed by me. No trees or bushes lined the sides to hide. But the store was within reach. The smell of freshly baked goods increased in intensity. I pushed through my urge to sit down right there and then.

I slammed the door open. No bell above the frame announced my arrival. My eyes searched for a sign. The sign that would promise me relief was nowhere in sight. On my right side, two white wooden shelves along the wall were all stacked with beautifully decorated cupcakes ranging through a rainbow of colors. In front of them, a young man served an older lady. On my left side, two small tables with two chairs each stood by the window.

In a frenzy, my head darted back to the starting point. My urges pushed me forward, sweat layering on my skin. A water pearl streamed down my right cheek. My eyes widened in fear of a possible accident. I patiently waited for the small talk in front of me to end. I tiptoed left, right, left. My hand balled and drummed in a nervous pattern until I couldn't hold my muscles back anymore. "Where is the bathroom?" I blurted out.

The woman in front of me and the young man

behind the counter sized me up. "I am sorry, but we don't have one," he said.

"You don't have one?" My incredulous voice pierced through the young man.

"You could try the restaurant around the corner," he offered.

My mouth gaped. This déjà vu moment didn't seem to end on a positive note.

Liquid dripped down my leg. My cleavage pulsated. My mind blanked. I turned around without a word to avoid the unavoidable.

I squeezed the liquid in, barely. I marched toward our home. *It's up the street, just up the street,* I repeated over and over and over. I focused entirely on my words, shuffling along. I reached the end of the row containing my apartment—my place of release. On the corner stood a papasan chair with a red cushion. *How random*, I thought as I continued home with my load of food dangling around my legs, ignoring the dampness.

Fumbling with my keys, I finally pushed the shaped metal into the lock and sank to my knees, barely containing the natural urge. The door unlocked, and I hurried in, leaving the groceries in the hallway, and stormed toward the bathroom while unbuttoning my trousers. *Aaahhh*, I released as I sat down.

Relieved and lighter and changed, I stored the food in the appropriate places. My relaxed mind wandered back to the chair on the street corner. The random encounter caused a memory to come back into the forefront of my mind. Guido told me that people around here always left stuff on the street. Was this the case here? I zipped up my coat again to check the situation out.

Twenty minutes had passed since I'd walked—I mean, *stormed*—by the chair. I checked left, right, and around the corner. My fingers itched, but my parents raised me well. What if someone screamed that I was a thief?

I couldn't just take the chair. Instead, I sat on the cushion, contemplating if I could manage to carry all three pieces: the seat, the cushion, and the base, one at a time.

I checked the stability of the chair. My friend Franziska had one sitting on her balcony in the spring, summer, fall, and winter. One summer, her kids played on the chair, and the base collapsed. Nothing happened, but I didn't want any passersby to see a show of a pregnant woman toppling over on someone else's chair on the street.

My bum fit in the chair nicely. I leaned back. I'd always wanted one of these, but I'd never gotten myself a papasan chair—it was too pricey for me. That was why I had difficulty imagining that someone would just leave this furniture out on the street like that. I crisscrossed my legs and closed my eyes.

"Mareike," a male voice called. I jumped. *Oh no, I fell asleep.* I tensed. Guido stood right in front of me. My cheeks burned. I lounged in the chair as if the street were my living room.

"Ehhmm, eeeeeehhh . . ." I pushed my arms to lift myself up. Unfortunately, physics worked against me. My body pulled back toward the cushion.

"Do you want to move again? There's way more space here if you don't mind the exhaust, dust, and people passing by," Guido teased.

"Very funny. I saw the chair sitting out here and was contemplating if we should take it home."

"Oh, I see. How long have you been sitting—I mean *napping*—here?" I shrugged my shoulders. "Oh, well, I think we should definitely take it then." Guido pulled me up. He swung the seat in his right hand and the cushion in his left. I carried the base.

Friday

The sun poked my face. The papasan chair stood right in front of the window. Three numbered paper boxes were scattered in the kitchen. With each Advent calendar box opened, the days brought us one step closer to the big two-four. Not just that, Nicholas came in three days. Yet my creative steam engine had puffed the last bit of energy out with the Christmas countdown decoration.

I flipped through my journal. The pages fell apart at my stroller requirements overview. From the day I'd learned about my pregnancy, strollers rolled everywhere. One baby buggy stood out. Big wheels, a bassinet, a chrome frame, and water-repellent baby-blue fabric pushed my heart to make an impulse buy. Yet my head zipped up my wallet.

First, I jotted down a list to compare weight, folding size, manufacturer warranties, practicality, width, and mobility. My sister urged me to list add-on features, like car seat base options, just in case, as we did own a car. The more I researched, the tougher the decision became.

I had dragged Ulrike into several stores to get a feel for the strollers on sale. The quest morphed into a reality check. The stunning design of my number one pick increased my blood flow, but the carriage's wheels didn't turn, the frame was un-foldable, and no suspension cushioned the precious cargo. Limited storage space prevented me from buying any stroller that I couldn't tuck away.

My mother suggested letting the child carrier stand in front of my door. The blood left my face. *Opportunities make thieves*, I'd reminded her.

In my quest to find the perfect fit for our family, I rolled, folded, and lifted several strollers in four different stores from Potsdam to Berlin. I bought none. "You dragged me around town for nothing," Ulrike complained after our fruitless stroller hunt.

"Well, I'm scared of buyer's regret," I confessed.

My statement still held true. Yet the need for a stroller increased. Suddenly, an idea blossomed. With no presents yet to stuff Guido's shoes and the needed baby equipment we still lacked, I could solve two needs with one deed.

Neither of us planned to carry the baby around the whole time. We had to get a stroller—not *the* stroller, just *a* stroller. And I had just the store in mind, but *when* was the bigger question for me to answer.

St. Nikolaus Day fell on a Monday. Friday had passed halfway already. Guido would be home on Saturday and Sunday. I needed a plan. Of course, I could have—should have—but I didn't organize or think about the surprise sooner. Perhaps I did have baby brain, as one of my colleagues predicted. Disarray in the apartment and the lack of baby stuff right in front of me every single day proved the change in my demeanor. There was hope, though. Once the baby said hi, everything would go back to normal.

A knock on the door interrupted my scheming.

"Hello, Henrietta," I greeted my neighbor.

She beamed. "Hey, how are you? I was wondering if you guys want to come over on Sunday to watch football with us."

"Football?" I let the word hang in the air. My gears turned.

"If you don't want to, you don't have to," Henrietta said.

"No, no, no. I am . . . I was just thinking Guido would probably love to come," I said. "I was just wondering if I could steal myself away and buy a stroller as a surprise."

"Oh. Where are you planning to go?" Henrietta asked.

"Just the secondhand shop around the corner." Admitting to anyone, actually to myself, that I shopped at a secondhand store turned out to be quite a hurdle. I never would have disclosed this circumstance to anyone. When I grew up, secondhand store interiors resembled run-down, crappy locations. Yet this baby store carried neat, flawless items; you could find gems. I wondered, however, if the stores around my hometown had also transformed like this.

I felt a new list coming along. *Places to rediscover at home.*

"I love that place! In fact, whatever Attila grows out of, I take it there. Perhaps from now on, I can pass everything on to you," Henrietta offered.

"Oh . . . Well, yes. Thanks," I stuttered, overwhelmed by her generosity.

<u>Sunday</u>

I inhaled the fresh wintry air. "Okay, all the boys are looked after." Henrietta stepped beside me. Tasked with purpose, we briskly strutted toward our target. We halted at an intersection for the pedestrian light to change from red to white. My eyes widened. I'd just found a pattern on the street.

"Do the streets named 'road' run north-ish?" I asked. Henrietta scanned the green street labels. I mirrored her gaze. "So avenues go eastward?"

"Honestly, I am not sure. I haven't really thought about it. These days, there are so many roads, avenues, squares, lanes, terraces, boulevards, drives, and streets."

"Huh." I hoped I'd found out a little nugget of information to drizzle under my sister's nose. Regardless, that also meant that an avenue wasn't an *Allee*, though, like I had previously thought.

On my lips hung a follow-up question based on the order of the house-numbering system. The secondhand store soon came into view. My mind shifted back to the goal of our quest. I pushed the door open. A baby cry alarmed the people inside that a new patron had stepped in. The store was stuffed with clothes, bags, toys, and the object of my desire: strollers.

Five were lined up right beside the cashier's counter. "Can I test them out?" I asked the shop owner.

"Of course," the woman said, approaching me. "Do you need any help?"

"I'm not sure yet." I scanned the options.

"Well, I just want to let you know this one has buttons inside the handlebar, which you need to push to unfold." The lady took the last stroller, a marine-blue one, and unfolded the frame with a seat now in the center of the construction. I rolled the stroller back and forth.

"It even comes with a bassinet," she added. She pulled a small baby bed out from behind her and approached me again. Detaching the toddler seat with a professional grip, she replaced the empty space with the bassinet.

"Thanks." I smiled at the woman. I liked the stroller. I pushed it around with the bassinet, replaced the seats again, and folded the stroller to check out its width and weight. I was smitten. "How much is it?" I inquired.

"Seventy-five dollars," she stated.

My breath got stuck in my throat. "Seventy-five dollars?"

"That's a steal," Henrietta said. My neighbor kneeled to inspect the wheels and integrity of the charcoal aluminum frame. I scanned the bassinet. No scratches on the inside or outside material or the soft mattress on the bottom appeared. Henrietta popped in the toddler seat. Only the washed-out black stains on the footrest showed signs of use.

Regardless of the original purchase price, this was exactly what I was looking for.

"I'll take it." My words echoed in the small shop.

"Great." The shop owner rang me up, and I pushed the stroller home.

"After such an easy purchase, I can't believe what kind of effort I put into my research."

"Well, I did the same. And then you realize so much stress isn't needed. And with the second one, you don't bother as much anymore," Henrietta explained.

"I hope you're right," I sighed.

She smiled as we walked. "It's a new thing to you. But you'll rise to the occasion and only bother with the real issues."

"Like?" I pressed with a laugh.

"Like removing your nose. You have no idea how kids can test you. But if you prevent them from picking everything off the shelf, unplugging all plugs, scooting behind the TV, and sprinkling a hundred cotton swabs all over the bathroom, your life will be less stressful," my neighbor explained.

The stroller glided over the pavement without hiccups and easily moved left and right. I pushed the front wheels up effortlessly and folded the frame in half at our doorstep.

"We can hide the stroller in our apartment. Tanner can prop it in front of the door when he leaves for work. I think that's before Guido goes to work," Henrietta offered.

"That would be wonderful," I said, beaming.

<u>Sunday Night</u>

Once we closed our apartment door after returning from the neighbors', my eyes fell on Guido's winter shoes. "Have you cleaned your boots yet?" He stared at me as if I were an alien demanding that he give a pee sample. "*Nicholas* won't bring you anything if you don't do it," I teased with a knowing grin.

"Just know that I haven't prepared anything for you," Guido confessed with puppy-dog eyes. His shoulders curled forward. Usually, Guido gave me some sort of treat on December 6 in the form of a massage, pedicure, or manicure gift card. In fact, one of them was his go-to present for me for any occasion. I couldn't have been more thrilled about receiving those gift cards. I never splurged on them myself.

But in this new town, neighborhood, and office environment, I understood why this occasion had slipped his mind. But we'd be back home in a few months, and Easter, my birthday, and Women's Day were still ahead of us.

"Don't worry about it. Nicholas will come to us anyway," I said, encouraging Guido to give in and put his cleaned boots next to the door.

"You shouldn't have." Guido shrugged.

"It's nothing," I countered, biting my lips. The gift wouldn't fit in his shoes, but I didn't want to spoil the surprise.

"Whatever you have planned, I hope you won't need to get up in the middle of the night again."

I grinned. "I don't." Well, so I hoped when I went to bed.

If you don't know, You don't know

WEEK 34

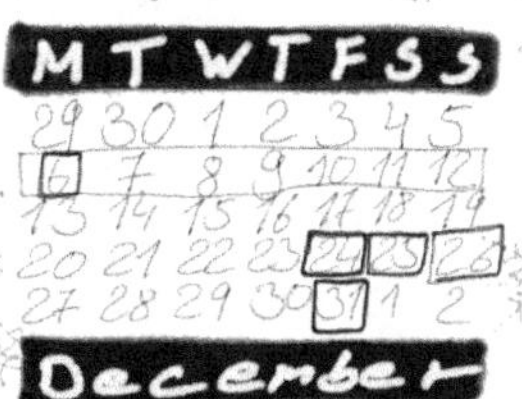

December

6 — Monday

Nikolaus

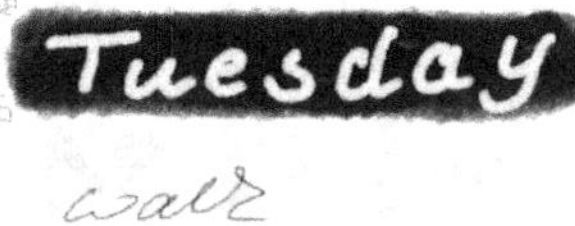

7 — Tuesday

Walz

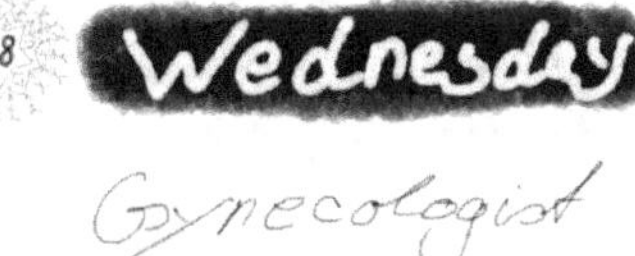

8 — Wednesday

Gynecologist

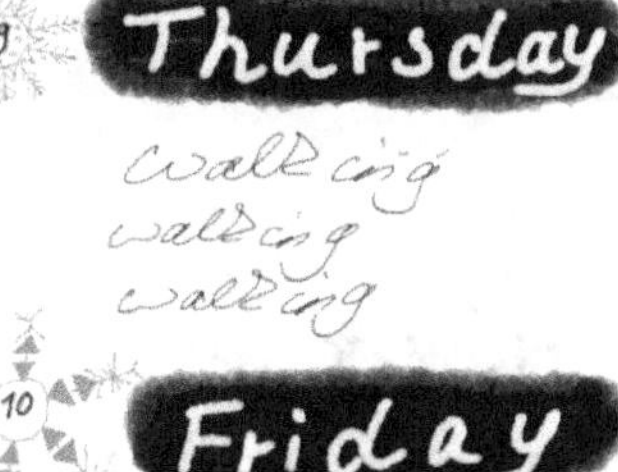

9 — Thursday

walking
walking
walking

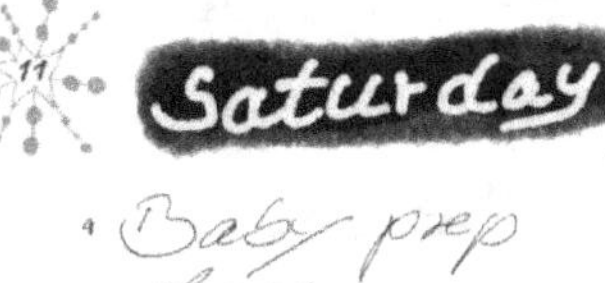

10 — Friday

Walz

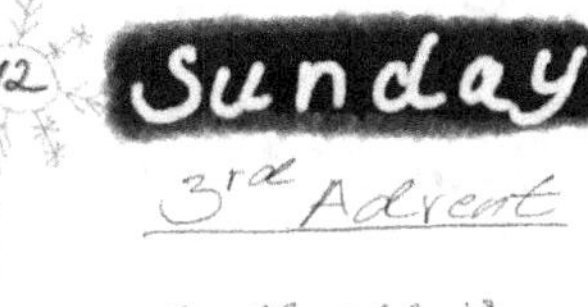

11 — Saturday

Baby prep class

12 — Sunday

3rd Advent

Call Ulrike

TO DO

Week 34

If You Don't Know, You Don't Know

<u>Monday</u>

How come Christmas developed differently in different countries? I wondered. I mean, we cleaned our boots for Nicholas. Milk chocolate Santa Clauses, along with jam-filled gingerbread hearts, were hidden in ours. Whereas here, people got their stockings stuffed on a mantelpiece, but on Christmas Day.

I loved Nicholas, but two men bore gifts in one month. Why? Additionally, how come Santa came on the twenty-fourth but around here on the twenty-fifth? I could joke a lot that Santa had to travel from Europe to the USA, but we probably would raise our child how we were brought up, so then the argument wouldn't make any sense at all, and as a kid, you'd figure out that Santa didn't exist anyway.

Why did we pretend to have Santa in the first place? Well, I knew why. He existed like the Grimms' fairy tales: to caution us to second-guess our behaviors, right? How often did I get warned that I would receive coal instead of presents if I behaved poorly? But I never got any coal, regardless of my behavior. Would kids these days even know what coal was if you threatened them with the word?

I still remembered three-foot-high coal bricks on the sidewalk for someone to shuffle into the basement. I dreaded being sent to fetch some bricks in a metal bin from the dirty, dark dungeons below street level. A shiver ran down my spine at the thought of the jet-black dust layered on my skin, clothes, and hair.

The other thing my parents encouraged us to write down countless times was our Christmas gift wish lists. Only one item had topped my list: a rocket to fly to space, just like Yuri

Gagarin, the first human to fly into space. My mother had constantly reminded me that the gift had to be wrap-able. So, in my neatest handwriting, I'd asked for a horse. My mom pinched her lips. I received a flute. I shook the memories away into the stillness of the night.

* * *

The smell of freshly brewed coffee woke me up. I pulled my cardigan over my shoulders and tightened the soft belt loosely around the baby.

Guido sat in the living room with a mug. Before him, on the table, jelly beans lined up like a pearl necklace. "I can't believe we never had them," Guido said.

"I saw them and hoped you'd love them. So, how are they?"

"Delicious. Thank you," Guido replied, munching a handful.

I kissed him. "You're welcome."

"Do you have any plans for today?"

"Maybe I should finally pack the baby bag and answer some emails." Out of the corner of my eye, I watched Guido move from one room to the next.

"What are you looking for?" My voice echoed in our former living room.

"My boots," Guido replied. "Please tell me where they are."

"Well, maybe Nicholas forgot them in front of the door," I said with a shoulder shrug.

Guido opened our front door. A gasp escaped his lips.

"Mareike," he squealed. Guido pulled the stroller into the house. "How? When?" A blue flower made from a paper napkin and a note hung on the stroller's handle.

"'Thanks for cleaning your boots this year. I considered shrinking the stroller to make it fit, but I thought you would get more use out of it in its normal size. Nicholas,'" Guido read out loud. "This is awesome. One less thing. Thanks, Mareike." Guido hugged me before putting on his boots to leave with a spring in his step.

Yes, one less thing. He was right. I pulled out my journal to cross out *the stroller*. Relief relaxed my muscles. A sigh escaped me. Slowly, the baby prep pieces fell into place. We were in good shape. With less weight on my shoulders, I went on to my daily walk.

<u>Wednesday</u>

A grin of accomplishment added to the brightness of the day, as I ignored for a moment that we needed at least one more important thing: a crib.

"Mrs. Korn!"

I followed a woman dressed in a lilac nurse's uniform. Again, I wanted to ask her if she came to work dressed like this or if she changed here. But my lack of communication skills and the worry that I'd seem rude kept my lips sealed.

A different woman with instruments on wheels came into my room. "Good morning. I'm Melissa."

How many people here had the same job? Or better, how big was this office? While this nurse did her usual routine of taking my blood pressure and everything else she had to check, I summoned the names of the previous nurses of my past visits: Joan and Karen. I patted myself on the shoulder that I still remembered that info—usually, names dissolved in my head like water at a hundred degrees Celsius. So far, all the nurse practitioners had been women, as were the nurses who took my blood pressure and pulse every time I came. Even though the word *nurse* had a female ring to it, at least to me, weren't there any men partaking in this job? I made a mental note to put on my list: *Search gender statistics on nurses.*

I waited for the nurse practitioner or doctor in the examination room. No voices, no alarms, no chimes bounced off the walls. I enjoyed the calmness of the space. Any area like this, honestly, invoked a sanctuary where one could calm any fears. A place where I reassured myself that everything would be alright.

A woman with almost white hair stepped into

the room. "Good afternoon. I'm Doctor Mitchel. How are you feeling?" she greeted me.

So, now I'd met Claire, Skylar, and Dr. Mitchel. "Hi, I am Mareike," I said.

Again, I lay on the cushioned medical bed with an elevated headrest, my shirt pulled up and pants unbuttoned. As usual, the warm gel on my skin and the motion of the ultrasound scanner increased my calm state. I lived for these moments—quiet, relaxing, de-stressing.

"Have you had any contractions yet?" the doctor asked.

"No," I murmured.

"If you feel something coming on, you could always call us if you're unsure. Braxton-Hicks can be a pain and be easily confused with real contractions. And the last thing we want is for you to go to the hospital only for them to tell you that you must go home again," she explained.

I digested her words. Questions interlocked in my mind, but my thoughts were jumbled. With zero experience with all this, could I differentiate the pain? Based on past experiences, I could tell if I had a cut or a bruise. But contractions were a whole new ball game. My spine tingled. My unpreparedness obliterated my good mood from earlier in the day.

The doctor did the same things as the nurse practitioners before her: measuring the baby and listening to his heartbeat.

"I saw you decided to have the baby at Brigham's and Women's." I nodded. "Have you visited the hospital already?" Dr. Mitchel inquired.

"Not yet, but we have signed up for a tour next week," I answered earnestly.

"Great. It's a big hospital. This will help you get an idea of where you need to go when it's time," she explained. A timid smile washed over my face to acknowledge her words. "And is your baby bag packed?"

Another question from this woman who seemed to sense I was unprepared.

"We're working on it." The bag was not even done in any way; it still sat where we'd left it in the living room, empty. I cursed myself, as I wasn't sure what was going on with me. Usually, I was organized and prepared. But since I was here, I had more time on my hands for the first time since tenth grade summer vacation, and I was behind on everything. My list of things to do seemingly grew every day. At least the baby wasn't here just yet.

"Would you like to have ultrasound scans to take home?" the doctor offered. Hearing the heartbeat gave me chills every time.

"Sure," I answered.

The paper strip crawled out of the machine with a printed picture of my baby. I cleaned myself up before covering up my naked belly.

"As you are in week thirty-four, the next appointment will be in two weeks. December twenty-second. Shall we make it for the same time again?"

"Sure." I nodded and prepared to leave after receiving my forms with the next appointment.

How quickly these appointments had become routine. Besides the couple minutes spent in the waiting room, the visits were quick, in and out, with the usual in between. Luckily, I add. Once my weight and pulse were taken and the baby was measured, I was sent off on my merry way with a new appointment in hand.

After zipping my jacket up to the top, I pulled my gloves out. Letters and cards tumbled out of the left one. Two white envelopes landed on the sidewalk. I hadn't seen a post office so far, nor mailboxes. I assumed I would just stumble upon one, just like back home. The bright yellow boxes with a black post horn would catch anyone's eye.

I trotted along Mass Ave. A word on a sign above a store caught my eye: *Bookstore*. The Harvard Bookstore contained rows and rows of books. Until now, I had restrained myself from looking at physical books around here. Guido and I had to take care of most of the stuff we owned—or were going to own while we were here but would have to get rid of again. Yet a little book would be more of a trinket to bring back. Perhaps my sister would like to read the book too. But what to get? I marched through the rows, scanning for the teen section. Labeled in all caps were the adult and young adult sections, but no teens.

"Excuse me," I interrupted a young woman who I hoped worked in this shop.

"Yes," she replied.

"I am looking for the teen section?"

"The young adult section is right behind you." I scrunched up my forehead.

Instead of voicing my confusion, I replied, "Thanks." On my way to the indicated spot, I marveled at why *Junge Erwachsene* was young adult, or why it wasn't, I guess. And what was the difference between young adult and new adult? Didn't it mean the same thing? New adults were young adults. Apparently not. Huh, I'd just learned something new. I guessed that that wouldn't be the last time, especially not with a book written in another tongue.

I scanned the titles in the young adult section. I reached for *Percy Jackson*, as I had enjoyed the German version. My eyes flickered to the spines of the other books on the shelf. However, *Percy* was a good choice. Since I'd read the book already, I knew what the words were supposed to mean. So maybe that would help me improve my English, and I could finish the book before we moved back home.

I made my way to the cashier counter. A turning shelf containing books on sale for parents-to-be stood close by. The covers showed happy mommies with happy babies and promising titles. A knot in my stomach formed again as I realized that time was pressing on and the baby's due date was rushing closer. I resisted the urge to look through one of these books. I already knew what we needed. I had a list.

I moved to the cashier counter to distance myself from the temptation. After I paid, the urge to purchase another book on parenthood faded away, but thoughts of the impending change to our lives rebounded.

"Would you like to have the book gift wrapped?" the young sales clerk asked.

"No thanks," I responded absentmindedly.

"I believe you bought these somewhere else," the woman pointed out after scanning my book.

My eyes darted to the counter, where my Christmas cards lay. "Mmmm, yes. Do you happen to sell stamps, or could you point me to the post office?" I inquired.

"Yes, we do, actually. First-class or international?" she asked.

First-class, I thought, staring wide-eyed at the woman. *Does that mean there are second-class stamps?* Instead of asking the question, I replied, "International."

"How many do you need?"

"Ten."

"That makes $13.30," the woman stated.

I placed a twenty-dollar bill on the counter. The woman returned the change to me. I bagged my shiny new book, stamps, and postcards.

The chilly outside air burned on my skin. A sign with letters that spelled out "Pastry" drew me in. My mind immediately twisted the word into "Bakery." I crossed the street with giant steps, trying to decide what to order first. Shortbread, cookies, pigs' ears, or a simple croissant. On the other hand, they might have some rum balls or a refreshing fruit cake. Honestly, though, I'd probably order my standard: a delicious cheesecake.

With wide, hungry eyes, I stepped into the bakery. Slightly taken aback, I stopped in my tracks. The white tiles with a blue pattern on the walls reminded me of an old-fashioned butcher, the one my grandma used to go to— not a bakery. Yet instead of liverwurst, sausage, or *Mettwurst*[1] behind the glass counter, piled-up cookies were decorated in intense colors along with interestingly shaped baked goods. I couldn't identify any of the goodies.

Upon closer inspection, some of the mouthwatering creations reminded me of the ones from the North End. I bent down to read the labels: *cannoli* and *lobster tail*. I bought two of each so that Guido could try these as well, just in case he hadn't already.

Before biting into the white, cream-stuffed afternoon treat, I pulled out the stamps, letters, and postcards. While I peeled off the stamps, I noticed that they were round. *How cool was that?* I supposed they symbolized the earth since they were international.

I gorged on the cannoli but was done after only eating half. The cream and shell combination filled me up faster than when I first experienced hunger. I placed the leftovers in the box and marched outside, holding the goodies in one hand and the Christmas letters in the other.

I scanned the sidewalk to my left, then turned right. Harvard Square buzzed despite the cold temperatures. No mailbox stood out. The cold crept into the seams of my coat. I trotted home with my eyes scanning for a letter collector. This mystery hadn't solved itself. I wondered if I hadn't passed a mailbox yet. They may have been placed in particular areas, like the center of the town, aka a square, to make it easier for the mail carrier to collect the mail. But I'd been to Union, Harvard, Porter, and Davis Square. How likely were the chances that I would keep missing the mailbox?

<u>Saturday</u>

The underground rumbled under Cambridge's streets on our way to the baby prep class. For whatever reason, they called the train "the T." In Berlin, *U-Bahn* stood for *Untergrundbahn*, or "underground train," and *S-Bahn* for . . . I wasn't sure. The *Strassenbahn* was not the S-Bahn, despite driving aboveground. So, the train could have been called the O-Bahn. So perhaps *the T* stood for "terra train"? But I knew that in New York, there was a subway, which indicated a train below, I supposed. Oh darn, I'd forgotten to bring my journal to add that question to my growing list of things I needed to research.

Since arriving here, I had used my purse less and less. I didn't go anywhere often anyway. And if I did go for my daily pregnancy sport, a walk around the block, the many pockets on Guido's coat provided space to store my phone and wallet.

My eyes wandered around to the other people sitting on the train. My head stopped at the hands of a young woman. On her left ring finger, a white transparent marble-sized stone dazzled. This was the first time I'd ever seen a diamond. I'd always thought these kinds of rings were part of the rom-com movie tropes.

I pulled my hands out of my pockets. My right pointer pushed the ring on my left ring finger counterclockwise. When Guido presented the engagement ring to me, I knew he was my long-term companion. Two leaves crossed over one another. The simple design still captured my heart.

The so-called "red line" stopped at Park Street. Guido pulled me up from the train seat to leave the subway. Above the public transportation, cold air welcomed us. Guido wrapped his hand around mine, and we strolled along the park.

"Perhaps we could go to the Prudential Center after the birthing class. They have a restaurant. We could grab lunch there," Guido proposed.

"Sounds like a good plan," I eagerly nodded.

We entered Boylston Street, and the whole environment changed. More cars, more people, and more shops lined the street. The livelihood of this new atmosphere took me out of my stupor.

Usually, I would have stopped at every shop window to note their inventory, but my feet and hips sounded a soft alarm of pain. My belly had grown so much. In addition to the extra water under my skin, my weight had increased, even though people still complimented me that they could barely tell I was pregnant. This was more of a curse than a compliment. Winter coats and sweaters covered my tummy even more, so nobody gave up their seat for me on the bus.

We rolled up the escalator before the Prudential Center building to enter the mall. Floor-to-ceiling glass windows displayed fancy clothes and gadgets.

"Are you sure we're in the right place?" I asked.

The glossiness needed to fit my idea of a place where one would learn about giving birth. Not that I needed more classes; I'd already gone to baby prep activities back home. But I wanted to hear the words in English. And of course this was an excellent activity for Guido to go through.

We zigzagged through the maze of shops. Eventually, the halls quieted down. We stopped before a glass door. A sign read: *Parents-to-Be.*

Instead of finding a sterile seminar room, we entered a baby store. Even though I'd already gotten my baby clothes fix at the outlets in upstate New York, I couldn't help but drift toward the doll-sized items.

Why did they make this stuff so cute? Argh.

Behind the hanging onesies stood three wooden baby beds. A maroon one bedazzled me, with its curved finished wood at both ends. I leaned over to fetch the price tag and almost fell in. My center of gravity must have shifted, or leaning forward wasn't the thing to do at week thirty-three anymore. I wondered, though, if putting the baby in and out of such a steep angle would be suitable for either my or Guido's back.

I scanned the price tag. The reversed punctuation marks to indicate the value of the numbers threw me off every time. A dot before the cents and a comma before three numbers knotted my brain cells together. The crib didn't cost two dollars and 430 cents. The cost equaled $2,430.00, plus tax.

Guido steadied me. He pulled me toward a room with chatting people. Six couples lined the walls in a beige meeting room, each occupying a seat. We sat in the two remaining chairs just before a woman in a zebra-striped one-piece stepped before the waiting people. "Good morning," the instructor greeted us in a husky voice. "My name is Vanessa, and I am a midwife of twenty-five years and counting."

I loved the word *midwife*. Every time my gynecologist said that word, I pictured a half-married woman, not a person who helped with pregnancies. The German word, *Hebamme*, didn't resemble its English counterpart, and I never understood what it actually meant growing up, as the word itself wasn't conclusive. As a child, I always thought she should be called a birth helper. Then, at least, everyone would know precisely what was going on.

"Since you all are here, I presume it is your first time welcoming a baby into your lives." Murmurs and nods sprouted from the future moms and dads. "As you undoubtedly discussed with your health-care provider, a midwife or doctor will deliver your baby at home or the hospital. If you haven't already, please tour the hospital where you plan to deliver your baby. So today you will learn about all birthing options. In addition to standard childbirth, some hospitals offer water births as well. And for you to better understand what childbirth looks like, we have prepared a video for you to see the different kinds."

I stared at the whiteboard behind the midwife. The video showed three birthing scenarios. One woman gave birth in a water tank. Another stood on her hands and knees. The third lay on her back. But the video didn't stop there. After ten minutes, the film continued to show an actual birth. I didn't think I was a prude, but I was not prepared to watch a baby's head slipping out between a woman's legs, ending up with the whole little creature coming out. A gooey cream or liquid-like stuff stuck on the baby's skin, wet hair gelled to the newborn's head, and the baby wailed. The mother's face grimaced, her body contorted, and her hands clenched onto the fabric beneath her sweating body.

I wasn't sure what shocked me more: the baby appearing, the screaming woman, or that I'd never seen a woman in such a position. Or, come to think of it, all of the above.

Once the video concluded, a somber silence flattened any questions anyone might have had. No one made even the tiniest peep. Vanessa continued the class. She informed us about the signs of labor versus Braxton-Hicks contractions, the length of labor, breathing techniques to cope with pain, epidural options during birth, potential complications, and how our partners could help during the process.

Honestly, though, fear consumed me thanks to the visual presentation. I mean, I sort of knew what childbirth was. I had been to several classes before. Countless people around me had given birth. I couldn't help but wonder why the process was that excruciating looking, though.

Suddenly, all the birth stories hit home. I didn't want to do this anymore. I was scared—scared out of my mind. Somehow, I'd imagined giving birth was just a thing to be done.

"You okay?" Guido asked with a soft squeeze of my hand.

"I'm scared," I muttered.

Guido pulled me in to bring me closer. "I'm here for you," he murmured into my ear.

Vanessa pulled out a bag with printed pink roses in front of her. "It will be very prudent of you to have your hospital bag prepared and with you at all times." She unzipped the bag to show us a sheet of paper in a plastic sleeve. "You should always have your birthing plan with you too." Then she pulled out a little white jacket. "Something to wear for your baby," the facilitator explained. She covered the outfit and placed socks on the pile. "Socks and something comfortable for the mother to wear." Then she popped yellow pajamas over the socks.

"These are just a few essential items, but there are many more to make your stay in the hospital more comfortable. We prepared a list of what you may want to bring and some samples and coupons you can take home."

Each couple grabbed a cloth bag stuffed with product samples and the promised hospital checklist.

"So, what did you learn?" Guido challenged me cheekily.

"That childbirth is still dangerous for women even in the twenty-first century," I pronounced somberly.

Not expecting my "I am not so thrilled about being pregnant" attitude, Guido tried again, "Let's get some food. Maybe you'll feel better afterward."

I trotted along with my hubby. He was right. I was one of those people who became miserable when hungry. But who wouldn't? Unfortunately, my hubby didn't. This was one of the few occasions when we just didn't understand each other.

I sighed. If that was the only thing, though, we were good.

We stepped into the elevator. Guido pushed the button next to *Top of the Hub*. I scanned the buttons just because and did a double take. The numbers increased by one but skipped from 12 to 14.

"There is a thirteen missing." I pointed at the display. Guido glanced at the buttons.

"You know, I noticed that at the Sheraton as well, but I thought it was just a fluke."

"How curious." I texted myself to check out the level 13s and to look up why commas and dots were exchanged. But I had no Internet connection.

A wide-open room lay before us when we stepped onto the restaurant floor. The dining area was enclosed by glass windows.

"How many?" a young woman asked.

"Two," Guido replied.

We followed the hostess to a table with a pair of chairs next to a window, and she placed menus in front of us. "Look, they have beef soup," I pronounced after skimming the dish titles.

"Wow, look at this!" I turned my head in every direction, surveying a city I had just started discovering.

"Would you like something to drink?" Holding a notepad, the copper-haired waitress stood next to our table, her eyes swinging back and forth between us.

"A lemonade would be great," I said.

"Me too," Guido seconded.

"Anything else?"

"Well, Guido, are you ready to order?" I pulled my eyebrows up.

"Yes, I'll take the steak tips," my husband said.

"Very well, and you?" The waitress looked up from her paper after writing down Guido's order.

"I take the beef stew, please. Thanks."

"I'll take these from you." The waitress cleared the menus off our table.

My eyes were glued to the ocean. This big body of water was so close, yet our current home felt so landlocked. Every time we went to the Baltic Sea, you could feel the closeness of the ocean miles away. The tree types changed, even the soil became sandy, and eventually, the air carried nano-sized salt particles. All signs concluded that we'd drawn closer to a significant source of water. Not like a lake, but more like a sea.

"We have to check out the ocean," I told Guido when my beef stew arrived.

"Absolutely," Guido agreed.

When we finished our lunch, I poured out the goody bag. A pacifier wrapped in plastic stuck on paper, a leaflet for a nipple cream with a tiny pouch glued on a booklet with baby coupons, and samples for baby bath products all fell out. I loved free stuff, but we'd already decided not to use pacifiers. My cousin's four-year-old still had one stuck in her mouth nonstop. Every time she lost her comforter, tragedy struck.

After we paid, we strolled around the restaurant. A couple of selfies later, we returned to the street level and returned to Somerville Ave.

I nodded toward the pharmacy. We should start stashing diapers.

"Sure, we can have a look," Guido agreed.

The faint aroma of freshly pressed plastic mixed with cinnamon swam in the air, and green, red, and white dominated the color spectrum of the seasonal items in the pharmacy. A fake lit-up Christmas tree with fake gift boxes decorated the cashier's area.

We made our way to the baby section. Two rows of diapers in various sizes were stacked on two shelves.

"So, which ones are we getting?" Guido inquired.

"I don't know." Different amounts of diapers and sizes marked the boxes. The bigger the diapers got, the less were contained in each box, but the cost per diaper increased.

"How heavy do you think the baby will be?" Guido kneeled to inspect one diaper box closer.

I rolled my eyes. "I can't look into the future." After a short silence, I added, "Let's get size one and two."

"Which brand?" Guido asked. He pulled out one box but stopped before taking a second one.

"I don't know. Maybe the one with the lowest price per diaper?" We both kneeled.

"Look, they have a deal. If we buy thirty dollars of diapers, it's five dollars off," Guido read from a display.

"Well, that's not bad. You know what? I think there was a coupon in the bag." I rummaged through the cloth bag to find the booklet. I flipped through the coupons until I found the right brand. I found three that worked.

We stacked the two boxes on the cashier's desk.

"Do you have a rewards card with us?" asked the man behind the counter.

"No," I said, while Guido answered, "Yes." Guido typed in his number. I squinted at his action.

The cashier said, "You have ten dollars in rewards points. Would you like to use them?"

"Yes," Guido replied with a smile.

The man scanned our diapers. The register displayed $59.98. Shortly after, the number reduced to $49.98. I handed two coupons to the man. He scanned the paper. The price decreased to $43.98. And Guido's store rewards coupons brought the total down to $33.98.

"Cash or card?"

"Cash." Guido pulled out his wallet.

"What happened to the tax?" I wondered.

"There is no tax on baby products in Massachusetts," the cashier informed us.

On our way home carrying our baby preparation items, I said to my husband, "We saved twenty-six dollars. That's a lot of money."

Guido replied, "Absolutely. This felt odd, though."

I beamed. "I know, but I felt slightly like a real

couponer. And we are now one step closer to being prepared for our baby."

<u>Sunday</u>

I doodled baby bottles, procrastinating until my sister called. Once I was done coloring the milk containers, I scanned my calendar. Only seven weeks to go.

The moment my phone screen lit up, I accepted her video call. "Good morning," I greeted Ulrike.

"What do you mean? It's past lunchtime," my sister joked. "What are you up to today?"

"Not much," I admitted. "What about you?"

"I'll go to Mom and Dad's for some *Stollen*," Ulrike informed me.

"Oh. Yeah. Right. Third Advent." My cheeks flushed red. Third Advent! I wasn't with my family during Advent for the first time ever. After wishing my sister a nice afternoon with our parents, I rubbed my right hand over my forehead to smooth out the folds of disbelief.

Besides the Advent calendar, nothing in our apartment screamed *Christmas*.

No one here celebrated Advent. A renewed blanket of unease fell over me. My free hand petted my cardigan—a touch from home—which wrapped my body. I realized what had caused my mood to gray out. I was lonely.

Emotion had tugged at my heartstrings before, but I brushed the sensation away. The adventure of being in a new town, a new country, had washed all other sentiments deeper into me. But now, the feeling bubbled up more often than I wanted. Back home, everyone was in a pre-Christmas mood. But here, jolliness didn't grow in my heart nor my mind.

Most days, I spent time alone, killing time, doing next to nothing. Yet moments like these, which let the truth peek out from behind the curtain, rattled my reality.

When I came here to be with my husband at this significant time in our lives, the decision was a no-brainer. Well, not immediately, but now, sitting in this unfamiliar apartment with no one to meet up with for a *Kaffeeklatsch*[2] or baby talk, my isolation was obvious. But I kept my feelings to myself. I was sure an argument would follow. This wasn't a hurdle; I was ready to jump. On the bright side, soon I would have company in the form of a little one in one hand and a plane ticket in the other.

Missing Christmas Spirit

Week 35

Missing Christmas Spirit

<u>Monday, Tuesday, Wednesday, Thursday . . . or was it Friday?</u>

The days melted together through non-thrilling daily activities. Walks and busying myself with envying my friends through videos and images they posted filled my schedule. Smiling faces, get-togethers, and group outings enriched their lives. I, on the other hand, soothed my aching body on a sofa far, far away.

For the first time in my life, never-ending time hung on my fingertips. When I was busy, stressed out, or just overwhelmed, a three-foot-long scroll with activity ideas rolled up in my head. Yet right now, I had plenty of time, but my head was a blank slate, and my energy flat. Only miniscule highlights enriched my life. Okay, the not-so-small one being: seeing my husband again and taking him along for the baby preparation ride, like on our hospital visit. The thought of this outing carried me through the mundanity of nothingness that was my week.

Saturday

A cold breeze brushed our faces. A handful of people passed us on the sidewalk. No cars drove by while we shuffled from foot to foot. Despite the low energy around Guido and me, excitement hung in the air. So much so that I didn't want to wait for our rideshare inside the apartment. Visiting the hospital brought butterflies to my stomach. I only wished that we would have been able to bring our baby into this world closer to home. At least one hospital was within walking distance of us. Unfortunately, even Guido didn't know why we had to travel across town for me to give birth.

An engine hummed closer. I turned to the vehicle, which stopped right in front of us. The window of the passenger door from the silver compact car rolled down.

"Good morning." A woman with wrinkles on the sides of her eyes looked up at us. "Are you Mareike?"

"Yes," I responded. I reached for the back door.

"Good morning," the driver repeated. Her red hair fell straight down to her shoulders, and her eyes fell on the curve of my jacket. "Congratulations," the woman continued.

"Thanks!" Guido and I exclaimed from the back seat.

"Are you off checking out your hospital?" the driver asked.

"Yes," Guido replied.

We buckled up, and the car zigzagged through the familiar streets. The houses, people, and air had grown on me through my daily walks. The car drove by new streets, new houses, and more traffic, but the containment of the car calmed my nerves. The stillness jolted my memory back to the moment when I learned of my pregnancy.

Six Months Ago

My constant tiredness indicated a change in my constitution. At first, I predicted a cold or even the flu coming on. My mother pushed me to make an appointment for weeks, but my energy loss was not drastic enough to propel me to see a doctor. I figured the feeling of unwellness would simply pass. I used the downtime to catch up on television. One of these TV channels advertised a new docuseries titled *She Didn't Know She Was Expecting.*

How could you not know that you are pregnant? It dawned on me in slow motion. *It couldn't be . . .*

Yet the realization didn't come with joy, happiness, or any other fantasy of positive emotion. Nauseousness pushed up my throat. We hadn't planned for a pregnancy. I mean, we weren't opposed to children. Guido and I were in a committed relationship. Friends around us had already taken their relationships to the next level. However, we never really talked about having a baby.

I needed proof. A hunch wasn't enough. The store-bought test displayed two blue lines. My eyes twitched. My mouth dried out. My knees softened. Perhaps the test showed a false positive? However, the doctor affirmed the accuracy of my condition. The new revelation sank in . . . I was indeed expecting. Ready or not, a baby would come.

The news didn't burst out of me. Days passed before I spilled the beans to the other person who should know. I wrapped a book titled *Don't Dad It Up* with a card congratulating Guido.

"Oh, thanks. What's the occasion?" Guido pulled on the spring-green ribbon.

"You'll see." I shrugged my shoulders. My face relaxed every muscle. The silver-striped paper opened up.

Guido lifted the card. "'Next project title: Addition. Start date: January fourteenth. End date: Eighteen years plus,'" Guido read out loud. His jaw clenched as he scanned the book's cover. Then he looked me up and down and reread the card. His mouth opened, then closed again. His eyes wrinkled up to reveal a beaming smile.

"No way." Guido embraced me.

"Yes," I whispered.

"How long have you known? Does Ulrike know? Or your parents?"

"No. You are the first," I assured him.

"I can't believe it! Shall we tell everyone? We can invite our parents over. Or order a table at *Zum Fliegenden Holländer?*"[1] Guido gushed.

"Yeah," I agreed happily.

My husband was practically beaming. "I can't believe we're going to be parents. What do you want to name him? Or is it a girl?"

"I don't know yet," I managed.

"What do we need to get for the baby? Oh, do you want to sit down? Do we need to make a room? Maybe we need to move? What do you think?" On and on he went with questions—which I had no answers to. His excitement lifted my spirits. But fear of the unknown gobbled up my glee.

A couple days before, I came to terms with the fact that there was a growing baby in my belly. Only to be dampened again by more news. His stint abroad came up only weeks after learning of our new addition. A couple days after that, the reality dawned on me that I might give birth by myself. Perhaps my mother would help me, but she didn't help make the baby, so it wasn't her responsibility. Only months later, the option of joining Guido across the pond crystallized out of the craziness life sometimes brought.

My headspace was filled with anger and confusion, and I had zero intention of joining him back then. I dug my heels into the sand. After all, he had left our home. Reflecting on that discussion, I realized I was easier to persuade than I thought. Ulrike's cons twirled around a *Litfaßsäule,*[2] but she used an ingenious hook.

"Remember when you couldn't go for your two-week exchange trip to Fredericksburg due to your appendix removal?"

"Of course. That would have been my first time leaving Europe," I said.

She smiled. "This is your opportunity."

Back in the Rideshare

"Here we are," the driver announced as the car stopped.

"Thanks," Guido said before he stepped out of the car.

"Good luck," she told us.

"Thanks, you too," I replied, scooting out.

I stretched my limbs as my eyes followed a row of glass reaching up toward the sky. A high-rise towered in front of us. I twisted around. Confused, I pointed at the glass building. "Is this the hospital?"

"Well, it says so." Guido nodded at the letters above the entrance: *Brigham and Women's Hospital.*

"It's so tall and un-hospital looking," I said. The

finished look of the facade rivaled a well-maintained residential house.

"Do you think you've entered the right address?" Guido asked, edged on by my insecurity.

"I think so, but let's check." I reached into my pocket for my phone, but only my gloves came out. I checked the other pocket—nothing. I patted down my jacket.

"What is it?" Guido asked.

"I think I lost my phone," I admitted.

"Just now?"

"I'm not sure. I ordered our ride. I got a notification. We put our jackets and boots on. I think I had my phone in my hand when we left."

"I'll call you," Guido offered.

"Sure." I pulled down the edges of my mouth.

Guido lifted his pointer finger to indicate for me to be quiet.

"I am sorry, but your phone doesn't have enough credits. Please reload it before continuing with your call," an automated voice informed us.

I inwardly rolled my eyes. "Why didn't you choose the option to get it to reload automatically when you reach a certain limit? Then you'd have constant reachability."

"It's really not the right time to give me that spiel," Guido scolded.

Instead of a clapback, I replied, "My phone wouldn't ring anyway, as it is not logged into the Internet. But we have to get it back."

"But how? It's not like I can just call a taxi."

"I don't know," I admitted.

"I know I told you to turn your GPS off on your phone, but did you?" Guido asked.

Honestly, I couldn't tell if that was a trick question. He did tell me several times to turn off my location finder to avoid a location stamp on digital pictures. But how would I use the map function if the device could not locate itself?

After throwing that argument into his face, the response I usually got was "a paper map," as we did before smartphones.

I really wanted to just yell at him: a) Who wandered around with a paper map on the street these days? and b) I always got lost with maps. I needed landmarks or someone there to tell me to go left or right, especially in a town I didn't know and a country whose language was second to me.

In a small voice, I admitted, "The GPS is still on."

"Great," Guido replied with more pep than I'd anticipated.

"Great?" I repeated.

"Yeah, so we can track it."

"How? With your phone?" I threw in way more sarcasm than I wanted. After all, this was my fault. He was the one who'd thought of a solution.

"No, we just have to find an Internet café," Guido proposed.

I couldn't hold my tongue. "You know, I think Internet cafés went out of style in 2010."

My husband gave me a pointed look. "That isn't helpful. Why don't you come up with a solution then?"

"How about we just ask someone to use their phone?" I offered the moment a gentleman in a suit marched by.

"I would never allow anyone I don't know to use my phone," Guido argued.

"What? This is an emergency!" I yelled.

"Precisely, and this is a tactic scammers use," Guido retorted.

Peeved by his declaration of what others do to misuse someone else's trust, we both just looked around. Then I noticed the magic words: *Public Library*.

Luckily, we managed to access one of the computers in the library. I actually remembered my password to the rideshare's online portal. I clicked my way through the menu to find my lost item. And, of course, the first prompt was to call the driver. I bit my lip. Yelling at the computer would cause more issues. Instead, I searched for another solution. Only five long, panic-stricken minutes later, I found a form to explain the situation, which led to a request for the driver to return.

Nervous, we decided to stake out the closest coffee shop we could find. Just around the corner, Seeds of the Earth invited us in with open windows. A strong aroma from my childhood had me standing up straight. Rose hip. I hadn't had this flavor since the Wall came down; I had swung back and forth between fennel and chamomile. Ha, what an odd correlation to have. Guido ordered a coffee, and I rose hip tea. I fell in love with the shelf of glass jars containing other teas, all by the same brand: *Xylem Sunflower*.

I inhaled the scent of my past as I drank some nostalgia. The flavor, however, was more aromatic than I remembered. Regardless, the hot beverage calmed my nerves with the help of the flower prints on the white walls.

Instead of Guido pocketing his wallet after he'd paid for our beverages, my husband counted his bills and coins. "I think we have to tip her when she returns. How much do you have?" he asked. Despite being surprised by his question, I copied him.

I put twenty dollars on the table. "How much do you have?"

"I have forty-two and a couple of cents," Guido said.

"Do you think that's enough?" I asked.

"I don't know. She has to come here if she's required to return your phone. After all, she can't accept other riders until then."

I nodded in agreement. "At least we didn't need to cross the city to fetch my phone."

The black hands on the clock on the wall below the tea shelf barely moved. I sipped periodically on my cooling dark red tea.

"What shall we do about the hospital tour?" I inquired.

"I think they have several tours throughout the day," Guido replied.

"But what if they're all booked up?"

My husband shrugged. "I don't know. Come back another day." I would have stated the obvious for his benefit too.

After minutes—no, *hours*—of sitting around, slurping our teas, snacking on CD-sized cookies, and pacing around the same spot the driver dropped us off, our nerves thinned along with any hope of ever getting my phone back. "All my pictures, contacts, and emails are gone," I whined.

"Nothing is lost. Everything is backed up. You just need to buy a new device if you want to salvage it all," Guido assured me.

I pressed my lips together. Usually, I would argue that my phone kept us more connected than before, but now that I was here with him, that wasn't true anymore. Bickering didn't make the time fizzle away faster.

As time passed, my hope that the driver would show up faded. I paced on the sidewalk, occasionally checking every crossing, stop sign, and intersection for the car. Suddenly, our rideshare pulled up next to us.

"Thank you so much!" I yelled at the woman through the open window. I pushed the money into her space and grabbed my phone out of her hand like it was my long-lost family heirloom. I wiped away a tear before Guido could see my emotional relief at having my phone back.

Holding my phone tighter than my soon-to-be firstborn, I joined my husband in finally entering the hospital two hours late.

"Oh, wow," breezed out of my mouth.

The inside of the hospital reflected the outside. The high ceiling of the entrance hall deepened my suspicion that a hotel architect had designed this care facility.

"A tour just started. We'll join them," Guido explained. Nervousness replaced my excitement at having made our way into the hospital and the elevator.

The doors slid open. A group of fifteen adults stood around an open door. I tiptoed to see over the shoulders of the expectant parents. A room for a single occupant with windows spanning from the left to the right side of the wall opened up in front of us.

"Look, you can even see the stadium," a female from somewhere on my left side said.

"What stadium?" I heard myself ask out loud.

"The Sox," a pregnant woman next to me replied. A picture of a pile of unmatched socks in my special lost bin for found singles popped into my mind. Instead of referring to this recurring mystery in our household, I turned to my husband.

"The socks?" I threw a confused grimace at Guido, who merely shrugged.

"Why don't you know the Red Sox?" my group neighbor wondered.

"We are Germans," I said apologetically, trying to cover up my stupefied cluelessness about the local sports scene—well, any sports scene in any country, county, or city . . . including my own.

"Oh, so you must like soccer?" the woman who had told me the stadium's name asked.

"I know nothing about soccer." I practically saw in the back of my head Guido's eye-rolling.

The woman gaped. Her husband mouthed the words she must have thought, "How can you know nothing about soccer? You're German."

Drilled to the floor by this assumption that being one specific nationality equals the interest of every citizen in a particular sport, my mind blanked.

Honestly, I had been to plenty of matches courtesy of Guido, but the most memorable ones were during the World Cup. To be honest, watching any game was kind of inevitable. Giant screens were propped up on several central points, even in parks. And suddenly, public viewing was born. The atmosphere brought out a community spirit in everyone. We met up with friends and made new ones.

"Yes, that's right. This is the Red Sox's stadium. That is why you have to keep their game schedule in mind. The streets can get really busy when they play, and you don't want to have the baby on the side of the road," our tour guide remarked before leading us to our next stop.

The expectant parents moved along to a wall with hip-to-ceiling-height glass windows. "And here are our newborns." Behind the window lay close to a dozen or so babies, who resembled pine cones during their nap, wrapped up in pink-and-blue-striped blankets. Each doll-sized human wore a beige beanie with either a blue or pink ribbon on the top. I patted my own pregnant belly.

"Why are they not with their parents?" a squeaky voice from someone to my left asked.

"We take care of the babies when the mom wants to sleep, and we bring them back when hungry," the guiding nurse responded. "Because most babies are swaddled, you can't see that every baby has a tag." The nurse pulled out a white band from her pocket. "This wristband should help prevent anyone from just taking a newborn, and it will be taken off when you leave the hospital."

The moment the nurse turned to move along toward the front desk, her words registered.

My heart rate increased. In the past, I'd heard about babies getting snatched. On the radio, on the news, somewhere far, far away. Nowhere in my sight. I squeezed Guido's hand to calm myself down.

The group crowded the entrance area of the newborn ward. All eyes fell on the nurse. "Please don't forget that you have to leave the hospital with an infant car seat and that we'll check that it hasn't expired."

"What?" My chin dropped. "We don't own a car. So, we won't be bringing a car seat," I blurted out.

"How are you planning to go home?" the woman beside me snarked.

"You know, walking, buses, and undergrounds are all options to transport yourself from A to B," Guido countered.

"Regardless of whether you own a car or not, you must leave the hospital with a car seat by law. That means we won't be able to let you leave without one." The nurse's words stunned everyone into silence. Before everyone left, the nurse continued, "Thank you so much for coming, and good luck."

"What way shall we go?" We stood in front of the hospital. This was my first time in this part of town. At first glance, no bus stop, tram, or underground station was visible, but this didn't mean anything in cities. There could be one just around the corner.

"I don't know." Guido shrugged.

"I feel slightly unprepared," I admitted.

"But that is why we are here to figure things out, isn't it?"

"True," I agreed.

"So, what do you think? What direction should we take?"

"I don't know either." I logged onto the city's website. "It looks like there is a bus stop around the corner. The bus would take us to Beacon Street, and then it's just a short walk home."

"Is there no T station?"

"Well, there is one just around the corner. The green one, I think," I offered.

"That's great. We'll take it to Park Street, then change to red. We'll get out at Harvard Square to check out the Christmas market," Guido suggested.

But . . . My vision blurred. My hand searched for Guido's arm.

"Are you okay?" His concerned eyes drifted into my focus.

"No, no. Not really."

Guido held me gently on my shoulders. "What's going on?"

"We are having a baby," I told him. When I wiped a stream of tears away, a smirk was plastered on Guido's face. "Why is that funny?"

"Well, you've been pregnant for a few months now."

"But . . . but it just hit me that we are having one. After I found out I was pregnant, I was excited for about five minutes, but then life went on as usual, plus a couple of throw-ups, restless nights, and pain here and there ... but all in all, my life went on as usual. Even the classes and gynecology visits were just part of a new normal for the past couple of months. But just now, it hit me that another person would be in our lives. Look at all this stuff we already got for him. And now we are forced to get a car seat. I am not sure if I am prepared to be a parent."

Guido squeezed my shoulders. "We'll manage it. Somehow, we'll be able to pull it together and become parents. We'll do our best, and that will be good enough. How about some gingerbread? That might lift your mood."

That Evening

Our bodies swayed along with the movements of the green line. "We still haven't really decided on one crucial issue," I cautioned Guido.

"What's that?"

"How will we go to the hospital and come back

home?" I asked. "We only hired a car to the hospital since we ran late."

"Still, we could use the same method for both ways," Guido said.

Yet, still, so many questions lingered. *What if the car took forever to pick us up? Or worse, what if my water broke in the back seat?* I cringed. Rumor had it the liquid from the baby bubble could fill up almost four cups. Could you imagine?

Regardless of what kind of water I produced, I wouldn't want my car seat drenched with someone else's bodily fluids.

"Where will we find a car seat?" Guido wondered.

"Maybe Target. I think I saw some there," I suggested.

"We'll just order one online," Guido stated as matter-of-factly as if he'd said the world is round.

"Order one?" I pushed my eyebrows together.

The man had never ever ordered anything online. Sometimes I didn't even understand how he could survive. Luckily, he had me. Even though he never really expressed that I should order something for him, he definitely profited from my habits. He didn't need to go to a store or make superfluous calls to get what he needed.

Even both of our parents were up to speed with the current trends and apps. Worst of all, my mother offered me her old smartphone when she got the latest model.

Guido, on the other hand, replaced his flip phones with more flip phones. He didn't care about staying up-to-date. He was blissfully ignorant. Guido not only used a computer for work, with all technological achievements, but chose not to participate outside of work. He had his friends, family, and a job he loved. What more could one want?

But I couldn't resist. All my friends were online. Unfortunately, the connectivity had brought out the dual personality in some of our acquaintances. Some comments and pictures they shared made my blood boil. So, we ousted them from our lives. For me, social media was just like intoxicated people. And you know what they say: Drunks show their true selves.

As we rumbled from one station to the next, I mentally added a car seat to my baby items list. If we got the seat, we would also have to buy an adapter for the stroller. I sighed—another thing to organize. On the bright side, we still had another four weeks to go.

Cold, sharp air brushed against our faces when we stepped off the escalator. The sun had already set, but the Christmas decorations strung from one pole to the next illuminated the packed square. People bustled around us.

We turned toward the center, but no Christmas market within the streets crisscrossing from north to south and east to west opened up to us. No tree stood in the middle of the square, no makeshift log houses sold fruitcake, gingerbread, or mulled wine.

"Maybe we should go around the square?" Guido proposed in a somber tone.

"I don't think there is one," I replied.

"This can't be. Let's go down Brattle Street. That could be the center of activities. Perhaps there were some space restrictions?"

His reassuring voice ignited my own hope. Perhaps he was right, but something in me doubted it. I scanned the area for a hint of Christmas market activities happening. Yet no one displayed a drunkard's walk. I checked people's necks for edible hearts with fun icing writing. None were visible. And worst of all, no Christmas carols spread through loudspeakers.

Despite the lack of festivities, we strolled down the street. After a short walk, the nonexistent Christmas signs proved this was not the spot. "How about we try Porter Square? Maybe that's the center of town?" Guido shrugged. "Walking or train?"

"Let's walk. I don't want to feel constricted right now." We turned around to begin our trek to the next so-called square.

We trotted along Massachusetts Avenue. My radar for new parents and moms-to-be kicked in. There were so many strollers out and about with different kinds of baby seats and beds. A couple of them even had car seats, which I eyed curiously. But it wasn't only strollers that I noticed but carriers too. Babies slept, watched, and cried in many styles on their parents' back or front. I had to put this on my list to check out, as Guido and I loved to be hands-free.

"You know, we still haven't decided on a name just yet," Guido said.

"Do you want to propose one?" I suggested.

"Well, the baby's name could start with an *A*, like Alexander, and then the baby would be A. Korn."

"Not bad," my husband laughed.

Alongside me, movement in the air above the rooftops caught my attention. The installation turned. Two more of the same objects appeared.

"What is that?" I pointed at the structure in the distance. My husband shrugged. When we drew closer, a pole at least twenty feet high poked in the air. On top moved three kitelike objects in the wind, just like a wind chime, right next to Porter Square's red line station.

No Christmas market–like area brought people together. "Nothing." The resignation in his voice reflected my own mood. He searched for some familiarity to bring him emotionally closer to home.

"Maybe they don't exist around here. After all, we are in a different country." Once I overcame my disappointment at leaving Harvard Square, I prepared myself for no festivities again.

"But they imported the Oktoberfest. If they did that, why not a good old Christmas market?" Guido pointed out.

"I don't know, maybe a lack of beer?" I answered honestly. We stared into the void of empty, cold streets.

"But there is mulled wine," Guido said, showing me his glove-covered palms. We moved along a bit more just to ensure we had seen all the Christmas vendors.

"True, but . . ." I acknowledged. All this walking, talking, and searching decreased my energy. I rubbed my belly. "Let's get some food," I proposed.

Guido nodded. "Yeah. Let's go to Davis Square."

"There are a ton of places around there that could satisfy us. There are restaurants. And there's takeout," I agreed.

"You will love this place," Guido promised.

"Will I?" I asked.

"Absolutely."

"Can we take a bus or underground this time?" Throbbing hips enticed my mood into getting public transportation. My thighs burned.

"Red line it is, then."

The entrance to the subway was only a five-minute walk away. Only one other person traveled down the escalator in front of us. The train arrived after another ten minutes. Wind traveled through the underground tunnels. With only a handful of people on both sides of the station, eeriness spread in my veins. I leaned against my husband's chest, and he wrapped his arm around my back. We disconnected from this peaceful moment only when the train arrived.

I sat down on the underground train's seat. My feet hurt. Unfortunately for my feet, but fortunately for my belly, the ride was one-stop long. I sighed but got up anyway. "Is it far?"

"No, only a couple of minutes."

In silence, Guido guided me across a street, a park, and another street until he stopped short in front of an old-fashioned train-like exterior with eight blacked-out windows. Guido opened a door with two steps leading up. A wall of heat that carried the flavors of cooked food hit me.

Pushed forward by hunger, I stepped inside eagerly. In awe, my eyes widened, and my tongue licked my lips. Moulin rouge–red seats brought back memories of the diner we'd been to in upstate New York. But this was upscale, classy, yet cozy.

A twentysomething woman dressed in a black top and black leggings approached us with menus in her hand.

"How many?" she asked.

"Two," Guido replied swiftly. I was still checking out the interior decor. The entire wall was lined with seats with cushioned backs on the left side. Approximately ten tables stood in front of the benches, with another chair opposite the wall. Every single chair was taken.

On the other side of the restaurant, an illuminated bar with two bartenders buzzed. Another fifteen seats were squeezed in in front of the bar. From my vantage point, each seat was taken. My growling tummy roared. My heart sank.

"We only have space at the bar right now. If you want a table, wait another ten to fifteen minutes."

"The bar is fine," Guido said.

"Yes," I chimed in. My knees buckled. The smell of food had lowered any remaining patience in me.

We followed the hostess. She sat us at the end of the bar right next to the wall and placed the menus in front of us.

"Your waitress will be right with you," she said.

"What are you having?" I asked my husband.

"I can't decide between the ribs and pulled pork." His eyes flickered back and forth.

"What's pulled pork?"

"I guess it's like pieces of meat taken apart?"

"I have so many questions. Anyways, I am going to have the cheeseburger."

A waitress arrived, and we ordered. Once our food arrived, I wolfed my dinner down. Ease returned to my bones, and the pain in my legs subsided. I stole a couple of Guido's pulled pork pieces. I stole another bite, pleasantly surprised by the tender meat and slight lemony flavor. As we sat there munching, I realized I had made the right decision. I wanted to be with my husband and go through this life-changing experience with him.

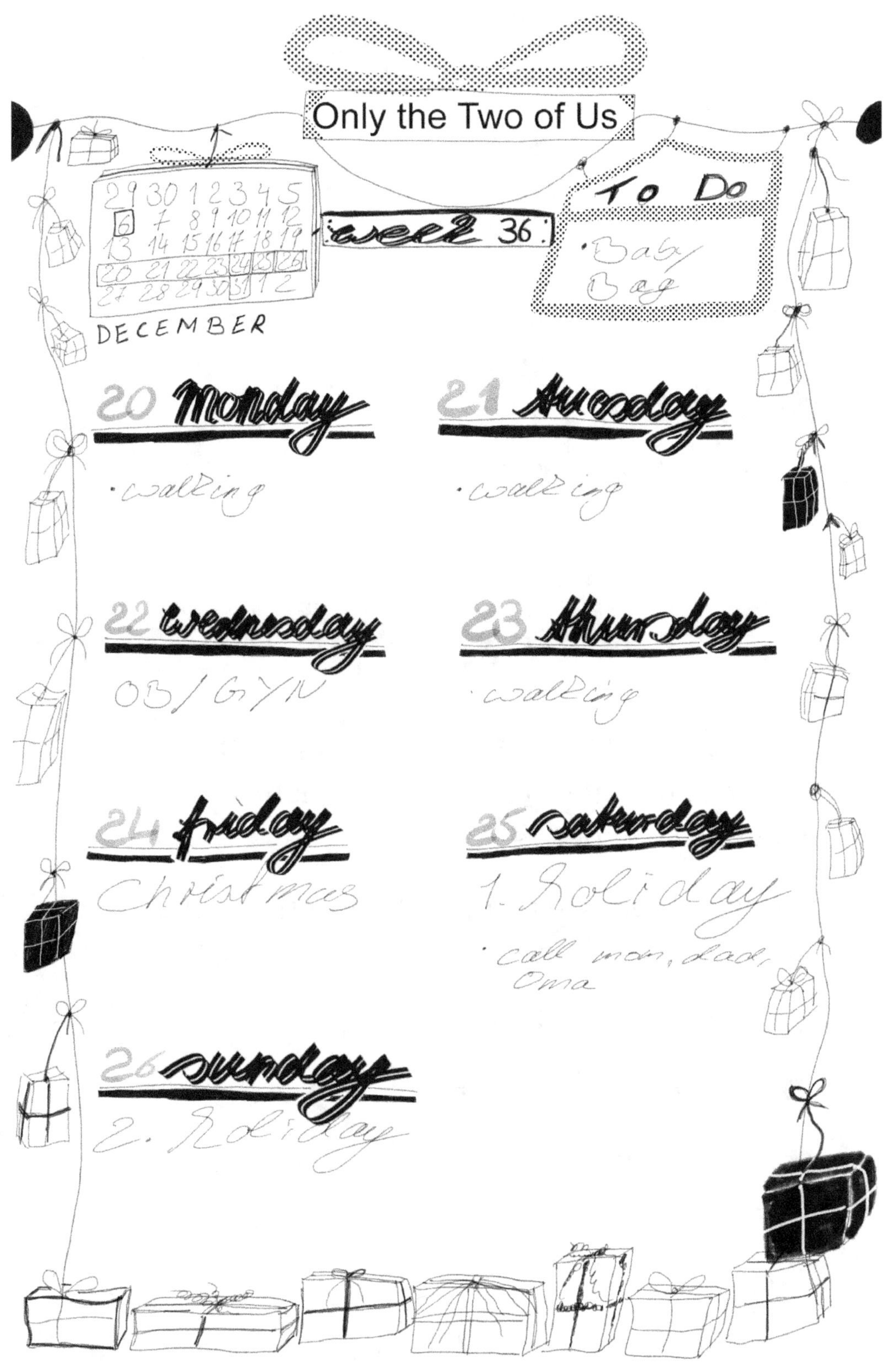

Only the Two of Us

29 30 1 2 3 4 5
6 7 8 9 10 11 12
13 14 15 16 17 18 19
20 21 22 23 24 25 26
27 28 29 30 31 1 2
DECEMBER

week 36

To Do
• Baby
  Bag

20 Monday
• walking

21 Tuesday
• walking

22 Wednesday
OB/GYN

23 Thursday
• walking

24 Friday
christmas

25 Saturday
1. Holiday
• call mom, dad,
  Oma

26 Sunday
2. Holiday

Week 36

Only the Two of US

<u>Monday</u>

I tightened my jaw, a scream lodged in my throat. A whimper escaped my mouth. I clutched my cheeks.

"I can't sleep when you toss around so much," Guido complained.

"My tooth hurts," I whined.

"Do you want an aspirin?"

I shook my head. "I don't know if I can take it."

"Why not?"

"I don't know if it harms the baby!" I exclaimed.

"Is there something else I could do for you? Maybe get a cold towel or something?" Guido asked.

"No. I don't know." My heart rate spiked while the pain exploded in my head. Instead of screaming, I imploded internally, but tears streamed down, wetting the pillowcase.

My hands kneaded the edges of our bedcovers. Guido's rhythmic breathing told me that he'd fallen back asleep. *How could he?* I reached for my phone to research a baby-friendly solution to kill this pain. My eyes skimmed over the results and clicked on every link, hoping to find one nugget of information to release me from my agony.

One of the endless entries suggested applying a pepper-water mix to the affected area. I whisked the paste into a cup in the kitchen and snuck into the bathroom. I opened my mouth in front of the mirror to pat the gray mixture on both sides of the base of my tooth. Much to my surprise, the pain vanished. Usually, most so-called hacks fell flat for me. Despite rinsing the paste out, I returned to bed with grains of pepper in my mouth, but I fell asleep shortly after.

Tuesday

The morning sun shot sharply into our bedroom. I blocked the rays out with a pillow over my face.

"How are you doing?" Guido asked when I stirred.

"I'm not sure," I said.

"Do you think you'll be alright?"

"I think so."

"Do you want to go to the dentist?" Guido asked.

"Maybe. I'll see. I'll just stay a little longer in bed. Maybe I can sleep some more."

"Call me if you need anything." Guido kissed me on my forehead. I closed my eyes again.

A searing pain woke me up again. I held my cheek to no avail. I redid the pepper-water mixture. The discomfort subsided, just like last night. Still, I knew I needed to visit the dentist, and the thought scared me. Besides being pregnant for the first time, this was my first tooth-related emergency.

Actually, my dentist was one of my favorite people. Since I could remember, Dr. Knoblauch had always been great to me. She never scared me with drilling, and I never had a filling or anything else on my teeth. Perhaps that is why my sister didn't like her as much as I did. From what I could gather, every second tooth in Ulrike's mouth contained some sort of metal.

The pain subsided again. I held my phone in both palms, and my right leg whipped up and down. Torn about what to do, I called my husband.

"Hey, I think I'll see if I can find a dentist," I said right away.

"I asked around for any potential dentist for you, but everyone keeps saying we should check with our insurance to see who they cover.”

“What? I don’t understand. I can’t just go to a doctor?”

“I know it is very confusing, but I am not sure if we have extra dental insurance.”

“An extra insurance? Okay, how do we find out?” I wondered. Why couldn’t things just be easy?

“I’ll talk to Nicole and let you know as soon as I can,” Guido promised.

I couldn’t believe that he didn’t know. *Argh*, the pain had infected my nerves literally and figuratively.

I breathed in deeply and exhaled. This was not the moment to tear down my husband. Would I have known if I were in Guido’s shoes? Well, I couldn’t say. I had never dared to work abroad at all. Guido had so much more courage than I had, but now, *right now*, I wished I knew more and could do more.

Tears welled up in my eyes. I couldn’t believe

how this pain inflicted so much disorientation and confusion.

My mouth pounded. Sweat coated my forehead. With shaking fingers, I typed "dentists near me" into the Internet browser's search bar. A list of offices filled the screen. One of the dental offices was within walking distance of us.

Just before I pressed the call button, I paused. What if we didn't have insurance, and I had to pay cash? I had zero idea how much a dental visit would cost, not even a ballpark. From the obligatory increase in monthly contributions to our health insurance once a year and the consequent discussions about the higher fees, I understood that doctor's visits were expensive. Yet I had never bothered to look up the price point for a checkup. Now that information would have been invaluable regardless of the country.

However, I heard through the grapevine that paying out of pocket wasn't uncommon around here. After a little bit more research, those whispers rang true. Scared to wipe out our savings, I'd urged Guido to figure out my health insurance before I arrived, just to keep our bank account in the black. I hadn't even considered that the dental insurance could be separate.

My phone rang. Only once. "So, we have Mass Dental. I emailed you the information," Guido said.

"Thanks," I managed to reply.

I returned to the list of dental offices after checking out Guido's email. I pressed the phone to my ear.

"Dr. Smiley's office. How can I help you?" answered a deep female voice.

"Hi, I want to make an appointment. I have a toothache," I stammered.

"Have you been here before?" the lady inquired.

"No," I managed to push out through the pain.

"Can you please give me your dental insurance information?" she asked.

"Yes." I proceeded to give her all the information she asked for.

She replied, "We have an opening in an hour. Would you like to come in?"

"Mhhh, sure," I mumbled.

At the Dentist

Only moments after I registered with the woman at the front desk, I was called in, and soon after, a nurse arrived. I expected them to tell me she would take my vitals, but she didn't. This nurse checked my mouth, asked me questions, and said, "The doctor will come shortly."

Enveloped by the quiet, my mind wondered how quickly teeth deteriorated. Was there already a brewing infection going on before I left? Or did harmful bacteria develop shortly after I landed?

"I am Dr. Bryan. How can I help you?" the dentist asked when she walked in.

"I have a horrible toothache," I explained. I knew this wasn't very informative, but this was the third or fourth time I'd had to explain what was happening. The first time was when I called. The second time was when I arrived, and the third time I explained the situation to the nurse and now the dentist. Honestly, this woman was probably the most important one, but I was exhausted from repeatedly explaining the same thing. And the more I did it, the more my pain story sounded flat.

Unfazed by my inexplicit explanation, the dentist numbed the left side of my lower mouth after examining my teeth. She left right after.

After hours—so it felt—the nurse returned to take an X-ray. Stunned, I lay on the seat, and things just happened. Shouldn't she have asked me? After all, I was pregnant. On the other hand, I'd almost died of tooth pain that very morning.

The nurse left. At some point, the dentist came back. She informed me, "You need a root canal."

"What?" I freaked out. How could this be? I didn't even have a filling the size of a breadcrumb. Instead of raising questions or getting up to leave, I stupidly answered.

"But I don't even have a filling," I protested.

"This can happen during pregnancies faster than during other times in your life. Your body reroutes resources to the baby."

The dentist drilled, the nurse sucked out my spit, the dentist drilled some more, the nurse dried off the inside of my tooth with cloth, the dentist poured some liquid into my tooth, and then they left again. Confused, I lay in the same spot with tears in my eyes.

Eventually, the dentist returned, filled my tooth, and left again. The nurse returned, smoothed out my tooth, and sent me on my merry way.

When I left the office, I checked my phone for the time. 1:00 p.m. Three hours had passed. Was I in a time trap? I guessed I was just in my very own twilight zone.

The numbness on my cheek persisted until dinner. My reflection reminded me of a one-sided chipmunk. Instead of being cute, though, my face gave the impression that the small rodent had a stroke.

Luckily for me, Guido always made ice cubes, which he usually put into his Coke and rum mix. Interestingly, since I had landed, his hand had been alcohol-free except at the Halloween party and Thanksgiving. Not just that, there was no Coke in the fridge, rum on the counter, or even empty liquor bottles next to the refrigerator.

When I first learned about my pregnancy, I'd teased Guido that he couldn't drink since I couldn't either. However, Guido had spent several months on his own, just like a *Strohwitwer*, and I sort of thought he would indulge himself just because I wasn't around. To be honest, I was very proud of him that he hadn't seemed to fall back into his old pattern of having an after-work drink to de-stress.

I nestled into the sofa, cradling the ice cubes wrapped in a kitchen towel against my jaw. My other hand went to the remote control. I flicked through the movie suggestions, which varied widely: *The Town, Ted, Mystic River, The Heat, Spotlight, The Social Network, Good Will Hunting*, and *What's Your Number?*

I had already seen most of these movies. I trailed through the suggestions one more time to pick a film that a) I hadn't seen yet and b) was fun to watch. And the winner was: *What's Your Number?*

Before I watched the flick, I made a new list titled *Rewatches*. But I couldn't leave it at that. In anticipation of the movie, my hand moved my pen to create another list: *Places I want to see in Beantown.*

Once done, I made myself comfortable on the sofa. There was just one thing that needed to be added: *Erdnussflips.*[1] These yummy peanut-based fluffy beans were my standard movie night snack. Of course, sweet popcorn was second to none, but who could pass up the peanut goodness?

This was the second time I'd watched an undubbed movie. I turned on the subtitles, though, and loved that I found them under the hearing-impaired section. It was so fascinating to hear the actors' actual voices, yet strange as well. I was so used to their German counterparts. Now the actors' mouth movements fit the words.

The movie slid by. I recognized some spots and patted myself on the back on my excellent memory. Some scenes set in the North End triggered my memory of the almost-pee debacle and created a hot flush of embarrassment on my face.

The list of places I had to visit grew steadily, even if I wasn't sure how to find them. Perhaps there were tours for movie locations? Why not? I thought to myself that these days, everything seemed to exist. Unfortunately, I was never the first person to have an idea. Yet.

The soon-to-be couple in the film stepped into the Public Garden, but I couldn't believe how quickly they went from there to the North End. I took out my phone and popped the landmarks into the navigation app. A car drive would take ten minutes, by foot around twenty-five minutes, and with public transportation, one hour.

After I finished the first flick, I continued in consecutive order of the streaming service's movie suggestions. In between, the swelling went down in my face. I turned on *The Town*. My sister had taken me to the movies for this one. I couldn't remember much of the plot anymore. I found the ending weird. How could you avoid justice by hiding out in another state? Why not at least leave the country? I was looking forward to rewatching the movie, not only to spot places I'd already been but to find new places to visit as well, and maybe I'd been wrong about my initial understanding of the ending.

My post-dental lazy day consisted of four movies: *What's Your Number? The Social Network, The Town*, and the oh-so-dark *Mystic River*, along with a long list of places I wanted to see while I was here, like the actual Red Sox stadium, which I'd sort of seen already from the hospital, but not really. Also on the list was Beacon Hill, which we'd wandered by, and an area called Brighton, which, so far, I'd always thought was a cute little beach town in the UK.

My list of places I wanted to see filled out a whole page. Satisfied with my new local destinations, I flipped through my journal. I stopped at my baby must-haves. My eyes focused on the "baby bathtub." Did we need one? My mother opposed buying one, as all babies were cleaned in the kitchen sink back in the day. My eyes flickered to the sink area. Perhaps the sink would be wide enough, but that would mean extra cleaning to make it hygienic.

What were the good old days anyway? Every time someone uttered this phrase, he or she never specified the time or time frame. Was it when your neighbor spied on you, and you could barely afford anything fancy? When you had to shovel coal from the sidewalk into the basement, can everything you harvested from your allotment or line up around the neighborhood to get one watermelon each summer?

We could buy a bathtub, but it would be one more thing we'd have to get rid of when we left. Perhaps a few wipes and washcloths would do the job. But we didn't even have washcloths. Maybe the pharmacy carried stuff like that.

<u>Wednesday</u>

The final stretch had arrived. My two-week appointment for my visit to the ob-gyn came up. Like the others before, I came, got gelled up on my tummy, and left with a new appointment in hand.

Instead of going straight home to bundle myself into the blanket on the sofa, I revisited the pharmacy. With a basket in hand, I strutted down the aisles. To my surprise, a pack of four pearl-white washcloths hung in the travel section. Nothing else landed on top of them. Proud of myself, I trotted home. I left any worries out in the cold. A sense of *getting there* lightened my shoulders. Slowly but surely, the feeling of preparedness set in.

"Hey, honey," Guido greeted me.

I dropped my plastic bag, slid off my shoes, and embraced my husband. "What a surprise that you are home already. How was your day?"

Guido wrapped his arms around me. His heat radiated through my clothes onto my skin. "Good, and I was thinking we could go out tonight. Just the two of us," Guido proposed.

"I'd love to. Do you already have an idea?"

"Yes. There is an excellent restaurant I think you'd like." We relaxed our embrace to look each other in the eyes.

"Okay." I nodded, put my coat back on, and pressed my feet into my boots. I was the last person to object to a meal prepared outside our house.

Despite the darkening of the sky, crisp air, and the coldness outside, other pedestrians passed us on the street.

We stopped at Beacon Street at a pedestrian light. The color changed from red for pedestrians. I stated, "Green."

"No, white," Guido corrected.

"I just can't get used to the different colors," I explained. Halfway through our street crossing, red numbers counted down from ten.

"Well, you learned your whole life that green means go not only for cars but for walkers too." Guido guided me down the street and turned left onto a side street.

"I think this is Cambridge already, but I am still unsure where the city line is," Guido explained.

We passed three-story houses. Each level had a balcony, and the houses were different colors. Overhead wires webbed from house to house. Nothing indicated a change in city boundaries.

"Just this afternoon, I marveled about how familiar everything has become," I said when we stopped at another light on Cambridge Street.

"I know what you mean," Guido agreed. "I suppose that is a survival skill. Adapting to the people around me helped me to settle in."

"Do you ever feel homesick?" I pressed him. We continued at a fast pace.

"Not really," Guido replied.

The tips of my ears burned. No hesitation marked his response. I waited for his question. Mine was just a prompt. An unplanned one, but an important one.

We crossed Broadway Street. My mouth opened, but I pressed my lips back together. If he had asked me, "Do you feel homesick?" my answer would have been *yes*, *yes*, and *yes*. But would my response make a difference? We were here now. And yes, I'd gotten used to my new environment, but this wasn't home.

Guido pushed the button of the pedestrian light on Harvard Street. Green—I meant white. Instead of opening up to him, I held Guido's hand tighter to steady myself. Emotional confrontations weren't my strong suit. And besides, only a couple of months were left until I would be *home*. Until then, I would just enjoy my temporary move to a foreign country.

"Here we are." Guido opened the door for me. We entered not just any eatery but a sports bar somewhere behind Harvard Square.

"Hi," we greeted the lady at the restaurant's welcome desk.

"For how many?"

"Two," my husband said.

The hostess guided us to a table with two chairs. Huge flat-screen TVs lined the walls of the dark-brown-paneled restaurant. Next to me, a baseball game was on, and behind Guido, two different American football games changed on the screen in intervals. On another screen in front of me, two men only dressed in shorts fought in a cage.

A waitress in a black shirt and leggings placed two tall glasses of iced water in front of us, along with menus. "What would you like to drink?" Her attention swung back and forth between us.

"Nothing for me," I said, pulling the water glass closer to me.

"I'll take a . . ." Guido's eyes scanned the bar to check the available beer on tap. "A cranberry juice would be great," he finally ordered.

Both of us scanned the menu. Everything sounded delicious. I ordered nachos along with a medium rare burger with everything. Guido looked forward to mozzarella cheese balls and rare steak tips.

The waitress slid the nachos and cheese balls under our noses only a few minutes later. At the sight of the appetizer, I almost fell backward. The bowl of nachos was the size of a whole dinner plate.

Guido dug into his mozzarella balls. I gazed over my food.

"Do you think we can cancel the burger?" I wondered.

Guido shrugged his shoulders. "I don't know. We just take it home," he suggested.

"Mmm, a cold burger for breakfast," I teased.

"I know you can eat it. Look at me. I got used to it."

I nodded my head. Guido had gained nearly ten pounds since he moved here.

Spicy tomato-red salsa combined with creamy guacamole rimmed my mouth. The thick liquid dripped off the nachos. But my focus zeroed in on the fighting scene on television. My mind was entranced by the two men, barely dressed, aggressively pouncing on each other. I hated it, yet the fight compelled my eyes. Veins popped. Blood smeared the fighters' skin.

"Here we go, a burger for you." The young woman pushed the nacho bowl to the side before she slid a plate with buns and burger meat combined with pickles, tomatoes, lettuce, cheese, and mushrooms in front of me. "Be careful. The plate is still hot," she said to Guido. My eyes bulged. The steak lay steaming on an iron skillet with cooking oil still bubbling up from the hot black metal.

"I am so full." After eating, I licked the last crumb of meat from my fork and wiped the meat fat from my mouth.

Guido placed several freshly printed bills in the night-black check presenter our waitress left on the table. My arms slipped into my coat, and I zipped the cold-weather jacket up. Guido copied me.

Winter air cooled down our warm faces. Stuffed yet satisfied from a good meal, we decided to take a detour on our way home. We crossed the now quiet town down the main street.

"Excuse me, excuse me!" The yelling voice compelled us to turn around. The street was ghostlike. Only the two of us occupied the pavement. We turned to the waitress, who charged toward us.

"Did we forget something?" Guido's thoughts mirrored my own.

She drew closer, out of breath and shivering. "Was something wrong?" the waitress stuttered.

"Wrong?" Guido's question lingered in the air for a short moment until she stabilized her posture.

"Yes, wrong. You just left barely any tip."

Guido's eyes bulged. My cheeks flushed. "How much did you leave?" My mind spun.

"Five bucks." Guido's answer sounded reasonable to me. The waitress extended the bill to us. My eyes ran the numbers up and down. $48.60 plus 6.25% tax. Guido had placed $55 on the bill. He rounded up. My mouth was about to form the word "So?" when I heard Guido say, "I don't understand what you are trying to say?"

The young woman stiffened. Her eyes flickered between us. "You gave me less than fifteen percent tip."

Hot blood flushed through my body. Guido, cool as a cucumber, pulled out his wallet. "Here you go." He placed fifteen dollars in the waitress's hands. I waited for Guido to say, "Happy now?" but instead he threaded his arm through mine and steered me away from her.

"This was one of the oddest moments of my life." We reached a small square with benches and leafless trees.

"I should have known better." Guido checked out the stars, which were nowhere to be found as the cape of streetlight beams illuminated the sky above the city. "During my introduction session, the facilitator mentioned that waiters expect fifteen to twenty percent tip."

My eyes widened after his announcement. "I guess I will not go out for dinner any time soon."

Guido cradled my bum. "Well, soon there will be a new reason to stay home anyway." We both leaned in until our lips touched each other.

It's Christmas!!!

I hummed and buzzed around despite spending our very first Christmas alone together. I meant together alone. Well, I meant just Guido and me. No family, no friends, no strangers. Just us in an apartment.

My phone and both our email accounts contained Christmas wishes from everyone and anyone. Some of them we called back. Our parents expressed how much they missed us, and friends with kids wished they could switch places with us. When we hung up after the last call, exhaustion from talking all morning offered itself up for a nap. But instead of hitting the sheets again, Guido convinced me to go for a walk.

The brisk air refreshed my energy, but something was missing. My family? Definitely. My friends? Completely. The Christmas spirit? Probably. All of the above? Absolutely!

An Advent calendar was the only Christmas decoration we had. We didn't have a tree—a mutual decision. If we had one, we would have been required to Christmas-ize the evergreen. This was a low-key Christmas event. There were no thrills, no decor, and no gifts. It was just a cuddle, a movie, and a bed.

My mind drifted to the past Christmases. I wondered if I would make the evenings as pleasant as my mother always had. She wasn't much of a decorator either, but the small touches made the evening exceptional. Especially her Christmas platters under the tree. Instead of just giving each of us the same thing, my mom remembered what my dad, sister, Guido, and I preferred. My plate was always filled with chocolate-covered gingerbread hearts, and my mother made *Kalter Hund*, a no-bake chocolate biscuit cake, while Guido's was piled up with marzipan and speculaas, along with my dad's homemade eggnog.

Saturday

Instead of driving to my aunt's for an hour, getting stuffed, and exchanging gifts, I bathed in the contentment of not having to go anywhere. I loved my aunt and her family, but these days were packed with the overstimulation of reconnecting with rarely seen family and acquaintances.

The only side effect of this year's uneventful days was the increase in being lethargic. I rolled with the flow. I doodled in my journal. After embellishing a piece I liked, I flipped from one random page to another. At the end of this week, I'd noticed I hadn't done anything for the New Year yet. Of course, I made a yearly overview to jot down important events, such as my due date and when I would return to work.

This never-ending baby prep slowly got on my nerves. I mean, I had peace of mind with the pile of baby stuff increasing in the house, but at least one more item still needed to be added to the mountain: a car seat.

I hadn't even considered purchasing one back home. But now, looking at strollers, I realized I didn't know if we should buy the most basic seat or one that could be used until the baby grew out of the seat.

My eyes flickered through so many options. My pen scratched the surface. My hands paused. Nausea bubbled up somewhere inside me.

I took a deep breath. I could do this.

We had to buy one more thing—a must-have, not optional—but my resistance didn't waver.

Guido's hand pressed gently down my shoulder. "What are you doing?" He leaned forward. "Oh, car seats. Why didn't you tell me? I'd be happy to do that with you."

A smile washed over my face. "I just wanted to get my bearings first and prepare a list for you of what I thought we needed the car seat to be, what the price options were, and to compare it with what's available and how much we should spend on it."

Guido looked at me, then at the screen and back. "Let's not sweat it. Buy the first one or the cheapest one. It doesn't matter."

"It doesn't matter?" I squeaked. "Why doesn't it matter? It is our baby. Our firstborn."

"Yes, and I doubt this company would sell anything to harm the baby or fall apart immediately. Imagine the bad press and the lawsuits. If you look at the first product listing, I am sure it will have thousands of ratings. In the comments, people will say good things and bad things. Plus, if you just get the first one you see, you can check the car seat off your list," Guido finished with a cheeky smile.

Dumfounded, I stared at my screen. Guido was right. The first car seat had thousands of ratings and comments. And the comments were mostly positive, and the negative ones were ridiculous. How was it the seller's fault that the package was delivered to the wrong address?

The pressure around my ribs loosened up. I pulled out my credit card and bought the car seat immediately without writing anything down. No weight comparison. No years-of-use comparison. No color comparison. No price comparison. No warranty comparison. No nothing. Would I regret this? I'd see soon enough. For now, this weight was off my shoulders. And I thought with that, we were done. And it wasn't even New Year's yet.

new resolutions
beginnings   A cozy Time   Happy NEW YEAR   Be In The Now
Week 37

1 2 3 4 5 6 7 8 9 10 11 12 13 14 15 16 17 18 19 20 21 22 23 24 25 26 27 28 29 30 31 1 2

Monday
27
walk

Tuesday
28
· walk
· plan the new year

Wednesday
29
walk   walk
walk

Thursday
30
let's walk

Friday
31
SILVESTER

Saturday
1
happy new year

Sunday
2
self care

grow intentions
Deep it simple
read sleep CREATE
keep it simple FOCUS
let go stuff
let go

date yourself Be Grateful

Week 37

A Cozy Time

<u>Monday</u>

"I can't believe New Year's Eve is only a couple of days away! " I said, more to myself than to Guido.

I flipped through my journal. A few blank pages were left in my weekly organizer. In general, this was a good thing. There wasn't a need to start a second notebook during the year and redo my calendars, trackers, and lists. This way, the year was compressed into one neat booklet and not spread over two journals.

But I was also a little bit sad. Most weeks had been empty. After I arrived, the white spaces increased. During the first three-quarters of the year, I was busy working, meeting friends, seeing my family, reading books, making plans, going to festivals, volunteering at the elder-care facility where my grandma lives, checking out new food trucks, watching street performers, and being all-around happy and content in my little bubble.

I'd felt like nothing exciting happened in my life until recently when I started thinking about the past couple of days and months and comparing them to the past few years. Rarely events exploded and lingered in my memory. Thinking about everything now, usually there was a lead-up to changing circumstances, which I might have missed. Or they were so tiny in their occurrence that I didn't recall them, just like right now. My monotonous life had zero zing, yet everything was different. Looking back on the past eleven months, I realized so much had happened that I would have never dreamt of despite letting the blank spaces in my bullet journal tell me otherwise.

In the past, Guido and I rarely discussed having a baby. The topic only came up when friends announced their baby news. Additionally, many people seemed to get pregnant around the same time, which I'd mentioned to my mom.

She replied, "Yes, life-changing events come in waves. First, everyone finds a partner. Then they get married, have a baby, and then people get divorced."

"Come again? Do you want to tell me something about you and Dad?" I gasped.

My parents had just celebrated their golden anniversary. Despite being an adult and forming my own family, I wasn't sure how I would handle it if my parents separated. Before my mother answered the lingering question, my sister said, "That is why I am going to do neither."

"You'll regret that. When it will all be too late," our mom forewarned.

"Well, Mareike is giving you a grandchild already," my sister pointed out to turn my mom's attention back to me.

I missed those moments when I could talk to them and just go home to my own four walls when I felt like it. Being surrounded by familiar things would have helped me settle in much better. But we never planned to stay here long enough to get our belongings shipped across the ocean. I could count the months, weeks, and days until I slept in my bed again.

I pulled out a pencil to outline a new calendar overview and planned the next year. In the new spread, I could count down the days until the baby's arrival, our return dates, my first day back at work, birthdays, vacations, bank holidays, and all other foreseeable events.

On the double pages, I had a spot for every month of the year, and I added the names and numbers of the days according to the following year with the help of the calendar on my computer. I looked at my electronic device and my weekly spreads in my notebook. I never realized that *Mittwoch*[1] was not in the middle at all. The week contained seven days, but the word *Mittwoch* literally means "middle."

"Guido, have you ever noticed that *Mittwoch* is not in the middle of the week?"

My husband pushed his eyebrows together. His gaze reminded me of my first-grade teacher. Despite there being thirty-six kids, not a peep escaped from any child under her stern expression.

"Well, actually, we just had a similar discussion at work," he began.

I sat up straight. "So?"

"I think I was explaining to Barret what bridge days are and stated something along the lines that Monday is the start of the week, obviously after the weekend, and he said no. The week starts on Sunday. I was irritated. A weekend is a unit, right?"

"Absolutely," I agreed.

"Barret countered that the week still starts on Sundays, but the workweek starts on Mondays."

"And what was the conclusion?" I asked.

"None. I had to answer a call, but now you are saying this. So this made me think he might be onto something."

"Well, my calendars all start with Monday," I stated. "Your computer is from here, isn't it?"

He nodded. "Yes."

"Why don't you open your calendar and see when the week starts there?"

Guido's fingers flew over his keyboard. "Well, what can I say? Sunday is the first day."

I was intrigued. I knew little about the origins of dates, times, and calendars. Western cultures were very similar to one another, yet those little itty-bitty details kept derailing me. That was not really true. They struck a string of curiosity inside me.

"Maybe the conclusion here is, other countries, other rules?" I underlined my excitement about this little nugget of discovery.

"You mean other countries, other customs," my husband corrected.

"It's not only that the week starts on a different day, but the heating has a different unit, Christmas is celebrated on different days, cars go different speeds, the size of milk is much bigger, the car drinks gallons, and even the pedestrian street crossing light changes into different colors," I explained.

"Well, that just proves my point," Guido said.

I didn't experience the culture shock I was warned about, but all those minor unexpected deviations made my trip exciting. I was glad I came, as I had learned so much—not just about subtle differences in different countries, which I would have never experienced if I hadn't moved. Visiting a country isn't the same as living in one, but I have grown and discovered myself. I understood my sister and her desire to travel more and more.

But this opportunity Guido gave me to live a couple of months in another country might be the last opportunity for the next few months. Maybe even years.

I rubbed my belly. Guido came over to sit beside me. After he placed his arm around my shoulders, I leaned into him. "Do you think we'll be good parents?"

"I hope so," he sighed. "We'll figure it out. What does the baby really need? He's going to have us. That's the most important thing."

Guido's heartbeat echoed in my ears like the baby's at the doctor's office. I was scared. Scared of the unknown. I opened my mouth but closed my lips again. I didn't want to tell him . . . but I feared I wasn't ready. I wasn't prepared to become a mother and suddenly act like one.

Throughout my pregnancy, similar thoughts ebbed in and out of my mind. For the most part, I pushed them out to clear my headspace for work and to deal with an absentee husband.

A monumental change in physical appearance shaped the new stage in my life. Unfortunately, the lack of Guido's presence sucked. After all, my uterus didn't suddenly implode to create an offspring on my own. I doubted anything and everything once in a while. The people in my life assured me that indecision was normal and that I wasn't alone. But I never asked for help. Everyone was wrapped up in their own lives and commitments, and to be honest, what could my mother do when nausea bubbled up in the middle of the night?

Ulrike offered to move in with me, but I wasn't sure that would improve our sisterly bond. We had no space for a long-term visitor, and she needed space. Despite working in a big studio with all the rooms she required, she preferred to work from home and turn on loud music while creating fabric patterns. She had countless samples, printouts of her designs, and a book collection in her apartment that dwarfed mine. The thought of her moving in, even temporarily, stressed me out. So I declined. Instead, I prepared some space for the little one.

"I dreamed that the baby would be coming, and we still didn't have everything," I said instead of admitting my emotional stress factor.

Some days, I believed I could climb mountains, smash any obstacle, or tear apart any problem. But during quiet moments when I considered everything rationally, a dark hole swallowed my positive outlook because change leaped with giant's steps. Well, actually, it stumbled with baby steps, but who's measuring? Even small changes would amount to big ones once chained together.

Guido patted my back. "There is still time."

"We don't even have a name for him yet." I shrugged.

"We can change that right now," my husband said.

"Now?" I questioned.

He nodded. "Now."

"Okay. What do you have?"

"How about Peter Alexander?" Guido proposed.

My voice exploded into laughter. I hollered so much. I hadn't heard that name of the late very poluar singer in ages. "Okay, all joking aside. We can shorten our list by one name a day until there's only one name standing. What do you think?"

"I was actually serious," Guido admitted.

"Oh," I managed to say.

"I thought Peter for my dad and Alexander for yours," my husband explained.

Stunned by his declaration, I had to be careful what and how I said the following words.

"That's so sweet of you. But why would you want to have double names?"

"Why not? It is both our dads. I wanted to honor them."

"Well, I don't understand how one can honor someone else by giving a child his or her name. It is more about how respectfully you treat that other person."

Guido squinted his eyes at me.

I quickly added, "Also, I never like middle names. I never understood their purpose. Unless their first name is hyphenated, like your mom's, nobody really uses them. Unless, of course, the parents get mad, and suddenly it's *Hanna Marie* or *Sofia Carolina*."

Of course, this declaration of my thoughts didn't bode well. Guido grew up way more bound by traditions, while I had questioned mine, with the help of my sister, since I could remember. Despite Guido's not being a conformist, some things were hard to shake.

"I have a middle name," Guido replied, as if that proved anything.

I challenged, "How often do you get called by it? And how often do you use it?"

I knew the answers to those questions almost as well as he did. Every time he had to fill out a form where he had to write down his full name, my hubby threw a little hissy fit. His middle name was Wolfgang. Not too bad, but unnecessary. And my husband knew that all too well. That was why I was surprised he proposed the idea, regardless of the thought behind it.

Guido clenched his jaw. "What do you want to do then?"

"I would like to keep the name simple, short. Evergreen," I explained.

"Evergreen," Guido mused. "That might be tough."

"But there are names that are timeless," I stated.

"Like . . . ?" Guido challenged.

"Like Max, or Leo, or Lars, or Niko," I proposed.

"Most of these are short for something. How

about classics like Walter, Mathias, Hans, Wolfgang, Jens, Sven?"

"I'm not sure," I doubted out loud. "A couple of these names are so old-fashioned."

"They're making a comeback," Guido interrupted.

"I'm not sure," I said. "We need a name that not only fits our last name but is also tease-proof."

He gave me an exasperated look. "You can't be serious."

"I am," I insisted.

"Kids tease."

"Let's write something down. We'll sleep on it and compare notes next year," Guido proposed.

I sighed. "That's a good idea."

I couldn't believe we managed to find ourselves in a name deadlock. Again. Why was it so complicated? Finding a name for another human being was really something.

Maybe we would follow my dad's advice. He said when we saw the baby, we'd know his name. But I was not sure if I could wait that long. I felt so unprepared, and I wanted to be ready. I wanted to know the baby's name before the baby came. Yet there I was, unsure of a name, unprepared for the birth, and uprooted from my home.

"You ordered the car seat, right? We've got a stroller, a bassinet where the baby can sleep, some clothes. What else does the baby need?" Guido asked.

I pursed my lips in thought. "I'm not sure."

"We still have over two weeks left to sort it out and prepare."

"Two weeks!" Both syllables came out with an edge. Two weeks. Fourteen days. Almost countable on both of my hands.

My mouth dried. I pumped air into my lungs and released the invisible gas. My muscles relaxed. "We can get everything missing from your list together after New Year's. We will zero in on a name then as well," Guido promised.

His words soothed my mind, but still, an uneasy feeling spread through me. How could it not? My rib cage tightened again. I thought we had this under control. I'd sort of forgotten about the impalpable baby things in favor of the tangible ones. I'd completely let the whole naming topic fall off the shelf.

I was done being pregnant. I was done making a decision for the baby and with my husband. I was just done.

Some Random Days of the Week

Over the in-between days, I went in and out of my stupor. The most irritating thing was that Guido had to work. "I only have ten vacation days per year."

"Ten days?" I hollered at him. I couldn't believe him. That wasn't true; Guido wasn't a liar. And I did believe him. I just couldn't comprehend the information.

"Well, actually, I only have five days, as I am not staying the whole year. But I had five this year and will have five next year, and I want to take them when the baby comes."

My brain froze. Air barricaded thoughts, reasonings, questions, and arguments. You name it. I had twenty-eight vacation days per year, plus sick days and maternity leave. So did Guido, back home. Well, he got paternity leave, obviously. So how could he only have ten days now? I didn't get it, but arguing with him about his vacation situation wouldn't change anything either.

New Year's Eve

Another telephone marathon. First, I called my friends when I woke up. I had at least ten messages wishing me a Happy New Year with inquiries about what we were going to do, as well as a short note on what everyone was doing back home and where they would spend their New Year's Eve.

"How are you doing?" Ulrike asked.

"Good, good. I'm going to go shopping later,

but I have yet to figure out what to use for lead pouring," I said.

"Beeswax is all the rage this year. I've seen it everywhere," Ulrike replied.

"What a good idea!"

Over the past decade or so, reports had bubbled up that lead is highly toxic. Back in the day, we popped a small piece of lead into a teaspoon and held a candle under the utensil to melt the metal. We dropped the liquid into the snow and guessed what the stiffened metal piece could resemble. The DIY fortune-telling tradition created a lot of fun each year.

I asked my sister, "Are you going to be with Mom and Dad later?"

"Maybe. Well, we might go bar hopping first and then swing by their house. And you?"

"It will only be the two of us, huddling on the sofa, just hanging, chatting, maybe watching a movie, and snacking," I stated.

"Why? This is the season to have fun and laugh."

Years ago, we stopped partying unanimously after joining the Brandenburger Tor crowd in Berlin. Never had I ever been so scared. Almost everybody was drunk, and random people let firecrackers go off within the sea of people. I begged our party to move to the edge of the gathering. Ulrike and her boyfriend at the time complained. They questioned why we came in the first place if we didn't see the performing acts' close-ups. The performers were Lego figure–sized from the middle of the crowds. The people around us squished the air out of our lungs. The installed big screens everywhere brought them closer to anywhere you watched on *17th of June Street*.

After one too many sardine-can-like squeezes, everyone but my sister and her date made their way toward *Tiergarten* neighborhood. We had zero game plan, just an escape from the massiveness of the event. We ended up finding a bench without bodily fluids on it and without stomach contents smeared all over the wood.

We waited for the clock to hit the magic number, signaling the dawn of a new year despite freezing our bums off.

The morning after, Ulrike came home telling us that she spent the night in the hospital since one random guy hit another next to her, only for her boyfriend to put on his "knight in shining armor gear" to hit another guy. A mass commotion broke out. Yeah, so much for setting the tone for the New Year. Shortly after, they broke up.

In the years after, we organized get-togethers in our houses, played games, made movie marathons, poured lead in the snow or cold water, planned the following year, and listed resolutions.

"I don't know. I just wanted to hang at home and be with my husband," I explained.

"Is Guido at least making some *Schmalzgebäck?*"[2] my sister asked.

"Actually, I volunteered to do it. As the batch will be small, I thought it would be a great learning opportunity."

My parents always made sweet fried dough when we were little. These days, Guido took over and made mulled wine at our gatherings. This year, I volunteered.

"I asked Mom for some recipes. I'll go shopping in half an hour, so I will return when Guido returns home."

Ulrike was surprised. "Why is he working today?"

"Don't ask me," I replied.

"Well, whatever you do, I wish you a Happy New Year, a relaxing night, and a painless start to the New Year!"

"Thank you, Ulrike. You too!"

Two Hours Later

The grocery store had doubled its shoppers compared to my previous visit. People zigzagged from one side of the aisle to the other. Despite maneuvering the cart out of other people's way, I still bumped into others until I found frozen pizzas.

When I stumbled upon frozen dumplings, a grin spread across my face. I loved pierogies and all the members of this food group. I didn't care if they were stuffed with veggies, meat, shrimp, or a mix; they all delighted my heart and stomach.

Once a couple of bags of premade foods landed in my cart, I eyed the frozen pies and tossed an apple pie on the top of the frozen pile. I drummed with my fingers on the push bar. I had too much stuff in the cart, and I hadn't even collected the "essential items" yet. A couple of rounds around the aisles later, the flour, crystallized and powdered sugar, oil, tea candles, and fireplace matches were a piece of cake to find.

I circled the aloe leaves again but didn't know how to process them. Did you cut them open, eat the meat, or apply the pulp to your skin and hair? I had so many questions. This was definitely something to figure out next year.

I marched on to my quest to find the beeswax. Randomly, the beeswax was stacked up next to the soaps. I made my way to the checkout but stopped in my tracks. My mouth fell to the floor. I read the words on a snack item. I reread them. Laughter bubbled up inside me, but I clenched my jaw. People here would not understand, but Guido and my sister would share in the hilarity of the bar, the fig bar. So I bought the snack.

Early Evening

I could not believe I was standing in the kitchen, making something. I heated a cup of water in the microwave and poured a spoonful of dried yeast and a spoonful of sugar into the white liquid. Per my mom's instructions, I mixed everything together and let the mixture sit.

I poured flour, sugar, and a sprinkling of salt into our soup pot before whisking everything together. After I spotted bubbles on the milky mixture, I added the liquid to the dry ingredients, along with an egg. The fork scooped the liquids into the flour. But my mom told me to use my hands to shape the dough.

I washed my fingers and cleaned under my nails, then lowered my tips onto the dough. A "Yikes!" escaped me. With every new attempt at shaping, pushing, squeezing, and rolling, a muffled sound of disgust echoed into the emptiness. After several rounds of pushing on the mass, groaning with every touch, the dough finally resembled Guido's and my mom's. I covered the pot with its lid to let the dough rise.

While waiting, I pulled out the beeswax and shaved pieces off. Next to them, I placed two small spoons and a water bowl.

"Are you kidding me?" Guido howled after he greeted me. My eyes fell to his hands. He held the snack bar. His laughter dripped over to me.

"No," I giggled. "I saw it and had to have it." I held my belly.

"This is too funny. Fig bar. This is hilarious." Guido wiped a tear out of his eye.

"Let me make some dinner. This is a great end to the year," he said, shaking with laughter. Guido sliced bread, salami, and cucumber, and pulled cream cheese, tomatoes, and hummus out of the fridge.

After dinner, the dough had doubled in size. After I drizzled flour on the kitchen counter, I pressed and stretched the dough out, fished out a knife, and cut lines horizontally and vertically, every couple of inches.

We layered the bread with parts of Guido's prepared spread. On the television, countless highlights and lowlights from the past year rolled. The summaries ranged from natural disasters around the globe to what captured people's attention to new species found and everything in between.

I turned on the stove to heat the vegetable oil, marveling at the town's quietness. No fizzing in the air, no gunshot-like explosions disrupting the sky, and no firecrackers foreshadowing this big night's event. Only a couple of cars vroomed past.

Back home, practically every house had New Year's Eve explosives ranging from noisemakers to rockets. My parents kept their stock in two plastic containers in the basement. They never finished what they bought. My sister and I also piled up our leftovers every first of January. However, we used to just collect them off the streets.

When Ulrike and I were little, we got up early while our parents still slept on the first of the year to follow our unofficial tradition. We scoured the streets for unexploded crackers, loading our Easter baskets yearly. The spirit of a treasure hunt kept us going longer than we should have. Eventually, we grew out of this activity. Interestingly, no adult ever told us off. As a grown-up, I thanked my lucky stars once I comprehended how dangerous it was. Oh well, different times, I guess.

Now that I was thinking about the New Year's celebration, I realized I hadn't noticed any crackers or rockets for sale anywhere. Back home, you could practically buy them at every corner.

Was it possible that you couldn't just buy them here? And that was why I couldn't hear them? That sounded like a reasonable explanation. I sorta-kinda liked that idea. The sudden increase in noise was loud and sometimes scary when everyone randomly decided to make stuff explode in the neighborhood. The streets and sidewalks were trashed the following day with all the cardboard, wrappers, and leftovers from the New Year's celebrations.

I dropped the squares into the pot. After a few seconds, I fished out the risen fried dough and drizzled powdered sugar over it. No smoke layered the air. No burned fumes rose up from the stove. No blackened oil crusted the inside of the pot. I patted my own back.

Guido turned on the countdown to midnight. Almost half the world had already turned the page to the following year. We dug into the *Schmalzgebäck*. A drone camera flew over the ocean to display the beaches and forests of the Line Islands. The footage continued with countries further west, like New Zealand, Mongolia, Tanzania, and eventually Germany.

Being in a foreign country made me suddenly realize that I always needed to understand different time zones. I got the concept—I learned it in school—but now I felt time, genuinely understanding the change. Everyone I knew was already fast asleep. While Australians had already eaten breakfast, Guido and I were still waiting for the first day of the New Year.

"Shall we do the wax pouring?" Guido asked after we'd stuffed ourselves with the fried dough.

"Sure," I agreed. We still had four hours until midnight.

Guido placed the plate with beeswax on the table, along with spoons, water, two-inch-long matches, and two tea candles. He lit the wicks. We scooped the wax onto the metal to levitate the shallow bowl over the golden flame. The shavings melted just fine. Guido dropped the liquid into the water and fished the lump back out. He laid his hardened wax on a kitchen towel. I copied his actions.

We repeated the process three times each to use up all the yellow wax.

Guido inspected his figure. "So, what do you see? I see maybe a bike and perhaps a cat or dog. The other two I am not sure. And you?"

"I see a baby," I teased.

"Do you?"

"Perhaps! Also, maybe a tree?" I laughed.

"Don't ask me," Guido said.

"Okay, let's say it's a tree, and hmmm . . . a deer, and perhaps a key, and maybe a stork?"

"So what does it mean?"

"I am not sure," I admitted, but I'd already pulled up my phone. Guido cleared up all used items. "So bike, I am not sure. I can't find it."

"Maybe a new one for me next year," my husband suggested.

"Maybe. Dog—you will receive unbelievable news. Tree—you will grow. And key means that I don't spill others' secrets."

Guido chuckled, "I was hoping for a new house."

"Perhaps we can talk about that once we are back home." I glanced at the screen again. "Stork—a baby is on the way! Oh, and deer means luck." I paused. "I like all the predictions," I chuckled.

Guido lined the wax shapes up. "What else should we do?" he asked.

"A movie?" I suggested.

"Sure," Guido agreed.

A yawn escaped my mouth.

"If you want, we can just go to bed," Guido offered.

I checked the time. "But it's three hours till midnight," I mumbled.

"Well, yeah. But we both seem to be tired. And why not start the year sleeping in?" Guido argued.

All my limbs screamed to go to bed. I stretched them out. "I think you're right. Let's just go to bed."

We tucked in tight with our coverless bedcover before the twenty-third hour struck, breaking a twenty-year-old tradition. Regardless, the first of the New Year had come in some places in the world already. With that in mind, any residual regret left my thoughts. My eyelids drooped. The heat from Guido's skin pulled me into the land of dreams.

A new Year
A new Experience
Week 38
1 2 3 4 5 6 7 8 9 10 11
12 13 14 15 16 17 18 19
20 21 22 23 24 25 26
27 28 29 30 31
What is left to do?
3 Monday
walking walking
oh & walking
4 Tuesday
· take a walk ·
5 Wednesday
more walking
6 Thursday
walk?
7 Friday
· kitchen science
lecture
8 Saturday
Don't forget
to walk
9 Sunday
probably hanging?

Week 38

A New Year, A New Experience

<u>Monday Night</u>

An awful sound made me sit up. I pushed Guido, shaking. "Did you hear that?"

"What?" My husband yawned.

"This sound?" I exclaimed. The noise emanated from Guido's phone again at several intervals. It made my blood run cold. Guido reached for his phone. "It's a storm warning."

"A storm warning?" I stammered.

"A weather emergency alert."

"What?" I couldn't believe it.

"It's a nor'easter warning," he continued.

"I don't understand."

"It's a winter storm. Probably with heavy snow," my husband explained. I pulled the blanket up to my chin. A storm warning? How? Why? Of course I had heard storm warnings before. But only randomly peppered throughout my life. In the news! Not on my phone. Not during the night.

Guido's chest moved up and down. Besides our breathing, stillness spread in the room, in the apartment. My eyes scanned the ceiling. My ears listened.

Outside, the wind increased its pace. Water hammered at the windows. Trash cans dropped to the ground. Metal dragged on the pavement. The wind slammed the roof. The glass of the window vibrated. I pulled my blanket up to my eyes. Eventually, a restless sleep overcame my body.

<u>Tuesday</u>

With a coffee mug in hand, I watched the grayness of winter, layering its mood on mine. A blanket of white crystallized water outlined the street, with parked cars forming hill-like structures under the snow cover. A few winter-embracing souls had left tracks in a perfect winter wonderland. Snow coated everything, even the overhead wires, which almost buckled under the frozen water's weight. A rumbling sound drew closer. A snowplow pushed dirty snow in front of its body. The cars' outlines vanished under the redistribution of snow.

Despite the minus ten degrees outside and the obstacle course, courtesy of last night, squirrels raced via the overhead cables from one house to the next. Besides the rodents, nothing moved much. Barely anyone walked on the sidewalk. Only the occasional car drove by, and some kids built snowmen.

I still wore my PJs myself. In my head, I ran over a list of things I still had to do: get groceries, make a list of baby items we still needed, finish up my yearly expenses, and take a nap.

The warmth of my coffee lifted my mood just a bit, and the caffeine soon kicked in. I stretched my arms up in the air. Out of the corner of my eye, I saw a white van rolling down the street. The unusual shape of the vehicle and its blue-and-white logo, which I knew now, gave its purpose away. Mail was getting delivered. Not just mail, I supposed, but perhaps packages?

As a kid, checking the mailbox was my daily highlight. Back in the day, I wrote birthday cards, holiday cards, letters to friends, and postcards from our family trips to everyone in my address book. This book was my life, my connector to everyone I knew. I wrote pages and pages for hours to my best friend and couldn't wait for her response, which always rivaled my page count.

These days, I might write a card to my grandmother. *Oh no, I still need to send her a Christmas card. Ugh, where's my brain?* My cheeks flushed red.

As the heat of embarrassment emanated from my face, the peculiar mail vehicle stopped in front of our house. A woman dressed in a blue oversized winter jacket carrying several letters, oversized envelopes, and a yellow package vanished under our down-sloping entrance cover. I stared at the black roof shingles.

It couldn't have been for me. Or could it?

I mean, a yellow package could only come from the Deutsche Post, or couldn't it? So far, I hadn't seen this kind of yellow associated with another country's postal company. This, of course, didn't say much. I hadn't been around the world, but no other European country that was twinned with the German post organization came to my mind.

There was another option. This package, potentially from Germany, could be for someone else. But come to think of it, how likely was it that another occupant in this house would receive mail from the country where I was from? Not so much, I would think.

The world was a curious place, though. When my class went to London, we traveled to the airport via the U-Bahn in Berlin. I could swear I only heard English when we were on the underground train. Then, in London, we walked across Hyde

Park, and many, I mean *a lot of people* who weren't part of our class, spoke German. Maybe the chance that the parcel was for someone else was way more likely than I wanted to admit.

Yet curiosity built up inside me. I had to know if my sister, mom, and dad surprised us with a package. I swung my cream cardigan over my pajama top. Once out of the apartment, I held my belly to sail down the flight of stairs, opened the house door, and froze.

The wind chill hammered on my exposed skin. Every pore instantly closed to prevent the formation of icicles—no wonder no one was strolling around. Anyone staying over five minutes in this cold would turn into an ice sculpture.

The yellow package sat inches away from me. I dared myself to push open the storm door. Despite already making my way so far, I was a moment short of turning around to wait for Guido to come back from work. Or I could get dressed appropriately. From how I stood in the doorframe, one could think that my experiences during winter involved palm trees.

I tightened my cardigan, which was useless in a winter storm, dared myself, and opened the flimsy last barrier to the outside world.

My arm stretched out to the parcel with a lump on top. I pulled the box to me. In fact, the yellow-dyed cardboard came from the Deutsche Post, and the label, written in my mother's handwriting, revealed the receiver.

I closed the apartment door behind me, and my muscles shivered uncontrollably. My mom's package slipped out of my hands. I stared at the parcel. My forehead folded into several waves of disbelief. The lump on top wasn't just any old thing deforming the cardboard. I carried the postal surprise into the living room.

I ripped off the plastic bandages. A sweet treat taped on top of the box greeted me. A blue partially transparent bag of Smurfs gummies was taped to the outside. I wrestled my phone out of my pocket, held the communication device horizontally over the unbelievable sight, and snapped a pic.

Under the bag of Haribos, a gaping hole in the box revealed itself. Christmas wrapping paper was pushed against the inside of the contained space through the broken cardboard. Automatically, I utilized my phone to make a video. I hovered over the top, moved forward, leaned to the side, and circled to get 360 degrees of proof that someone had ripped the package open.

Carefully, I leveled a scissor blade through the hole and sliced the uneven tape open. A rectangle gift greeted me. Under the floppy present lay a mix of crumpled-up German newspapers hiding the treats. My heart warmed. My shaking hands pulled out the goods. The result was: five bags of Haribos, half frozen; six Ritter Sport squares, ice-cubed; four bags of gingerbread, hard as bricks; two bags of Russisch Brot, sweet, crispy snacks; two tins full of homemade Christmas cookies, crumbled everywhere in the parcel; two chocolate Christmas calendars, squashed; two Stollen, fallen apart; three bags of Knusperflocken, chocolate covered crispbread, pulverized; four bags of Gelebananen, banana flavored jelly covered in chocolate, squashed; and three books in Japanese. *Hmm*. My Japanese was nonexistent. Was Ulrike pranking me?

I opened the messenger app, attached the pictures and videos, and wrote to my sister:

Thanks for the Christmas package. It just arrived. It came with a couple of surprises. It was opened. Is something missing? It also came with interesting literature.

I peered at the chocolate-filled calendars and drew one of them closer. Without further ado, I ripped the top off. Twenty-four small chocolates showed me their flat backs. I pulled the first one out of its plastic form. Chocolate imprinted with reindeer images lined the inside of the calendar box. My mouth melted the sweet between my teeth. I unplugged the remaining twenty-three chocolates. The pile ended up on the table before me between the other treats and the wrapped gift.

Ding. I opened my messenger app.

OMG, Ulrike responded. *I didn't put the books in. Why would I? Do you know how expensive the package was? Why should I make it heavier with something you can't use?*

Ulrike. That's hilarious. But is anything missing? I asked.

My sister replied only a moment later:

I don't think so. That is hilarious. But why would someone open a package and put books in?

I don't know. At least nothing was taken.

Yeah, I know. Well, enjoy, and call Mom after dinner. She'll be happy to hear that her surprise worked.

I will.

After putting my phone down next to me, I shifted my eyes back to the pile of chocolate waiting to be devoured. The lock turned, and Guido pushed the door open. Caught in a sugar rush, I froze. Guido stood in the doorframe. "What are you doing?" His wide eyes nearly popped right out. His pupils scanned the mountain of food before me, wandering to my chocolate-smudged face.

"What are you doing here so early?" Only two hours ago, Guido had left for work.

"We had a power outage," Guido explained.

"Did a squirrel bite the dust again?"

He chuckled, "No. A tree branch fell on the cable. But before that, I signed us up for a talk on Friday, part of a series called Kitchen Science."

"Because I am so good at it?" I joked. My cooking skills only prevented me from getting scurvy. I wondered if sometimes Guido tried to challenge me to get more active in the kitchen without saying the words aloud.

"It just sounds fun. This talk will be about how we eat with our eyes and how we taste if we can't see or identify the food. It takes place at Harvard," Guido explained while joining me on the sofa. He reached for chocolate. I threw the second calendar into his lap before he got into my pile.

"Here is your own."

"But you know you must share everything else, right?" Guido said.

"I know. That is why I am sharing the second calendar with you."

He laughed. "How generous of you. What's in the gift wrap?"

I shrugged. "I don't know. Do you want to open it?"

"Sure." Guido tore the paper apart.

I gasped. In my husband's hand was my favorite kind of linen. The percale elephant tusk, white cotton fabric glided smoothly between my fingers.

Guido read the note from the folded fabric: *Just donate it before you return home. I have more. And they are ready to use. I washed them. Merry Christmas, Mom.*

My mother always had spare linen. She had received a ton as her dowry, and once her mother passed away, a whole cupboard-full was added to her household. Ulrike was the only one who had actively defied Mom by buying her sheets the day she moved into her own space.

Guido unfolded the cloth. "Shall we put it on?"

"Sure."

We piled into our bedroom. Guido reached into the inside-out cover, holding up the protector's corners. I offered him the blanket's corners. Together, we covered up our duvet. He and I shook the comforter to make the fabric fit into its soft casing, but the blanket stayed bumpy in my mom's linen. We both nodded and stretched it, but the blanket remained uneven on the cover. Guido even went inside the linen to smooth out the comforter, to no avail.

"Let's do the pillows then," I proposed.

Guido held up the case. I popped the pillow in. His incredulous face mirrored my confusion. The pillow was half as wide as the case my mom sent me. And I couldn't believe that this difference had gone over my head. When I first came, I didn't think twice that the pillows back home were square and probably twice the size of the ones Guido had. I just accepted that.

"Perhaps the blanket has a different size as well, then?" Guido wondered out loud.

"I don't understand."

"Do we have a measuring tape?" Guido looked at me as if I knew every single household item in the apartment. This place's inventory was scarce, but I hadn't acquired everything. Most of the items weren't acquired by me at all. And we'd already had that topic of discussion a couple of weeks ago.

I shook my head. "Do you want to measure the cover and blanket?"

"Yes. But we could also look up the sizes," my husband proposed.

I pulled out my phone. "What size is the blanket?"

"I don't know. I got it on the bed."

I scrolled through the information given on my screen. "Okay, so a twin size is sixty-six by ninety inches, a double is eighty by ninety inches, a queen is ninety by a hundred inches, and a king size is ninety by a hundred and eight inches," I read off the screen.

"That means twelve inches are roughly thirty centimeters. That makes ninety to a hundred inches, two meters, and twenty or so," my husband calculated.

"Or so," I echoed.

Guido's face displayed the same inner status as me: cluelessness. I was unsure if I'd ever bought sheets or checked the size of one, thanks to my mom and her endless supply.

This set had never been used. I unbuttoned the cover, turned the protection inside out, and searched for some indication of my mom's cover's dimensions.

"What are you doing?"

"I am looking for the label." And I soon found the information. "So, this will never fit regardless of the size of the comforter. 155 by 220 centimeters."

"What do you want to do?"

"I don't know." I shrugged. "How about we try it out now during a nap? I could use one."

"Sounds good to me."

If the unevenness of the blanket within the cover annoyed me, two options remained. Option one: sucking it up and having no covers. I had managed the last couple of weeks without them. I did complain a lot, but I would try to swallow my dismay for the remaining time.

Then option two would be the most sensible one. Just buy new covers!

And while I was out and about, a measuring tape. An argument with myself would ensue. I could do without a fitting cover. I wanted to keep our stuff minimal, only to break down a week before I returned.

I was annoyed by my own predictability and that I couldn't get over myself to just buy the damn thing immediately.

We proceeded to put the cover back on and lay down. After my hubby snuggled up to me, my eyes closed regardless of the waves in the blanket.

<u>Friday</u>

Restlessness overshadowed the last three nights, not because of the unfitting cover but because pregnancy sucked out my energy. Unfortunately, my daily walks vaporized thanks to ice and piles of snow blocking crossings and thinning the width of the sidewalk.

Unbalanced without physical activity, my back ached, and my head throbbed. Sweat coated my skin despite the chilliness in the apartment. I scooched up to my hubby, but his side was already empty. Confused, I called to him, "Guido?"

"I'm in the kitchen," he answered.

"How did you sleep?"

"Well, I moved onto the sofa at one point," he admitted. I couldn't blame him. He had to go to work somewhat rested. He could only take paternity leave once he was back home. Until then, he had to soldier through the pregnancy.

On the other hand, he was more of a spectator or a hand-holder who could only take away part of the pregnancy burden. His body didn't deform. Besides the growing belly and poking baby, I could feel how my organs shifted. Nobody could have prepared me for this physical change, adding to the emotional drainage.

"The coffee is done and waiting in the kitchen. Do you want to meet me at Harvard Square, or do you want me to come home first?" I squeezed my eyebrows together to help wake up my brain. "The food talk at Harvard," Guido prompted.

"Yes, the talk," I repeated slowly. "Let's meet there. Five forty-five?"

"Yeah. And we can grab dinner afterward."

"Sounds good," I said, falling back into the bed.

Excited to go out, I looked forward to being around unfamiliar people, which increased my energy.

I felt so low after flipping through my journal. Most weeks were so empty. If I put on a coat, I went for my daily walk to get my blood flowing, and my mood lifted by decompressing from the apartment walls, which seemed to be closing in on me if I didn't strap on my shoes.

After breakfast, I dressed and prepared for my new routine: a walk around the block on an iceless circuit, which Guido had preapproved.

I was about to close the door behind me when my belly rumbled. No, that wasn't rumbling. Perhaps it was pulling itself together. Or was the pain in my stomach at all? The pain stung, cutting into my lower stomach. But the painful sensation left abruptly. I leaned against the closed door. Shallow breaths streamed out of my mouth. My shoulders loosened up.

I pulled myself up on the doorframe. Timid steps pushed me forward. Shaking limbs carried me to the sofa, only for the pain to reappear—a sense of foreboding set in. I inhaled through my nose. The air pushed down into my lungs.

My mouth pushed the air back out. Instead of resting, I walked back and forth in the living room. My body released the pain back into my nervous system.

Was this it? I drilled my fingers into the back of the sofa to release some of the sharpness. I had to talk to someone. I had to know.

I fished my phone out of my winter coat's pocket and dialed the hospital.

"How can I help you?" the nurse asked.

"Hi, my name is Mareike, and I am pregnant. I don't feel so good. I started to feel pain, and I'm unsure what to do," I explained.

"When are you due?" the nurse asked.

"Fourteenth of January," I replied.

"Since you are still ten days away from your due date, you might only have Braxton-Hicks," she explained.

"Okay," I murmured.

The nurse suggested, "Why don't you take a nice warm bath? That could help you relax."

"Well, okay," I said stupidly.

"Call your health-care provider tomorrow morning if the symptoms don't fade away."

"Okay, thanks." I hung up. I continued walking through the apartment, trying to sit down and relax, but the pain increased.

I clenched my phone and, at some point, decided to call Guido.

"Hey, maybe we should stay home tonight. I don't feel so good."

"What do you mean? Do you think you are having the baby?"

"I don't know."

"Do you want me to come home?"

"No, I don't know. I just wanted to tell you that I don't feel well and don't want to go out."

"Call me again if you want me to come home immediately. You could also call the hospital and tell them that you don't feel well," Guido suggested.

"I already did. They told me it might be Braxton-Hicks since I'm still ten days away from my due date."

"Okay, well, I'll come home ASAP," Guido promised.

I showered to wash away the pain, relax, and distract myself from the situation. The warm water drizzled on my skin. I leaned forward, and the water landed on my shoulders and streamed down my back.

Pop. What just happened? I turned off the shower, my hand shaking. I dried myself off and put on sweatpants and a sweater. Then I stumbled back into the living room, holding my belly.

"How are you doing?" Guido said, now home from work.

My limbs shook, and my voice quivered. "I'm not sure, but I think my water broke." Goose bumps spread over my skin.

"Do you want to call the hospital again?" Concern layered Guido's voice. He moved forward to hold me in his upper arms.

Pain seared up and down my muscles. Which ones, I couldn't tell. Sharp darts of distress punctured my thinking.

I finally nodded up and down after a wave of needles in my lower back subsided.

I dialed the number. A different nurse picked up. "This is Nurse Jasmine speaking. How can I help you?"

"Well, I am pregnant, and I just took a shower, and I heard a pop, and I think my water just broke."

"You won't hear a popping sound when the water breaks."

"But . . . but I did," I stated, unsure of myself.

"How much water broke?"

"I don't know. I was in the shower," I repeated.

"Okay. When is your due date?"

"January fourteenth."

"Do you have any pain?"

"Yes."

"Do you have cramps?"

"Maybe. I guess."

"What is the interval of your contractions?"

"Well, it's every ten minutes, I think."

"As you are due in ten days, this pain might last until the end of your pregnancy."

"What?"

"Even if your water broke, I don't think you'll have a baby now."

"Why not?"

"You still can talk to me," the woman on the other side of the phone declared.

"Mmmhhhh," was all I could say, comprehending what the nurse indicated.

"Why don't you come in tomorrow morning around seven, and we'll have a look."

"Um. Okay."

"Have a good night," the nurse said before hanging up on me.

"What did they say?" Guido wanted to know.

I stared at Guido blankly. "They said the pain could stay for the remainder of my pregnancy, and I could come in tomorrow for a checkup."

I clenched my hands and took a deep breath in and a deep breath out. I strode to the window. The thin pink silver lining of the sky rounded out the light for the day. I turned and marched to the other end of the living room. I tightened my upper arm muscles and leaned forward.

Guido held my arm. His other hand rubbed my back. "I think I want to go to the hospital now so they can tell me in person that I will not have the baby yet."

Guido straightened up and patted down his shirt. "I'll get Tanner."

I barely registered the streetlights, passing cars, pedestrians, piles of blackened snow, and plows. The recurring pain increased with even shorter intervals. My jaw clenched to suppress screams. I squeezed my facial muscles together. Whenever a red light stopped the car from moving forward, my eyes bulged out of my sockets. I breathed in and out, in and out.

With the increase in pain, the drive seemed to last for hours.

"I'm sorry we're going so slow, but the snow piles have forced one-lane streets," Tanner explained.

I leaned to the side. My eyes made out rows and rows of red brake lights. My right hand squeezed the bridge of my nose to control my body's tightness. I rubbed back and forth, breathing in and out, containing the pain, the panic, the angst.

"Can I do something?" Guido offered next to me.

"No," I moaned.

I just wanted the pain to stop. I just wanted to fall apart. Tears welled out the sides of my eyes. I no longer cared if I had the baby in the back of the car. I just wanted to rid my body of this pain. My muscles tensed. Short reprieves brought out hope that I could push through the slow-moving traffic. My skin moistened.

I dug my fingers into the seat and saw it—our destination, the high-rise hospital.

"Good luck!" Tanner yelled as we stepped out of his car right in front of the hospital entrance. The sliding doors opened.

I hobbled alongside Guido, who had the brainpower to remember the baby bag. I would have just left with the clothes on my body.

A young woman behind a three-foot-wide desk pointed her hand right behind a pregnant woman in front of her. When the other woman left, we stumbled toward the receptionist.

"I think I am having a baby," I stammered.

"You can reach the maternity ward via the elevator." The lady in front of me lifted her arm and pointed right behind us as if this was just another Friday for her. Well, I guess it was. For me, not so much. This was a first-of-its-kind Friday for me.

The elevator lifted us to the fifth floor. I held my belly. Guido guided me toward a row of chairs.

A nurse behind her desk sized me up. "Are you checking in?"

"Yes." My words barely came out as a new contraction occurred only minutes after the last one.

"It will be a second. Someone else is being examined at the moment."

I adjusted my body in the waiting chair to find the most comfortable position. The pain in my lower tummy increased. I got up to move: ten steps in one direction, then I turned around and took ten steps back in the other direction.

"How are you doing?" Guido's leg bounced quickly up and down. His nervousness wasn't even close to my angst.

"I don't know. Not well." I went to my knees. The pain came from everywhere. Guido held my shoulders. He breathed in and out to guide me. I could barely concentrate on anything other than the pain.

After the last wave subsided, I let myself be pulled up by my husband. I leaned against a bare wall, took a deep breath to relax my thighs, and breathed out. Instead of air, vomit came out of my mouth. The bodily fluid splashed on the floor. The puddle of my ejected tummy contents was unidentifiable. I couldn't even remember the time of my last meal. "I'm sorry," I mumbled through gritted teeth.

Guido jumped up. "Nurse. Nurse!" Quick footsteps rushed closer.

"Jasmine," called the approaching nurse to another. "We need a wheelchair."

I didn't object to being sat in the four-wheeler.

I gripped the cushioned armrests. My heart rate increased. I'd completely lost control of my body. I may not have been in control of my body since the previous night. I supposed birthing a baby was ultimately out of the mind's power. My brain fogged up, attempting to make sense of the whole situation. But at this point, I just went along. I couldn't even stand it anymore.

I was brought into an examination room and asked to wear a hospital gown. Only with Guido's help was I able to undress.

I lay on a cushioned hospital bench. Eventually, an older lady I hadn't met before entered the room.

"I am Dr. Caine," she said. I only nodded. The intensity of the contractions made it hard for me to use my vocal cords.

The doctor's face vanished between my legs. I barely heard her words through my waves of pain. But one sentence registered: "You'll have a baby tonight."

Guido squeezed my hand. I returned his gesture before a nurse pushed me on the bed out of the hallway into another elevator. On another floor, I was moved into a birthing room.

A different nurse came and tried to make me comfortable with the cushions. But I shook and cried, "I just want the pain to disappear."

"I'm so sorry. I was told it's too late for you to get an epidural."

"But . . ." I managed to say. Oh, the irony. "I want this pain to go away!" I cried.

Guido replaced the nurse by my side.

"Please make it stop," I pleaded through shallow breaths.

His pale face answered me. Of course I knew better. But I wanted him to do something. I had to share this pain. I couldn't bear it much longer. The pain filled out every sense I had in my body. The cramps drowned out my whole environment. And this wasn't even it. This was the precursor to the actual birth. *No, no, no, no.* This had to stop. I couldn't do it. I didn't want to do this anymore. And a realization made itself apparent. I voluntarily admitted it. I didn't want to feel a thing. I wanted to be numb.

A nurse pushed me onto the bed, and the

doctor positioned himself before me. The nurse kept saying, "Breathe in and breathe out."

I couldn't care less who birthed the baby with me at this point. I just wanted to get it over with. I wanted this pain to stop.

"When you have another contraction, push as if you need to use the toilet."

"What?" The instruction threw me off. I didn't know how to do this. This was the wrong position. I was lying, not sitting down. I had no control over myself. But I tried anyway. I had to. I wanted to make this stop. But instructing my body to do something different was hard. My energy faded.

"Keep on pushing," the doctor repeated, "I can see the head."

Accelerated by his words, I pushed. I pushed every time a cramp filled my shaking body. Four, five times, and an outlandish cry filled the room.

Tears of exhaustion watered my eyes. The nurse placed the baby on my naked upper body. "Do you already have a name?"

"I ... I ..." I stumbled, not comprehending what had just happened. The pain was gone, now replaced by a baby.

"We haven't decided yet," Guido said.

"We thought we still had time," I added.

The nurse nodded. "So Baby Korn, until you know."

"Little B," I cried in Guido's embrace with our baby in the middle.

German Words in Alphabetical Order

Allee is a city street with trees lined on both sides of the street.

Ampelmännchen is a former East German figure on pedestrian crossings.

Apfelschorle is a mix of primarily carbonated water and apple juice.

Broiler is grilled chicken.

Döner is a kebab.

Ebay Kleinanzeigen is similar to Craigslist, just on Ebay.

Erdnussflips are peanut puffs.

Fasching is a day of celebration in February when people dress up in costumes.

Frau Holle is a German fairy tale collected by the Brothers Grimm.

Goldmarie is the main character of the fairy tale *Frau Holle*.

Hebamme is a midwife.

Intershop was a former store in East Germany where people could buy products from West Germany with D-mark.

Litfaßsäule used to be an advertising column.

Mettwurst is cured or smoked raw minced pork.

Mittwoch is Wednesday.

Mürbeteigplätzchen are classic German cookies.

Nürnberger Gingerbread is a brand specializing in Christmas-related treats.

Paulaner is a German beer company.

Quark is a creamy dairy product.

Quarkkeulchen is a sweet dish made out of flour and quark.

Rollmops is pickled herring.

Rote Grütze is a red jelly-like dessert.

Schmalzgebäck is fried dough.

Schnapszahl are numbers that are repetitive. For example, 11/11/2011 (11/11/11), or the same number on two or more dice.

Schwibbögen are arched frames with candle holders and decorated with Christmas motives displayed in windows.

Sternentaller is a German fairy tale collected by the Brothers Grimm.

Stollen is a traditional Christmas fruit bread.

Strohwitwer is a man who lives temporarily without his wife.

Thüringer Bratwurst is a mildly seasoned sausage that comes from Thuringia.

Torte is a multi-layered cake.

Tropifrutti is a Haribo variety featuring colorful gummies.

Waldmeister is a green lemonade.

Wernesgrüner is a German beer company.

Wiener is a sausage similar to a hot dog.

eBook: 978-1-7365806-9-1

Paperback: 978-1-7365806-8-4

Footnotes

Week 26

1. **Strohwitwer** is a man who lives temporarily without his wife.
2. **Ebay Kleinanzeigen** is similar to Craigslist, just on Ebay.
3. **Ampelmännchen** is a former East German figure on pedestrian crossings.
4. **Allee** is a city street with trees lined on both sides of the street.
5. **Hebamme** is a midwife.

Week 27

1. **Intershop** was a former store in East Germany where people could buy products from West Germany with D-mark.

Week 28

1. **Fasching** is a day of celebration in February when people dress up in costumes.
2. **Schnapszahl** are numbers that are repetitive. For example, 11/11/2011 (11/11/11), or the same number on two or more dice.
3. **Wernesgrüner** is a German beer company.
4. **Paulaner** is a German beer company.

Week 29

1. Quark is a creamy dairy product.

Week 30

1. **Tropifrutti** is a Haribo variety featuring colorful gummies.
2. **Apfelschorle** is a mix of primarily carbonated water and apple juice.
3. **Waldmeister** is a green lemonade.

Week 32

1. **Stollen** is a traditional Christmas fruit bread.
2. **Sternentaller** is a German fairy tale collected by the Brothers Grimm.
3. **Goldmarie** is the main character of the fairy tale *Frau Holle*.
4. **Frau Holle** is a German fairy tale collected by the Brothers Grimm.
5. **Nürnberger Gingerbread** is a brand specializing in Christmas-related treats.
6. **Thüringer Bratwurst** is a mildly seasoned sausage that comes from Thuringia.
7. **Currywurst** is steamed, fried sausage. Sold as fast food.
8. **Broiler** is grilled chicken.
9. **Wiener** is a sausage similar to a hot dog.
10. **Döner** is a kebab.
11. **Quarkkeulchen** is a sweet dish made out of flour and quark. Delicious!

Footnotes

12. ***Rollmops*** is pickled herring. Yum!
13. ***Rote Grütze*** is a red jelly-like dessert.
14. ***Mürbeteigplätzchen*** are classic German cookies.
15. ***Torte*** is a multi-layered cake.

Week 33

1. *Schwibbögen are arched frames with candle holders and decorated with Christmas motives displayed in windows.*

Week 34

1. ***Mettwurst*** is another type of sausage.
2. ***Kaffeeklatsch*** is a social gathering usually including baked goods with coffee, tea, or hot chocolate.

Week 35

1. ***Zum Fliegenden Holländer*** is a restaurant in Potsdam.
2. ***Litfaßsäule*** used to be an advertising column.

Week 36

1. ***Erdnussflips*** are peanut puffs.

Week 37

1. ***Mittwoch*** is Wednesday.
2. ***Schmalzgebäck*** is fried dough.